Mixed
CONNECTION

Published by Independently Published

E-Book ASIN: B0DGWQ2KLM

Paperback ISBN: 9798339107187

Alternate Paperback ISBN: 9798284812433

Cover Design by Nicole Devonne, Art by FlashFryed
Editing by ReJoyce Literary Editing Co

For more information, visit: www.nicoledevonnebooks.com

content advisory

negative comments about the FMC's body
(not by MMC), emotional neglect from
parents, death of parents due to drunk
driver (off page), light breath play, break-in,
on-page sex scenes

dicktionary

The below chapters have explicit on-
page sexual scenes.

Chapter 12
Chapter 13
Chapter 16 (after page break)
Chapter 23

playlist

Return of the Mack by Mark Morrison
Gbese by Majeeed feat. Tiwa Savage
Complete by T'neeya
Hold On by Navy Kenzo feat. Fireboy DML
Journey by Sam Cross
Black Like You by Joseph Solomon
Three Hour Drive by Alicia Keys feat. SiR (A Colors Show)
John Redcorn by SiR
Jeans by Jessie Reyez feat. Miguel
ICU by Coco Jones
Lose Control by Teddy Swims
Peace of Mind by kust and Bertram Kvist
Addict by Don Louis
Grateful by Mahalia
Met You At A Bar by Jaz Karis feat. Tone Stith
Until Morning by James Vickery (A Colors Show)
Garden Kisses by Giveon
Another Sad Love Song by Toni Braxton
Hrs & Hrs by Muni Long
Feelings (live) by Dre Scott
On Purpose (wedding version) by Ni/Co

To those who struggle with giving themselves a *yes*,
it's time to give yourself permission to live.

This is my love letter to *yes*.

1

Cassidy

> You know, I could turn around and no one would be the wiser.

Lo

> Get your fine ass in the car and call me when you get there.

The reunion invitation might as well be putty in my hands with how many times I've folded and unfolded it. When I was a teen, this place made my skin crawl. I didn't have a great high school experience, my last year was a tough one, being constantly ridiculed by other students. Granted we were all kids, trying to figure out who we were becoming, but the interactions still left lasting impressions on me. Let's just say being fat, in a hormonally raging teen fest, wasn't easy for me.

A balmy breeze ruffles my curls, conjuring memories of the last few weeks of junior year, right before summertime fun would take over and it would be pool days from then on out with Paloma and Janelle. I miss those days.

"Why the fuck did I RSVP to this again?" I mumble, in an attempt to keep my voice low, as more people walk up the weathered concrete steps. I fumble with the thick cardstock, remembering the promises I made to myself after graduating. Determined I was done with allowing the bullies to win, done with not loving myself, and vowed to work on choosing me first in all areas of my life.

Forcing myself to relax my shoulders, I finally notice the old school sign and shake my head. Cypress Lake High School still has its raggedy sign in the entryway of campus, the deep-red letters are washed out and almost pink from years of the natural elements taking their toll. One would think it would have been replaced after all these years but apparently the administration hasn't, and I'm not going to hold my breath that they ever will.

"de Que hablas Willis, *why did you RSVP to this.*" My best friend's face scrunches up at me, before she continues with the pep talk I don't want, but need. "Cass, you can do this babe. Just walk in. Besides, we made a pact to say *yes* to more things in life, even the stuff that makes us uncomfortable," Paloma reminds me, her face filling the screen of our video call as if I need her throwing my own obligations back in my face.

The pact was something Donna, my therapist, suggested, and Paloma was happy to support me as an accountability partner. When we agreed to this effort almost a year ago, I promised to say yes to more things that would bring me joy. My early twenties were filled with moments of second guessing the importance of making myself a priority given my parents couldn't fathom doing so. I knew I didn't want to remain stagnant by being stuck in a cycle of second-best or the abandonment issues I was beginning to form prior to starting therapy.

After many sessions along with building trust with my therapist, it was suggested that *just maybe*, I needed to start by being the first choice for myself and move away from placing my worth in others, especially my parents. Removing the insecurity that I wouldn't be anybody's priority because I already was, to me.

Taking a deep inhale I tease, "You know, you were supposed to be here with me but you bailed." I watch her eyes roll and can read her expression that says, *I should cuss you out right now.*

Silent conversations and Spanglish sass are our love language.

"Carajo!" She laughs. "I would be there if I could, but I'm sick as a dog right now." Her shoulder-length, magenta hair is currently pulled up into a messy bun, lumpy from curls not brushed down, while a few wispy stragglers hang freely in the back, far too short to fit so high on her head. It's exactly how I know she's sicker than she lets on, it's her, I-feel-like-shit hairdo. Shifting my shoulders slightly, I consider turning around and going home, not wanting to do this alone.

This is a place of such disdain for me. I kept in touch with maybe two other people, and we're not even that close. The music from inside grows louder as a few people enter. I know I can't stand out here much longer before I begin to look like a creep. *Fuck, I look like a creep.*

"You know I love you, and you can do this. These people, this place, they don't have control over you anymore." She slips out the last words right before a coughing fit hits. She pulls a tissue into view and I swear I can smell the menthol and eucalyptus from the vapor rub through the screen. Any time Lo is feeling under the weather, she slathers herself in it. Balling the tissue up, she tosses it out of view. Her nose is rubbed raw and looks as though it can illuminate a Christmas Eve night.

I can hear how tired she is and decide to take her advice. "I hate that you're right. I love you. Now go take some medicine and ponte vicks," I say the same words she tells me the moment congestion is a contender.

3

"I'll text you when I make it home later. Promise."

We say our final goodbyes and I disconnect the call. She's right. Why allow the anxiety of yesterday to bother what could be a great night in the here and now? Besides, I don't have to be here long. I'll pop in and say hi to those I remember and get the hell home.

I wiggle my toes, imagining my cozy bunny slippers.

In and out.

Being at Cypress Lake High isn't all bad, I guess—I did meet my best friends here after all. And I'm proud of where I am in my life. There is nothing and no one stopping me from walking through those doors but myself, and I'll be damned if I get in my own way.

I grab the cold, brass handle and pull open the door; my eyes go wide and a sense of awe presses in on me as I take in the decor.

Though the outside of the building looks the same as it did ten years ago, the reunion committee did an amazing job transforming the dilapidating interior into something worth having some school spirit over.

The inside of the main hall is completely revamped, the theme for this year being Botanical Oasis. The surroundings are decked out in shades of deep green with a combination of faux shrubs obstructing what I can only imagine are unsightly walls and baseboards still trapped in the eighties. Large, leafy, potted plants are arranged in clusters along with flowerpots throughout the space, and I think I may even hear the sound of rain playing softly.

Wanting to see a bit more, I stand on my tiptoes and peer over the shrubs. There are couches and chairs in small groupings so everyone can lounge about when they aren't dancing or eating.

I dip into the bathroom to make sure I look my very best and to quell the bits of anxiety that are still seeping into my psyche. I'm met with a full-length mirror as soon as I walk in, a wall sconce adorns the top casting my reflection to look more like a framed piece of art. This perks my mood up a bit, ridding me of any remaining jitters. Swallowing a laugh, I tuck a loose strand of hair back into place. My deep-chestnut curls are perfect tonight. I gave myself a heavy side part and allowed them to fall where they may, cascading over my shoulders and fluffed to perfection.

My strapless bustier top glitters under the fluorescent bulbs. It has a dainty floral pattern embroidered into it and I knew it would be the perfect piece to bring my outfit together. I opted for exaggerated wide-legged, olive pants that flutter as I move to complement the form-fitting bodice—one that gives me enough cleavage to feel sexy but allows me not to worry about flashing anyone the goods. Giving it one last adjustment, and righting the skinny black belt that beautifully matches my thin choker, I feel a bit more settled in myself again. Taking in a deep breath, I smirk at the reflection because I feel fucking amazing, I'm not going to let this night get the best of me.

I remind myself of the pact Lo and I made, emphasizing that personal growth and inner joy can come from moments of discomfort. Leaning into the uneasiness of experiences we wouldn't normally indulge in, might help release ourselves from the possibility of regret. We can live and enjoy, and learn from our mistakes and successes, but we won't be stuck wondering what could have been.

Pulling open the bathroom door, I take my first step out and then another, and another, my heels giving me a bit more sway in my hips and I let that drive me forward. I told myself I was going to have a good time, that I would dance, and try to experience more joy. I'm giving myself permission to do the things I might regret not doing later—this is another *yes* I need to give myself.

By the time I step back into the hallway, the lighting has dimmed slightly to allow the colored LED lights to illuminate a more relaxed mood before the DJ takes over for the night. The smile dancing on my lips feels good but is short-lived when I hear my name.

"Wooooww, Cassidy? Girl is that you?" Her voice still grates against my skin like it did all those years ago. Before I falter further, I hear the words my best friend told me before walking in, *"These people, this place, they don't have control over you anymore."* She's right, they don't have control over me anymore, especially not her.

"Vanessa, how are you?" I respond, hoping she can't detect the disdain in my facial expression. I watch her nose scrunch regardless. I was not expecting to see her so soon, but God must have a twisted sense of humor today.

"Girl, I'm doing great! I have been looking forward to this reunion since I got the invitation, but I was not expecting to see *you* here." Her gaze is calculating as she looks me up and down, just like she always did.

"Why, exactly, wouldn't I be here?" I question her, letting my annoyance slip through my tone.

My question doesn't seem to stop her as she continues speaking. As if I didn't say anything at all.

"I'm living the good life. Traveling the world for work. You know how it is."

I, in fact, do not know how "it" is. She spoke of traveling the world often in high school, to literally anyone near enough to hear, and now she does. Immediately after graduation Vanessa applied to be a flight attendant. Living in a small town, well, everyone ends up knowing everyone's business. I also don't like to admit that I saw it on her social media pages.

But she seems as though she wants to chat and maybe saying *yes* this once with her can be an olive branch. We're adults now, after all.

"That's great. I've finished adding a new space to my bar where I ca—" I begin, quickly realizing she doesn't give two shits to the wind when she interrupts me.

"Mmhm, that's so interesting. You know, if you would wear a shaper then that pudge on the side wouldn't be so full." She reaches out but hesitates, something very unlike the Vanessa I remember from high school. I make it a point to step back, giving her an assessing gaze. "Oh, you don't have to be so sensitive. I thought you would have grown out of that." Her sickly-sweet tone coats my skin and only furthers my embarrassment, and anger heats my face. This is why I don't want to be here; I have barely made it inside and I am already making heart-eyes at the exit.

"And here I thought you would have grown out of being such a bi—" As I'm about to finally give her a piece of my mind, someone knocks into me so hard I lose my train of thought and I know I am going to hit the floor. I brace myself for the impact of the cold floor, squeezing my eyes shut but it never comes. Hands suddenly reach out, holding my arms to steady me. And whoever these hands belong to smells incredible, like the smokiness of a rich bourbon.

The owner of the strong grip ends his conversation, pulling only one of his hands away to tap on the bluetooth hidden in his ear as his eyes lock on mine. Craning my head back, I look at the offending bulldozer that knocked me off my feet, saving Vanessa from my fury in the process. He has to be at least six feet four inches, if how far I need to lean back to look at him is any indication. Wide shoulders and a strong chest have to be beneath the shirt he wears with the way the material stretches and wrinkles with his movements.

He gives me a warm smile I will not soon forget, one that tugs at teenage memories I'm having trouble placing, and all I can do is nod my head. It looks like he wants to say something before frustration slightly clouds his features. "Um, I..." he mumbles and my lips tip up slightly, welcoming him to say *anything really*. Instead, he gives me a tight lipped grin before he mumbles something I don't quite catch as he releases me, his gaze never leaving mine, even as Vanessa waves her hand in a flourish of *pick-me-energy*.

"So are you going to pretend like I'm not here?" Before Vanessa fully finishes her sentence, he has already turned on his heel, making his way toward the main hall. I can't hold back the smirk on my face, shocked by his blatant disregard for her, I bite the inside of my cheek to hold in a chuckle. He totally snubbed her, didn't even acknowledge her, and the petty part of me loves it a little too much. When I twist to look back at her, her face is fixed in a grimace and her shoulders sag. I take the moment to look a bit more closely at the person standing in front of me. Watching her fold in on herself makes me question if I know *this* Vanessa, the one who is all grown up and no longer the bully from our teens.

That is until she notices my eyes on her and she quickly puts on the facade she is clearly carrying around. "We had a little fling back in the day, clearly he isn't over me ending it." She shrugs as I choke on a laugh. I know she's not trying to pull that sorry card. *Girl, please.*

"Mmhm, that must be exactly what it is. I'll see you inside." As I start to turn, I look over my shoulder. "Oh and Vanessa?" She looks at me then and I say, "Just for the record, we might be inside Cypress Lake but this is not high school anymore. You need to grow the fuck up and start focusing on yourself."

"Cassidy, I—" she begins, but I wave my hand, not wanting to hear anything else she has to say.

"Just... don't, Vanessa. Save it. We had four years together and I don't want, nor do I have the time for, anything else you have to say."

Shaking my head as I spin around, I internally give myself a high five for finally standing up for myself. I understand hurt people, hurt people and some people need time to heal, but I am not going to be anyone's punching bag. I gave enough of myself to her motives a decade ago and I don't have it in me to give her any more of my time.

I focus on walking as I even out my racing heart. I want to say I hate her, but I refuse to give her that much power over my emotions ever again.

I shake off the negative energy and walk back into the event space thinking about Mr. Tall, Dark, and Shoulders wide enough for a hell of a ride.

The main hall is even more beautiful than the outer lounge area, vines with small flowers are cascading here and there from the ceiling. There is a soft glow that lights the room and pulses to the thump of the music, creating a welcoming ambiance with the scent of rosewater in the air. Clusters of chaises and chairs are grouped along the walls like in the outer area, but in the back of the large room, there's a bartender near a full buffet. After my introduction to the night, I am going to reset it with a cocktail.

As I get closer to the bar, I take in a wide set of shoulders, and I think of the man who ran into me earlier. I'm staring at a tailored pair of brown pants that rest on this man's trim waist, where a crisp white shirt is tucked in. Oh, it's definitely him. The shirt is folded at the widest part of his biceps and I can't stop the sigh as I notice how the fabric grips his deep-umber skin. His hair is cut low around the sides, and freshly twisted locs are wrapped in an impressive bun on the top of his head.

As though he can feel my perusal, he turns his head slightly to the side. The lights are dim enough that he would be able to tell if someone was walking up behind him but I'm just far enough away that there is no way he can see me checking him out. The bartender must have called his attention back as the mystery man faces the bar once more. Grabbing the short glass of liquid the bartender slides to him, he turns—nimble on his feet for such a large man—before he walks toward a cluster of chairs. I can't help but watch his long strides, and the way his thighs power him forward as I settle up to the spot he was just standing in.

"Um... Miss? What can I get for you?" The hum of a voice behind the hightop pulls me from the naughty images of my thick legs tangled in his... naked. He walks with relaxed confidence as if nothing bothers him, something I enjoy in a man.

Wow, I shake my head at myself. What is it I find so captivating about him? It's been a long while since I've laid my eyes on someone who fits my visual package so perfectly.

"Yes, sorry about that. Can I have a cherry bourbon sour, with champagne instead of soda?" The bartender nods, gives me a wink, and turns with a flourish to begin working on my drink. It's one of my favorites, and I find myself smirking about my specialty titled, *One Bed*, the first drink that inspired Shaken Tropes.

My best friend and I opened the bar a few years ago and the business immediately took off. Patrons can come in for a drink, mingle, and read, though our specialty is hosting blind dates. Customers can share what they are in the mood to read and we'll make a magical pairing of a beverage and a book, just for them. They are welcome to borrow the book while they drink and even buy it when they come to get a refill. And we never worry because they always come back for a refill.

The bartender hands me my drink and I lounge my back against the bar to take in the crowd around me as I spot a familiar face, one I haven't seen since graduation.

"Janelle?" A giddiness overtakes me as I set my eyes on the side profile of an old high school friend, one I regret losing touch with. Her waist-length, box braids are parted down the center and sway with her movements. I lightly snort watching her hands move as fast as her mouth while she talks with another attendee. Janelle's eyes sweep the crowd, waving goodbye to the former students as they part ways before she locks in on me and in a few quick strides, closes the distance between us.

"Oh my God! Cass! I'm so glad you're here. I was hoping you would be." She looks at me with a huge smile splitting her face as she stretches out her hands. We give each other a squeeze before laughing at the bits of awkwardness that waft around us.

We tried to text and call while she was away but life happens. Janelle went into the military after graduating and I was still struggling with the loss of my parents while starting university classes. I blame life circumstances on all the time we missed, but being here now—my chest warms recalling all the sleepovers Janelle, Paloma, and I shared.

We would pick whose house we would all head to Friday after school, stuff ourselves with junk food, and stay up far too late singing ourselves hoarse to music videos. Saturdays during the summer were spent at her parents' pool. Paloma sunburned so badly one year, I thought she might turn into a tomato. I scrunch my nose up remembering the scent of aloe vera gel. *So much aloe vera gel.* Curling my lips into themselves I hold back a laugh. Being here with Janelle now makes me realize how much I missed her, we may have to do a real-deal girls' night while she's here.

"I know, it's been a lifetime." I return her smile, giving her arms a squeeze before letting go.

"It really has been, how is everything? Come sit with us," she says, ushering me toward the back corner of the room. There is a grouping of chairs I didn't see, hidden behind a large plant and sheer, ruby curtains. Crossing the space, we catch up on some of the last decade. I tell her all about Shaken Tropes and why I decided not to move out of state like so many of our classmates. We each pick a plush chair to sink into as she begins to fill me in on her life.

Janelle has been active duty in the military since graduating. She reminds me that her entire family is either retired or still in one branch or another. "Growing up it felt like I didn't have any other choice, it felt like it was expected of me, and in some ways, I guess following the legacy of my parents and joining the military was a hope that, someday I would, you know?" I shake my head at her as I sip my drink, but stay quiet so she'll continue. "Over the years, I learned that I really love the Army. Now, I can't imagine doing anything else." She has a soft grin that stretches across her cheeks, it lights up her face in a way that I know she truly loves what she does. "I'm going to be in town for a little while. I can't wait to experience this book boyfriend pairing at the bar, tell me, are they only fictional?" She wiggles her eyebrows suggestively, but my words get caught in my throat and in place of them, I laugh-snort, unable to hold back; Janelle joins in with her own loud and joyous laugh.

She nudges me with her shoulder before her gaze leaves my own and her grin grows wider as she stands to greet someone. "Jameson! I was wondering where you ran off to, or with whom. I swear you're never a stranger no matter what room you're in."

All of a sudden, the same rich bourbon smell from my run-in with Vanessa hits my senses. The handsome bulldozer stands with the same confidence from earlier, he was definitely the stranger walking away from the bar. My fingers twitch as I eye his wide shoulders, putting his broad and muscled chest on display. I've never been more glad for Janelle to be a social butterfly than I am at this moment.

2

Cassidy

sends picture Blast from the past!

Lo

Who's the guy in the background?

Is this eye candy *eyes emoji*

"It's been too long," Janelle says, greeting Jameson. Genuine interest dances across his face, along with something else I can't put my finger on. His eyes meet mine, his gaze burns with mischief and intrigue, so much so that I want to reach out and touch him. The way he looks at me makes me take a sharp breath, he eats up my form like it is his first and last meal—a starved man that has finally found his nourishment.

Or he could be eyeing my body for completely other reasons, you get used to that mindset when you are a fat woman... a fat kid honestly. Though with the way this man is looking at me right now, I can tell it's the former. I straighten my shoulders, remembering that I stopped placing my value in other people's opinions of me and started focusing on what I thought of myself. But I can't take my eyes off him, allowing him his perusal of my full figure. Who doesn't shiver beneath a wanted gaze?

"J-Dog!" Jameson breaks eye contact with me, I fold my lips in to stop myself from laughing at the nickname he's given to one of my oldest friends. "What's up girl?" he says, pulling her in for a hug.

I take a moment to peek at this bulldozer's face, his cool umber skin reminds me of brown quartz beneath red and orange mood lighting. He has a thick, but manicured beard that enhances his pronounced cupid's bow. I can tell he left the barber's earlier today by how sharp his line up is, and I also catch the glint from the small, gold hoop earrings he has in his ear—one at his earlobe and two more at the very top of the same ear. That alone has me crossing my legs. I love a man who takes care of himself and shows pride in his appearance.

Cocking my head to the side a bit, I look a little deeper at his handsome face. My eyes widen further when I realize who he is and an excited flutter fills me. I watch as a slow smile spreads across his face, the action forces my gaze away from his lips and back to his almond-shaped, hickory eyes. Eyes that are focused back on me. The intensity in the way he looks at me quiets the surrounding noise, even if just for a moment.

"You are a fool, you know that?" Janelle playfully taunts, her laugh is infectious and has my own lips turning up into a soft smile. "Jameson, this is my friend Cassidy. Oh wait...Do you guys know each other? This is *our* reunion after all." I smirk at her, she rambles when she's excited. Glad to see nothing has changed.

As I begin to say we don't know each other, Jameson reaches out his hand, lowering his voice a bit as he leans in toward me. "Pleasure to meet you, officially, Cassidy. I remember seeing you around the halls here and there but I don't think we have ever been properly introduced." I stand to take his hand, but instead of shaking it, he holds it a bit, rubbing his thumb over the back of mine. "It's a shame we didn't meet sooner."

Biting the inside of my cheek, I meet his focused gaze with my own and internally squeal, like we're still in high school.

"It really is, but it's nice to meet you all the same now," I respond. I find I don't want to pull away, enjoying the warmth of his hand on my own. "Officially, of course."

My hand remains in his a few seconds longer before Janelle interrupts whatever moment we are lost in. "Do you guys want to get refills on the drinks and dance a bit?"

This would be my cue to step back and sit, protecting myself in the comfort of the chairs, in the guise of some fake truth. My phone chimes at that moment and in the spirit of "saying yes" more often, I surprise myself by agreeing quickly and excusing myself to grab my clutch from our cluster of chairs.

Lo

Just checking in on you babes

Hey babes, I'm having a really great time, actually!

OMG! Guess what?

Lo

As you should be! Any eye candy there?

Of course she wants to know about the eye candy, her question urging me to lift my eyes to find a certain man on the dance floor. She's right, he sure is yummy. My best friend has always been a serial dater, her focus has been on building skills and not on finding Mr. Right when Mr.

Right-Now suited her needs just fine. She met someone before going for her MBA who I thought may be something more than a fling. I remember crawling up on the couch with her and wrapping her in my arms as she sobbed after she made their breakup final. Right person, wrong time, and too much trauma mixed together. Since then, she's gone back to being a singleton, *enjoying life* as she puts it, and I'm here for her finding what she wants. I only want her to be happy.

Lo

Chisme? What is it!

LOL! No Lo.

I ran into Janelle

Lo

OMG! OUR JANELLE!?

Yep, the one and only.

Lo

Make sure you tell her I said hi and I miss her.

I will! I love you, thank you for checking in on me. Get some rest!

Lo

So there is eye candy!

Let me see! *eye looking emoji*

Lol. Bitch I am not snapping a pic, I will call you in the morning.

Lo

FINEEEE!

Feeling lighter than ever, I laugh at my best friend's antics. Now, I just need to get another drink of liquid courage before I go find Janelle and Jameson on the dance floor. Stuffing my phone back into my clutch and snapping it closed, I shake my head still thinking of Paloma's crazy that I love so much. A pair of deep-tan boots come into my line of sight and I snap my head up to find Jameson holding our drinks.

"You have a lovely smile Cassidy." The compliment in his smooth, deep voice causes a blush to spread across my cheeks and I find that his cheeks are now a deeper shade as well.

"Thank you," I say softly, as he clears his throat before handing me my drink. His fingers brush against mine, sending warmth up my wrist and making the want burn hotter. "And thank you, for the drink. How did you know what I was drinking?" I question him, needing to know.

He twists around, waving at the bartender who holds both thumbs up. "I told Charles over there I needed a drink for a beautiful woman but didn't know her drink order. I pointed you out and lucky for me, he remembered." Jokingly, he drops his smile and squints his eyes a bit. "Though, maybe that means I'm not so lucky." He turns back around, making eye contact with the bartender once again and points a finger gun at him. Charles mockingly clutches his chest and I laugh so hard my face hurts. Jameson has a lightness about him that brightens up every space he's in.

"You're pretty smooth for a bulldozer." I emphasize the sound of the

19

't' in pretty before asking him, "And what are you having? Wait... let me guess." His smile looks genuine as he watches me make up my mind. "Whiskey, with maybe...club soda."

His laugh rumbles his chest, stretching his shirt over the muscles beneath it, a shirt that I would much rather be non-existent. *Get your act together girl!*

"You're not far off, it's called The Godfather. Charles had a nice small batch of scotch whiskey that I wanted to try, it gave me the perfect reason to order my favorite. The amaretto in it makes the flavors lighter than you'd expect." He nods his head behind him, toward the rest of our class dancing to whatever the DJ is playing. "So about that dance floor over there," he says, rolling his shoulders. "You ready for my moves?"

I move my head to the side and quickly look in the direction of the dance floor. "Bring it on!"

Jameson and Janelle dance like they're the stars of the show, where one of them bounces and rocks their shoulders the other is shimmying their hips to the beat of the music. At one point they both worked their way lower to the floor facing one another, their heads bopping back and forth to the beat. Watching the two of them goof off together leaves me questioning whether he was coming on to me when he brought over my drink or if I imagined the tension I felt between the two of us, and honestly, I'm still not sure.

I'm not going to let my confusion stop me from having fun; the dance floor is packed and I can't believe I haven't taken more chances at dancing. It is something I deprived myself of for way too long. It allows me to take up too much space, to be seen, watched, and allows my insecurities to be louder than what I know to be true for myself. Being out here, on the dance floor with Jameson and Janelle, seems to chase all those doubts and worries from my mind, giving me the chance to experience peak joy. It's a feeling I'll never let go of.

Now we are in the center of the dance floor, sweat glimmers against my skin from the exertion. There is steady warmth from all the people gyrating, surrounding us in their own separate worlds, and I've never felt lighter. I lean into our little trio, shouting over the music that I'm going to grab some water. Just as I make it to the edge of the dance floor, "Return of the Mack" by Mark Marrison comes on. Before I get the chance to turn back around, it's like Jameson is thinking the same thing I am as he grabs my hand, tugging me back to the dance floor.

"You can't go yet, this is my jam, girl!" Janelle yells over the music as we both join her. Thoroughly in her zone, she throws her head back and sways her hips without a single care.

Someone squeezes past me, waving their hands in the air, pushing me flush against Jameson. Both my palms now rest on his chest, one of his arms is wrapped around my middle. I can feel the searing heat of his hand pressed against my lower back and can do nothing but stare up at him. My chest rises and falls quickly, my heartbeat thumping in my ears muffles the music surrounding us. I can't be the only one feeling this connection between the two of us. He raises an eyebrow at me, his eyes holding a flirtatious gleam to them before releasing me slowly. I'm definitely not the only one. This could be awkward but it feels so natural, which is throwing me for a loop. My gaze darts to our feet, not wanting to show my uncertainty that's playing clearly across my face and I try my best to catch my breath.

Jameson slides his finger under my chin, tilting my head back so I'm forced to look at him. The focus this man has as he searches my face leaves me breathless. "Let's not let J-Dog steal the show." He smirks and as if on cue, Janelle bumps her hip with mine and Jameson spins me.

Every single time I brought up water or wanted to grab another drink, another song came on that was one of "our songs." I can't stop dancing when it's my song playing. We've been dancing for so long that Janelle, the dancing queen herself, lets us know she is heading out, giving each of us a hug and a kiss on the cheek.

I nod to Jameson, lifting myself on my toes, I press a palm to his chest and lean into him. "I'm going to walk her out. Don't you dare find another dance partner!" I tease him as he throws his hands up in the air.

Janelle and I exchange numbers and I promise her I will actually stay in touch this time. She lets me know she will be by Shaken Tropes some time before her leave is over. Waving her off, I can feel my anxiety rise up, my palms are sweating a bit as I make my way back into the hall that has become a club scene. But I don't return to the dance floor, instead I go back to the bartender and grab a water.

Fuck me. I want to give Jameson my number but is that too forward? Do I care if it is? Asking myself that question, I find that I don't care one bit. I release a breath and reach into my clutch to grab a pen before scribbling my number down on the back of the invite. Goosebumps erupt down my arms, as I stand stunned in my own assertiveness. I don't know if I can do this but I know if I don't, I'll regret it and fuck regretting things. The worst thing that could happen is he says no. I would be mortified. But I would live without the regret.

Walking back into the main event space, I scan the dance floor before spotting my dance partner off to the side. He's leaning against the wall, sipping on a drink. My skin is still slicked with sweat from dancing as I make my way over to Jameson. His gaze lifts to mine and he points toward the chairs we were sitting in earlier in the evening, and I nod in agreement.

He holds out his arm for me to go ahead first. There's a gleam of mischief that shines in his eyes and a growing smirk as he drinks me in. I can't lie, it does something to my already secure confidence. I sink my hips deeper into each of my steps and I can feel his eyes track the sway of my ass. The bass dies down and cool relief hits me as I take a seat. I couldn't be happier to step out of the range of the speakers and the thick heat of the crowd.

"Are we going to ask those boring *what have you been doing with your life* questions, now?" I say, lifting my brows and pursing my lips.

"It's only boring if you don't want to know. And I'm definitely interested in learning what you've been doing for the last ten years." I stop myself from swiveling my head around, wanting to find the cameraman of this dating episode because this man cannot be real. He's too good and so right, so I tell him so.

"You're right!" Leaning forward, I take a sip of my drink before continuing. "What's the best part of the last ten years for you?"

"Without a doubt, working with my best friend. I went to school for design architecture but I wasn't sure where I wanted to go with it until my best friend called me up one day asking for help on a project. The rest is history."

"I co-own a business with my best friend too!" My shock is both audible and shows brightly on my face. "I opened Shaken Tropes with my closest friend almost five years ago now. Some people say to be careful about mixing business with friends and family, but it's been the best decision I've made."

"What is Shaken Tropes?" he asks with genuine intrigue.

"Oh, it's my bar." A wide smile climbs up my cheeks at remembering our earlier conversation. "Paloma, my bestie, and I are both big romance readers and we really wanted to have a place where we could share that love with others. So, we thought what better way than books, cocktails, and fictional love interests. Each of our drinks are named after book tropes, we have shelves filled with books within every genre of romance to ensure everyone feels included. It's right on the outskirts of downtown, and it's been a dream come true."

"That sounds really dope. I don't think I've heard of anything like that before," Jameson says, his arm wrapping around the back of the chaise he sits on in a relaxed nature, his focus solely on me. *God this man is effortlessly gorgeous.*

"Yeah, the cherry bourbon sour is my favorite and it's one of the first drinks we created for the bar."

"What's it called there?" I should have known that question was coming.

"Oh! Um...it's called One Bed." His eyes never leave mine but now there is a deeper look of something within them. "It's the name of a trope and is a fan favorite with romance readers. It's when there is only one bed and the main characters are forced to share the same bed. One of the main characters always decides they'll sleep on the couch or floor and then eventually, ends up in the bed with the other. My favorite sub-trope of a one-bed scenario is when they're enemies, but they are actually obsessed with each other, and they *refuse* to sleep anywhere else, *but* in the bed. And then they end up having..." I stop myself and realize I've been rambling. Heat slowly creeps up to my cheeks, staining them a deep shade of pink. "Having, um, a really good time."

I'm not a prude by any means, but there is no way I am going to go into heavy detail about that scene. Clearing my throat, I lean back a bit and ask, "Why is it we never met? Janelle was one of my best friends during school and I don't know...I'm kind of shocked she never introduced us." There were several occasions I saw him walking the halls, but my younger self just didn't have the nerve to approach him. It wasn't until tonight that I realized he knew someone I was so close with.

"I find that interesting too." The hint of intrigue in his voice has me doubting which part he is responding to. "But I'm not complaining now. When we were in high school, we were all running around trying to figure out who we were, while also being horny little shits."

A laugh easily falls from my mouth. "We were horny little shits. I have never been so glad to be an adult as I am now. Ugh! I couldn't go back. I don't know about you, but there is this freedom in being myself as an adult. Not having that ever-present feeling of not being enough. And maybe, being a horny little shit isn't totally a teen thing." He sputters and all but chokes on his drink before he laughs. "Tell me more about you, about this business of yours?" I ask him, wanting to know more about him.

"After I finished my bachelors, I started flipping houses...Well, no. That's not entirely accurate. When I was a teen, I helped my best friend during the summer months and learned a lot about house remodels. I didn't start doing it on my own until after college. That's why I'm here actually. I'm starting a new project that's in the area while I wait to finalize on another." He rubs his hands together like he can't wait to get started on it. "I want to know more about this bar of yours."

Time flies by, talking with Jameson is easy. I can completely be myself, but as we talk a yawn works its way free. The music is still thumping in the background, but the crowd seems to be slowly dwindling.

I start to gather the napkins I've used, stuffing them in my empty plastic cup. A few servers started passing around small cups of water about an hour ago. Owning a bar drives me to clean up after myself, making it easier on the servers that will ultimately fret over my mess. I look over at Jameson who is slowly nodding his head to the beat of the music, piling up toothpicks from the hors d'oeuvres into his own cup. I take the opportunity to run my fingers up his arm to gain his attention.

"Jameson, thank you for hanging out with me tonight. It was really great to meet you, *officially* of course. I...Well. I didn't think I was going to have much fun, but you and Janelle really made this night worth it." This man is so fine and if I am going to say yes to anything else today, it is going to be to myself. And I know exactly what I want.

"I feel the same way." His smirk is devilish and disarming, which only rattles me more as I clench my thighs together. His fingers brush against my own as he continues to help me clear our table. Knocking over my napkin-filled cup, my gaze snaps to the exit as my nerves start to get the best of me as I assess how to get out of here quickly.

Jameson leans over, I watch him as he picks up the mess that fell to the floor and looks back up at me with a soft smile. His deep-brown eyes meet mine and it's as if the room quiets completely. I could drown in him, and there's no way I can walk out of here without trying. Before he can say anything more, I interrupt him not wanting to lose my nerve.

"I have to head home, but..." My thoughts stall. *It's now or never Cassidy! You are a grown-ass woman and this man is so into you!* I shift my weight a bit, nervous about the invitation that is burning a hole in my clutch and finally pull it free. "I hope I'm not being too forward, but here's my number."

I wanted to be forward and give my number to him; I needed to have it written down and ready to give him because I was bound to talk myself out of doing so. I hand him my cell number that I scribbled on the back of the reunion invite. "Call me, sometime, if you want. Have a great night!"

Quick on my feet, I'm already walking away as he takes the invite from my hand and smiles. *Hopefully I didn't read this situation wrong*, I think to myself as he starts to stand, but I am already waving goodbye and moving toward the exit. My nerves are very much getting the best of me. I know he is as into me as I am him, but I don't want to wait around for the possibility of a no. I can hear the beat of the music slowly fade as the click of my heels becomes louder.

Pressing the metal bar that will release the lock, I take a deep breath and open the door and I'm met with the pleasantly warm night air that pebbles my skin. I may be standing here now, ten years later, but seeing him again is like I'm right back in the heat of teenage dream bliss, I have hope that the flirty glances we shared turn to something much more. A crush that I never acted on, never let myself dive too deep into, but tonight feels like it could be fate... or good karma, whatever it is they call it.

Unlocking my car door, I climb in and press the locks before turning it on. I pull out of the parking lot and roll the windows down to enjoy the evening breeze whip through my curls. Nothing short of death could steal away the effect he left on me.

3

Cassidy

> I can't wait to see you babes at Benny's! OOH, that's a good group chat name.

Group chat name has been updated to Babes at Benny's

The alarm from my phone sounds in the background, letting me know that if I don't get my ass moving I'll be late. I slap my hand at it, knocking it to the floor in the process. Setting multiple alarms should help me stay on time and on track of when I need to leave—what it actually does is give me a false sense of security, blanketing me in my own lies. Kicking my legs at the tangled sheet, I truly feel like a toddler at this moment. Throwing a temper tantrum because my sandwich wasn't cut the exact way I wanted. Today is just one of those days that I would rather stay in bed, but I have things I need to get done. I peel the duvet back, sit up, and force myself out of bed.

Living upstairs above the bar, allows me extra time to get my day started and saves me a good sum of money in rent and utilities. When I first thought of Shaken Tropes, I knew I was going to want to have my own business near town, instead of downtown. Instead of needing to pay for two separate mortgages, I opted to buy a building that could work in both capacities. It didn't hurt that I stumbled on a construction company nearby that could accomplish everything on my wishlist. The owner is a goliath but a softy at heart, we became fast friends during the design portion, and created my own sanctuary that encompassed my business too. I have future plans for my apartment when Lo and I decide to expand; he worked up mocks of future remodel possibilities.

Folding the sheet and duvet over my bed, I straighten my satin-covered pillows and pour a glass of water from my bedside carafe. The sky is all blue; not a cloud in sight. At least, not from my bedroom window. It's going to be a great night to stargaze from the rooftop deck... one that is all mine. There is nothing that fills me with all-encompassing joy than when I get to enjoy a cocktail while I send some much needed wishes up to the moon.

I take in a deep breath at the thought of holding a cafe con leche, and the scent of bourbon hits my nose from downstairs. It takes me right back to being introduced to the boy I had a thing for all those years ago, who is very much a man now. *A sexy one,* my inner voice reminds me.

Jameson's thick, muscled arms felt like a comforting weight as he wrapped them around my center stopping me from falling on my face after he ran into me. He was gentler than I expected for a man of his size—limber too, with all the dancing we did. The way his hands ghosted along my waist with feather-soft touches left me almost panting with a deep want to know how his hands would feel in other places.

My phone dings, pulling me out of my thoughts and reminding me of those *worthless,* and possibly forgetful, hands. Hands that couldn't bother to call or text me. Not even once. It has been two days since the reunion and I'm not one to rush anyone but, *come on*. Two days is enough time to say something, anything. He seemed so interested. I'm frustrated, convinced the attraction was one-sided.

Shrugging and shaking my head, I guess spicy romance really is taking over my mind and...well, I find myself looking for romantic scenarios. What girl doesn't want swoon-worthy love? I shrug my shoulders up to my ears at no one but myself. I guess I could have imagined it, spicy romance has quickly become a *not so* guilty pleasure, because I don't feel guilty for enjoying something so damn good. I can't even count how many fictional relationships I have right now. But no matter how fine they are, they are not keeping my sheets warm at night. At this point, my bed might as well be frostbitten.

Since the reunion, Facebook's *people you may know* feature has continued to push him in my face. I know I should remove the pop-up, but I can't force myself to, not after all the years of crushing on him during high school. Not yet, at least. He has a handsome face I want to throttle, but he doesn't truly deserve my energy if he's not interested. *On to the next* as Paloma would say. I'm a crippling romantic and I am holding out, hoping for my whirlwind romance.

Flicking on the bathroom light, I dig underneath the vanity and grab my hair dryer, along with my favorite curly hair attachment, and plug it in. Before clicking on my diffuser, not trusting my internal clock, my eyes snap up to check the time in the corner of the vanity, and it looks like I was right not to trust myself. I needed to be out of here five minutes ago, so it looks like I am going out into the world looking like a waterlogged rat instead.

Putting the blow dryer down, I sweep my hair back in a low ponytail that's parted down the middle and apply a swipe of red lipstick. Wiggling my hips I pull on my jean shorts and button them before pulling on a soft white t-shirt that is slightly oversized. These high waist shorts are soft from years of wear, a clear favorite in my wardrobe, they hug my curves just the way I like. I tuck my shirt in a bit and pair my outfit with sandals the color of dark mustard, and head out the door. Just as I am walking down the stairs, my phone chirps with an incoming video call and Paloma's bright, caramel eyes and wine-colored hair fills my screen.

I swear this woman is probably the only person I will answer a random video call from. "Hola, babe! How are we feeling this morning?" She wiggles her eyebrows at me and the large, gold hoops that dangle from her ears twist back and forth as she bounces in her seat. My lips twitch, cracking my resting bitch face as it always does when we're talking.

"Today is going to be a good day," I declare. "I refuse to focus anymore on Mister Tall, Dark, and Bulldozer-y."

"Forget him babe, if he isn't going to call you then it's his loss. You are a fucking catch! On to the next one," she chirps from the other side of the phone.

"I know, I know. I just felt this chemistry with him and it's bothering me," I respond, letting my annoyance seep through my voice. I circle my hand in a flourish instead of expressing how ridiculous I feel for wanting this connection so badly. Okay, maybe I am going to focus on him a bit more. One night at a reunion and I am stuck on him. And for what? "I'm heading out the door right now to meet you both for brunch. Are we still meeting at our spot?"

"Of course we are! They have these new waffles I want to try," she says, almost dancing in response. Paloma loves waffles, at this point, I think she's in a relationship with them.

"Okay babes, I will be there in ten..." I sing-song the last few words to her.

"Do you want me to swing by and pick you up?" she offers, causing me to lean back and peer at the clear, blue sky from the side door window. It's a perfect day.

"Nope, it's only a ten-minute walk. I think the fresh air will do me good. But you can drop me back off because I am going to need to be rolled out of there," I say.

"You and me both!" she replies before we disconnect the call. I push open the door to the bar, locking it before turning on the paved sidewalk on my way to Eggs Benny.

Swinging the heavy wood door of our favorite brunch spot open, my eyes immediately find Paloma who must have walked in moments before me. Her arms are outstretched to me and a high-pitched squeal catches us both by surprise, freezing us in the moment. Paloma and I both look toward the upstairs foyer where the squeal originated to see one of our oldest friends. Janelle's joy is contagious.

I couldn't contain the elation I felt when she called me yesterday, saying she was free today and really wanted to get together with us since it has been a decade since she last saw Paloma. Our screams and giggles quickly follow as we rush up the stairs, pulling each other into bear hugs.

"Oh my freaking God, Paloma! It's so damn good to see you girl." Janelle's voice is an octave higher than normal as she pulls back from Paloma, just enough to look into her face. I can feel the joy radiating out from all of us.

"I know! And it already feels like the summer pool days!" Paloma answers, pulling Janelle into another hug; each of us giving each other kisses on the cheeks.

I turn to pull the red, leather-upholstered chair out and lounge into the pillow-soft seat. My eyes take in our surroundings, noting the small changes Benny has made since the last time we were here. I take in the plush decor while my two best friends do the catching up they missed out on at the reunion. Eggs Benny is an interesting spot—soft, eclectic maximalist is what I would call it. There are booths of different shades in every color palette, mis-matched chairs, and tables of different sizes and materials. Everything somehow blends together so well.

I drop my head back, swaying my shoulders to the soft music playing in the background, and allow a lazy grin to form as I look up to the ceiling. The light fixtures are full of art pieces that were installed around bulbs. Some have half a red painted chair, others with the sexy lady leg lamp from that Christmas movie everyone loves. Sinking deep into the plush cushions of the seats, it's like sitting on a cloud and I consider for a moment how I can sneak it out of here. I know just the place for it in my apartment. I think he figured if the chairs were soft, people would eat more and not conspire to steal them. If I could fit it in my bag, he'd have a real problem on his hands.

I stifle a giggle noticing the comics on Paloma's newspaper-printed chair cushion. "What's so funny?" Paloma asks. I point toward her cushion, she tilts her hips slightly, looking down at her seat before joining in with her own snicker. Almost as soon as Janelle's butt hits the seat, she stands, brushing her hands against her ass.

"Tell me if I have a whole poodle on my butt?" She turns around, bending slightly to give us a view of what the offending faux fur chair may have left.

"You're good babe! No poodle butt for you today. Not yet, anyway!"

I wiggle my fingers, making grabby hands at her. I love the vibes at Eggs Benny, and I love it even more, now that Janelle is here to share it with us.

"What can I get for the most beautiful trio of ladies I have ever laid my eyes on?" Benny greets the table. He's an older gentleman who bought this building with his husband a few years ago and we fucking love him. The previous owner was a grouchy old lady.

Paloma purses her lips and says in a teasingly mocking tone, "You are laying it on mighty thick this morning, Benny Boy."

He throws his hands up in mock defense, his fingers wiggling on either side of his head as a sassy smirk causes his cheeks to point. Leaning forward, he kisses each of our cheeks. Both sides. Benny loves a flourish and it's my absolute favorite thing about him. He isn't scared to be himself, fully and without apology. Claiming right here at this moment, I want to be like him when I grow up. "How are you girls this morning and who is this?" He wiggles his brows.

"Benny, this is Janelle. We all went to high school together and she's visiting for a little while. Janelle, this is Benny, he is scandalous. Believe nothing he says." I giggle, introducing them.

With theatrical flair, he clutches at his neck, as though reaching for a strand of pearls in a feigned display of offense. Rolling his eyes slightly, he bends at the knee and covers his mouth to whisper to Janelle. I giggle as he begins speaking loud enough for Lo and I to hear as well. "I'm a proud tease. I'd flirt with a biscuit if it would talk back."

Janelle reaches out her hand like an eighteenth-century dutchess and bats her eyelashes at Benny. "It is a pleasure to make your acquaintance, Lord Teaserton."

"Oh, the pleasure is all mine," he says as we scooch back into our seats.

At this point I don't even bother with a menu; I look at Janelle, knowing it's her first time. Her shoulders are relaxed even while reading over the item descriptions, intermittently pausing to share some juicy gossip with Lo about people from the reunion, their dance moves something of the future. They were zig-zagging all over the floor, stepping on toes, but the joy on their faces was everything. I still made sure to keep my toes far away from those foot crunchers they called feet.

When Janelle looks up at me, a twinkle in her eyes, it's all the confirmation I need as I knew she'd love it here, it's like she's always been a part of our trio, even during the ten year hiatus. And the feeling of rightness, in this moment, with the crew back together, it'd take a nuclear explosion to pry me away.

"What can I get you ladies?" Paloma orders the honey and lime fried chicken and waffles and Janelle opts for a Tex-Mex omelet with toast. Both rattle off their orders so we can get to girl talk and stuff our faces. Benny then turns towards me with a knowing look as I hand him the menus I've gathered.

"Benny, can you ask Ralph to make me something new…surprise me!" We have tried every single item on the menu since they opened. So, I started pushing Ralph, the head cook, to create new things. He always creates something amazing, he literally can not make anything bad. "And a pitcher of your sunrise sangria, pretty please." I can already feel the bubbles on my tongue from the lemon-lime soda, the tart citrus flavors that make me forget there is red wine mixed in to create the perfect brunch drink.

He shushes me and walks off with our orders, waving goodbye for the moment. Off to tend to other customers or flirt with his hubby. The girls and I take the time to catch up on life. It doesn't take long before we all feel as though we never lost touch. Some people just click, and it's always been that way with the three of us.

"Sooo, Lo, who are you seeing right now?" If she wasn't my best friend, I probably wouldn't catch the slight tightness in Lo's shoulders at Janelle's question. It's a question she's asked often when we're with friends or when her mom calls, but she's never been the relationship type. It has been years since Paloma actually dated anyone seriously. She may have had a few casual flings here and there, one that resulted in an actual boyfriend, but it fizzled out as quickly as it started.

"Men are not on my radar. The bar has all my attention," Paloma responds, her voice confident. I eye her from the top of my glass of sangria that I have been drinking like juice. Benny garnishes the glass with a fresh slice of orange, making the entire drink that much better. "I know it may not be the norm, but I don't want to date around. Cass and I have worked so hard to build, not just Shaken Tropes, but the brand around it." Her eyes skate to me for just a moment before continuing, "I'm kind of hoping we get the chance to expand in the near future. I don't want a relationship to take my focus away right now. It's not worth the heartbreak or the effort."

Janelle moves to grab her sangria, taking a sip before responding, "Hey, I get it, Lo! Do what feels right for you. I'm not dating anyone either. I mean, I'd like to put myself out there and I have, but being active duty doesn't give me much time aside from online dating. I know it works for so many, but I've not had any luck with it." She shares her own reasons for singleness and continues, "I'm proud of you for standing in what your needs are and I am so ready to see this bar of yours. Cass told me a bit about it at the reunion and it sounds incredible!" Then her eyes turn toward me, but before she can ask the question that I know is sitting on the tip of her tongue, out comes Benny with our food.

Paloma's eyes widen into saucers as soon as she sees the chicken and waffles, and I can't lie, it looks absolutely delicious. So does Janelle's meal.

He sets my plate in front of me and I do my best not to drool. "Ralph wanted to try something a little different for one of your favorites. Chorizo gravy and biscuits with a sweet potato hash and a honey whipped butter."

"You tell your husband that I love him." I point my fork at Benny's chest to ensure he knows how serious I am before I holler toward the kitchen, "Ralph I love you!" Knowing Ralph can hear me from this distance, I can see in my mind's eye the smile that I know he has on his face.

We all enjoy the food, sampling from one another's choices. At one point, Paloma almost took out my finger when I attempted to grab a bite, she gets a bit stabby over waffles. We joke and people-watch those around us.

"We should plan a trip!" I say, and Paloma's gaze turns to me, honey drips from her mouth as she stuffs another bite in, nodding her head in agreement.

"Gol, yuspft," Janelle tries and fails to speak. We all make eye contact and burst out laughing—yes, we all somehow understood what she said.

"Fuck, that was way funny!" Holding my face from the pains of laughter, I grin and continue, "Janelle, I know you'll have to give us your schedule but I think we should, it'll be like old times."

"I am so down! Ooh, let's go on a cruise!" Paloma exclaims, clearly excited by the thought of it.

"But isn't that more like a couples' kind of thing?" I furrow my brows in question. For whatever reason I imagine a cruise with a significant other. You know, drinking our fill while going on excursions that turn steamy, someone to snuggle in the sheets with. Never did I think of a cruise as a girls' trip.

"Girl, no! There are all types of cruises. Maybe we can find one that's adults-only and all-inclusive. One that stops at a lot of good beaches!" Paloma says, waving off my comment.

"True! We could also rent out a badass house instead. Ooh, on the beach in Tulum or something." Janelle then adds, giving us both a judgy look through her lowered lashes, "Just remember I need time to put in the request! I will not be missing this."

"Now, that is a couples' thing. I love y'all, but if I am in Tulum, I want to be getting my cheeks clapped under the stars." I pinch my lips together before Paloma slaps the table with the palm of her hand and squeals. We all start laughing again, clearly we've had our fill of sangria. This is exactly why we choose Benny's upstairs deck when the days are nice. It's a covered deck and all the surrounding, sliding glass doors are open, allowing the warm breeze in. We've been here for a couple of hours and even I am feeling far past tipsy.

Pushing my glass back, I grab a piece of my remaining biscuit, stuffing it in my mouth as if that is going to help soak up the alcohol. Eventually, Janelle brings up how much she missed Paloma at the reunion.

"I have to know"—Paloma looks at Janelle—"what is up with your boy Jameson?" My eyes go wide and I turn my head, blatantly staring at her. After hanging out with both Janelle and Jameson for most of the night, they seemed like they were as close of friends as Paloma and I, and I told her just that. I just didn't think she would bring it up.

"What do you mean?" she asks curiously.

"Aren't you two good friends?" Confusion is written all over Paloma's face.

"I mean, we were close in high school. I kind of lost touch with everyone once I enlisted," she says. "Cassidy, you two were eye fucking the entire night, what happened with that?"

I look around for the exits, why am I suddenly under attack?

"All that *eye fucking* and your girl here can't even get a text back." Maybe it was me frantically throwing my number in his lap, but I know he was feeling the pull just as much as I was. "I gave him my number, but no call or text. I guess he wasn't as interested as I thought he was," I respond, absentmindedly pulling my wine glass to me and realize it's empty. I shrug my shoulders, and run my finger over the rim of the glass, giving one of my hands something to do.

"Babe, you called me and told me the man looked"—Lo purses her lips— "hmm, how did you put it... Depraved!" She snickers and a blush sneaks up my neck and cheeks.

"Cass, I don't know. He was eating you up. There is no way that man just up and ghosted you, not that I don't believe you, because I do. But there has to be an explanation. Do you want me to call him? Kick him in his shin? I'm up for either option," Janelle offers, toeing her foot softly at my shin.

I shake my head, huffing a frustrated sigh under my breath. "No babe, I'm fine. I'm going to chalk it up to a fun night with friends and those heavy-poured cherry bourbon sours," I answer, letting her off the hook. If he wanted to connect, he would have. No matter what I say, I can still feel the sagging in my shoulders and the bits of hope I was holding on to flutter away.

Paloma grabs my knee and squeezes. "Enough about men, when are we going to the pool? We can plan our trip while tanning."

"Lo is right! My parents changed it to a salt water system a few years back and let me tell you... my skin feels as smooooth as a baby's butt when I get out," Janelle exclaims as she wraps her arms around herself and rubs them in fake seduction.

Benny walks over, placing a hand on my shoulder before he lays the check on the table. I look down for a moment before snapping my now-narrowed eyes back to him, immediately stuffing my hand in my pocket to quickly pull out my wallet; I decided to come only with the necessities since I walked here. I can hear bits of commotion at the table as I struggle to pull out my credit card. I dare a peek at my best friends, hoping I beat them to the bill.

They are both furiously digging in their bags for their cards. "Trying to pay the tab first I see," I tease, with a menacing voice. Whipping out my credit card, I slap it in Benny's outstretched hand as whispered curses and laughs are released around the table. He knows the drill, Paloma and I are constantly attempting to pay the tab before the other.

Before Janelle gets in her rideshare, she looks over at Paloma and me, smiling brightly. We promised that next week, we will get together for a pool day at her parents' house. We'll flesh out our trip a bit more and pray Paloma doesn't become a lobster. I make a mental note, as I wave goodbye to Janelle, that I will pack extra sunscreen just in case.

Paloma drops me off at the bar but doesn't come up since we will see each other later to open up. Just as my hand reaches for the door I notice a blue and white notice attached to the door knob, I snatch it off and sloppily place it on my desk before making my way upstairs. I'm tipsy and really just want to relax before my shift. It's probably something new happening at the Night Market. I make a mental note to read the advertisement or review their social media to confirm the events—I love that place.

Lo cut herself off at one drink early into brunch as she knew she would be driving, we are both very serious about drinking and driving, as in, we don't. End of story. There are too many stories about drunk drivers and accidents, we don't intend on being a part of the problem.

I strip my clothes off for an oversized Shaken Tropes t-shirt that I cut the neckline out of for more slouch, a pair of comfy shorts, and my bunny-eared fuzzy slippers that I should probably throw away, but I love them too much. All the others I tried to replace them with broke instantly and I don't want to splurge on a new pair either. They are slippers for God's sake, let me be comfy. The slap of my slippers against the hardwood floors echoes as I open the fridge and grab a bottled peach tea. I lift my laptop from the bartop counter and plop down on the couch.

The space I created on the top floor of the building is my own personal sanctuary. Plants are hanging all over the place, others set on shelves, really any place I can rest them. I made sure to place hooks along the border of the bay window, giving my favorite spot a place for my pothos to grow.

Though I didn't want my home and business to be downtown, I still love looking at the skyline once the sun sets. I get a beautiful view of the town day and night.

Floating shelves sandwich the window, all of which house a few of my favorite reads, candles, and plants. I kick off my slippers and dig my toes into the soft, dark-green rug in my living room while I open my laptop to do a last minute inventory before getting down to the bar.

Social media is my Achilles heel and I catch myself scrolling after working through last minute inventory changes Paloma sent over. My eyebrows lift at seeing Jameson cross my screen again and before I can stop myself, I click on "add friend" and promptly slap the top of my laptop down, closing off the heat I feel rising in my cheeks. Sure the FBI is watching me through my camera as I buy more smut, but they will not be catching me blazing with embarrassment over digitally befriending a man, my old teenage freaking crush. I need to draw the line somewhere!

"You know what, it's fine. So you sent him a friend request after he didn't bother to text or call you. Maybe he lost it," I grumble to myself. Though isn't losing it just as bad? My phone pings with a notification showing me that Jameson accepted my friend request. Hmmm.

Then I notice the time and realize I must have had my head down in the wine order for longer than I thought. I really need to start getting ready. It may be a slower night but we love book club, which is always a hoot. It was an idea from one of our regulars. One night a week to come together, get out of the house, and talk spicy reads together. Paloma ran with it and now we host Toasted Book Club every week!

I know she can handle book club, but I want to be there in case Paloma wants to head out. Kicking off my slippers by my bedroom door, I grab one of the many black Shaken Tropes t-shirts I own and a pair of linen shorts.

> Hey babes! Are you already downstairs?

Lo

> Yeah, the last minute shipment for the case of wine just came in.

Ooh yummy! Maybe it'll be slow enough to try it out.

Lo

Mmhm, but you know how the girls at book club get. Lol

Don't I know it. Coming!

I slip on my sneakers before walking towards slipping through the door to head downstairs. As soon as I close the door I can hear Paloma unlocking the front door of the bar and welcoming our book club patrons. Tonight it's all about secret identity with a splash of childhood sweetheart. The group is brimming with excitement to chat it up, their laughter filling the room causes me to smile too.

As I'm lining up the tart cherry tequila shots that I dubbed Crimson Bonds after the blood-red color, and also the name of the book for this month, one of the girls comes over. "Hi Cassidy, thank you again for hosting us here."

"Toya! You know I love hosting as much as you enjoy coming." Delight flitting through my tone. "I hear you ladies are switching over to dark fantasy next month? Maybe I can come up with a new drink for you... just let me know, okay?"

She hums to herself before saying, "Maybe something with fire and whiskey! Our female main character loves whiskey."

"Say less, babe!"

The night wears on, but no new customers come in who aren't already here for book club. Once Paloma finishes unpacking the crate of wine, she walks over, hands me a bottle, and all but pushes me out of our bar to relax.

"You are here every moment of every day, take your ass home and don't come back down, girl. Try the wine and let me know if you think it works for Shaken. Bye bitch!" She blows me a kiss and I swear my eyes are going to get stuck in the back of my head with how hard I roll them.

I take her advice and tread back up the stairs knowing the wine is going to be incredible. My fuzzy bunny slippers are calling my name.

Three glasses of the sweetest red wine I have ever tasted later, and everything feels too hot. When I came upstairs from the bar I just wanted to breathe. Forgoing changing into my tank and pajama shorts, I threw my clothes in the laundry room and wrapped myself in my soft cotton robe. Though even the deep purple robe feels too warm against my skin.

I notch the air conditioner on and untie my robe before turning up the old school R&B music that is pumping through my speakers. I catch a glimpse of myself in the floor-length mirror in my room as I sway to the song. The smart lights glow and flow smoothly, pulsing along with the beat of the music in deep pinks and dark oranges. The set of lingerie I have on is my favorite, and I wear it often because it makes me feel damn good. The panties sit high up on my hips, the outline of my belly prominent, as is my cleavage. I take the opportunity to bend over, twist, and move my body to the music as I dance, and snap full-body pictures along with favorite areas of my body.

Lying over the edge of my bed, my hair just barely touching the floor from the height of the frame. I roll over, pulling my sheets over me, wanting to scroll through the pictures I took. Wanting to get rid of the ones I'm not fond of. I click on the photos app but my phone pings with a reminder, drawing my attention to something more interesting.

Send your new friend Jameson a message!

The notification stays there for a few moments before I decide I will, in fact, send him a message, and show him exactly what he is missing. Flicking through the pictures, I look over a couple I snapped while on my bed, my heart skipping a beat as I hover over my favorite before clicking share. I rattle a message to him, pouring a bit of brat into it as my fingers move rapidly over the keyboard. The moment I hit "send", a wave of clarity along with the heat of embarrassment overtakes me, climbing up my neck, face, and ears. What the fuck was I thinking? Sending a man I barely know racy photos of me. My gaze slowly drifts to the empty bottle of wine and I consider how I feel. I'm a grown-ass woman and I can send photos to whomever I please. It was a *yes* that, when I sit here and think about it, I'm proud of. I hope he drools himself into oblivion for what he's missing out on. Satisfied with myself again, the wine finally hits my system, and I doze off.

4

Jameson

Mama

We're rollin' with the homies, as you kids say.

Pops

Honey, no one says that.

laughing emoji Take plenty of pics Mama.

Music thumps from the bluetooth speaker that I set on the vanity. I packed a couple of speakers with me to bring to this project. I knew I was going to be staying here until the tenant was out of my parents' place and then I would make that my temporary home.

My mom often talked about traveling the world in their *'suped up* camper as my dad called it. An RV that neither of them owned until I was halfway through my freshman year of college. Once I was settled into college life it seemed like those two made a beeline to the closest RV dealership, they couldn't be out of there quicker. "A push present to Mama," Pops said. I remember telling him that she pushed me into this world eighteen years ago and he quickly said he'd push me right out the door too if I kept up my back talk. We laughed, but I knew he was somewhat serious.

They left the house to me after they got the tricked out camper and said to *treat her right,* and that's what I've been doing. I knew they thought I would flip her and use it as a starter fund and in a way, I did. But instead of selling it to someone else, I kept it and worked on it when I had down time before renting it out.

My parents bought this land and the tiny house it was sitting on. Throughout the years they remodeled, building on rooms and enlarging others, they really made it something of their dreams, I couldn't put a price tag on sentimentality.

They've been all over the place, and are currently somewhere close to the Glacier National Park, getting their sights in. I shake my head, knowing I'll be getting a load of pictures of the same mountain from my mom soon.

The water is starting to run cold, so I turn it off and step out of the shower. My plans were to flip this house, one I very much need a name for. I always name my projects something that evokes what the house could feel like to potential buyers, and bring quick cash flow into Crew Construction and Consult. But the more and more I work on this particular property, the less I want to sell it. Making it a short-term rental property may be the better way to go; I'm not sure why I never thought of it for this house.

I pull my lips in as I consider the other property I bought at the same time as this one—it's in a better area to sell. It's a two hour flight from here, which is great since I'll need to go visit that location when I'm about halfway done with this one.

Tucking the towel in tightly around my waist, a notification interrupts the music only for a second, reminding me I need to get a move on. Project management needs to start for this new house if I am going to stay on target to finish in eight weeks. It's tight, but it is possible given the house has great bones and doesn't need much work, it's all cosmetic and add-ons.

Being back in my hometown is most definitely a blast from the past, this place holds a lot of great memories for me. I've come back occasionally for meetings at Crew's home office but I wasn't staying for fun. More in and out to get a job done before I'm needed on another project.

When I got the reunion invitation in the mail, I knew I wanted to be here. Not because I wanted to relive any of my past, but because I knew I would get a chance to catch up with people I hadn't seen in years. And yeah, okay, maybe show off a bit. I've changed a lot since high school like everyone has, I assume. I'm proud of the life I've built for myself; my confidence wasn't sky-high during school and now, I feel pretty damn good about myself.

My phone chirps through the speakers again, reminding me to check my messages and notifications from the night before, I reach for it and lean against the vanity. My lips twitch when I see who has been messaging me. I got a few friend requests the other night from old friends after the reunion, one being from Cassidy. Considering she gave me a faulty number, I'm surprised to see she sent me a request at all. Could it have been a mistake?

Of course it was, she was the one who offered it to me, I didn't even ask for her digits. I'd wracked my brain trying to remember her last name, I didn't catch it at the reunion. I rub my hand down my face, realizing I could have reached out to Janelle but I didn't consider that at the time. I wasn't going to make a fool out of myself.

At least not again.

I thought I made it pretty clear how attractive I thought she was and how interested I was in her. When we went to high school together, we didn't know each other but I saw her. Everywhere. She was beautiful even then, always clutching one of those zip-up purple binders with a book or two, but now... she's stunning. I haven't been able to get her off my mind. She has this soft energy that evens out her loud infectious laugh and quick wit. And the kind of curves I would gladly cherish, I wanted to kneel at her feet and get my fill of her. Though I don't think I could ever get enough of a woman like her.

Clicking on the notification, the app pulls up her messages and my mind scrambles, almost dropping my phone in the process. The picture is framed by a gold mirror that's on her floor, but fuck if that is where my eyes are. She is lying on her side in nothing but a sheer lace bra and a sheet covering the apex of her thighs. Her breasts spill over, giving me a hint of the dark rosy areola. I follow her lines, seeing how the valleys and hills of her hips create a space where I want my tongue to explore. She has the sheet draped over where her panties are and I find myself wanting to peel back the sheet with my teeth. My eyes squint as if that will help me see through the deep-green fabric that covers her but also enhances the warm tan of her skin.

Fuck.

Her thighs are large and even through the picture, I can tell they're soft. I palm my cock through the towel as I force myself to scroll up, wondering if she sent a message along with this, telling me that these are just for me. Even now, I don't want to consider these being for another man. I don't know what I did to deserve this but I plan on making it up to her the moment she gives me a chance.

Instead, I'm met with another picture and I groan at how hard I am.

This time she's laying down with her head hanging off the end of her bed, her eyes staring straight at the camera, at me, and fuck if that doesn't make me relive past fantasies. Her ample cleavage spills over and out of her bra, and her legs are spread but I can't see much from the angle she is at. What I can see is that one of her hands is gripping her breast and then slides down then back up, gripping her breast again, in a boomerang loop. I involuntarily stroke myself at the thought of where that hand is going, at it being my hand.

When I finally pry my eyes off of her and scroll a bit more, I finally get her message.

Cassidy Heart

> This could have been yours but you never texted me. *peace sign emoji*

Oh, this woman has no idea what she just started. I swipe my hand across the fogged mirror to clear the condensation, water droplets stick to the glass, just enough for her to see exactly what I want her to. I take a few steps back towards the door. Angling my camera at the mirror, I grip my aching cock through the plush material. This causes my makeshift garment to partially fall away behind me. I stroke myself slightly before tossing the towel to the mirror as I take a Live Photo, obscuring her view completely. My locs hang down the front of my chest as I tip my head forward slightly and snap a picture, only for her. I want her to see exactly what she does to me.

> I would have taken those pics for you if you gave me the right number, Babygirl.

Chuckling, I set my phone down to fully dry my hair, getting lost in my thoughts from the night of the reunion. When I opened the front door of Cypress Lake High, I was stunned by how well the inside of the building was decorated. Looking at the outside, I felt like I was suddenly stuck in the past. Curls caught my attention and I scoured the main hall to determine who I thought they might belong to, who I *hoped* they belonged to.

I lost them as soon as I saw them before an old acquaintance called my name and clapped his hand against my back. We caught up on some small talk before Anderson, my best friend, saved me by returning an earlier missed call I left about a house remodel. He all but forgot that I wouldn't be on the property since I was coming to my ten year high school reunion. I gave my old classmate an apologetic headnod before throwing my thumb over my shoulder towards the gym where the main area of the reunion was happening. I made my way towards the gym and ran into the girl I had a crush on throughout all four years of high school.

I quickly ended the call with Anderson, just in time to catch her by the elbow. I let my gaze fully assess this woman who had taken over my thoughts at random throughout the years. She was stunning, her clothes melting into voluptuous curves that would make anyone stare, and I was—staring, that is. It was a hell of a task to force myself to look at her eyes. But when I did, I was met with her deep-brown gaze which held more surprise than shock, enticing me to lean closer.

It was definitely her; I never caught her name all those years ago and somehow I was tongue-tied at the worst time. Unable to think of asking for her name, I pulled on my normal, calm, confident demeanor like a warm coat. She probably didn't even know who I was and possibly nervous that a stranger just barreled into her but she smiled back at me, giving me a gentle nudge towards ease. I gently released her from my grasp, made a parting comment I can't even remember, turned on my heel and made my way into the gym. Music and the sound of rain bounced off the walls, but all I could hear was the erratic thumping of my own heartbeat. I was too nervous to ask for her name all those years ago and I let my teenage nerves flatline my chance just a moment ago, but I wouldn't be letting that happen again, not a third time.

Bumping into Janelle was a highlight of the night, she was an amazing friend. We tried to date, and by try, I mean we went on one date to a diner all the kids would go to, we shared a cheeseburger and a double order of fries before making our minds up that we were far better friends than whatever we thought we could be romantically. The experience strengthened our friendship, we were each other's shoulders to lean on, or we ended up roasting each other to bits.

As soon as Janelle waved me over, I spotted those long, chestnut curls swaying back and forth as she chatted away with her friend. I didn't take my eyes off her for the remainder of the night. She was funny, easy to talk to, and downright sexy. Cassidy. And right now, these pictures are going to do me in.

Seeing her bountiful thighs in this picture, absently I bite into my bottom lip imagining how sweet she must taste. Cassidy had this way about her all night and I wanted to get to know her more. So, when she quickly gave me her number, I did my best to remain cool and not show just how excited I was that she beat me to it. Except, when I sent her a quick text, telling her I hoped she made it home safely and to save my number, my smile quickly fizzled out when the response that came back was from Alma, an eighty-seven year old woman who was up late watching Criminal Minds.

Alma

> Oh honey, you have the wrong number. I wish I
> was about 40 years younger, now my walks on
> the beach are a lot slower. *winky face*

I couldn't help but laugh at Alma's advances. I let her know that I might just take her up on her offer.

Now that Cassidy messaged me on social media, I'll put the ball back in her court. My ringtone sounds from the countertop, pulling me out of my thoughts completely. Anderson Jones' name shows on the screen of my phone, a picture of my niece in place of what would be his face. I hit the green button to accept the call.

"Anders, what's up?" If it wasn't my best friend I may not have bothered answering at all. Anderson and I have been friends since birth, our parents were close. And of course that made us what we are today, following in our parents' footsteps. I wouldn't have it any other way.

"What's going on man!" The joy is evident in his voice. "Just checking that we are still meeting up tonight to chat it up about the house you bought. I'm really glad to be flipping a house together, it's been too long."

Anderson has been a general contractor for years, his grandfather worked in housing construction and we would spend the summers with him when we were teenagers. *Becoming men* as his grandfather would tell us. Now we co-own Crew Construction and Consult, also known as Crew, or even Triple C as we sometimes call it.

Though we own it together, I own forty-five percent of the company and manage all the consulting clients we bring in. He fought me on being an equal partner, but Anderson was the one who built this company from the ground up. I came in later when he was ready to add a new wing to the business—back when it was just Crew Construction. He wanted more, and our partnership felt natural.

I bought this house in Cypress Lake on a whim, knowing it would be a great property for us to work on. Something about it really called to me, I couldn't pass it up. A few weeks after I signed the paperwork, a purple envelope showed up in my primary residence's mailbox—an invitation to my high school's graduating class' ten year reunion. It felt like a happy coincidence that the new project would be in my home town. I flew in a week early to enjoy the reunion and check on the tenants that were renting my childhood home.

"Yeah, man! But let's meet at this local bar I recently found out about a few days ago. There's someone there I need to check in with," I say. We agree to meet around seven; I disconnect the call and finish getting ready for the day.

If I am going to stay on target for this house, I need to finish up the budget for both the selling potential and the marketability of it as a short-term rental.

When I was younger I always thought I would wind up playing football and be some kind of NFL star. Don't get me wrong, I love the game but now that I am really working within my passion, I couldn't imagine being a professional athlete.

Shaking my head, I pull my locs back and pull on a deep-green beanie that matches my tracksuit before spraying my favorite cologne. If I'm going to get my truck detailed and oil changed before meeting up with Anders, my gaze snaps down to my watch, I *needed* to head out the door about five minutes ago. Toeing on my white sneakers, I rush out the front door.

With the maintenance for my truck out of the way I was able to make it to the bar a little earlier than Anders, looking around the parking lot to ensure I don't see his SUV, I make my way to the front doors.

Shaken Tropes has a lime green neon sign out in front, with large leafy green plants that line the walkway of the brick building. From the outside I can see the history of the building, the aged brick is something I have learned to love since I started flipping houses. This building reminds me why I fell in love with flipping and buying properties for possible clients.

The new builds we do for Triple C are beautiful but there is something about older buildings, there is a charm to them that is nearly impossible to recreate, and people will pay top dollar for character.

Cool air greets me as I pull open the bar's front door; the inside is modern with a cozy feel to it. Creating nooks for readers to lounge in while they sip their drinks. Edison bulbs hang from the ceiling allowing a sultry glow that pulls me closer towards the bar.

If luxury living and the coziness of a winter cabin had a baby with a library, this would be the vision, and I can't lie, I'm feeling it. The bar top is smack dab in the middle of the space with low back barstools that beg to be sat in, and I would do just that if I didn't have ulterior motives for being here.

Grabbing a booth in the back corner, I don't have to wait too long before a door swings open next to me and those wide hips come swaying out. My hands strain at the effort it takes for me not to reach out and grip them, to not slide her onto my lap. Those pictures she sent me are seared into my mind and now that I'm here she is all I can think about. Like the creep that I apparently am, I continue to watch her.

I can tell this is her happy place, she smiles at all the customers and laughs with her friend who's behind the bar. She looks oddly familiar, but I don't spare her another glance as I am focused on Cassidy. I have it bad for a woman who I have had two conversations with, if I can even count the messages as a conversation.

I get up and start moving before I really know what I am going to say. But I do know one thing, I haven't gotten her off my mind since literally bumping into her, and I don't see that changing any time soon.

5

Cassidy

J-babe

Is "let him read your recs" code for sexy time?

Paloma doubles over in laughter as she wraps her arms around her stomach. I just finished showing her the message Jameson sent me about his old-lady girlfriend. "I don't think I have laughed that hard in months! So, you're competing with granny now, huh?" She laughs again and this time I join in.

"Imagine her coming out like, hold my bag, Helen!" She imitates what she thinks an old woman sounds like and sticks her tongue out, holding back a laugh. "I, for one, can't believe that is the same guy from high school. Age has done him more than good, babe!" She licks her lips and I playfully nudge her arm with my own.

"He is most definitely a cold glass of yummy I'd like to sip on. But I don't think he lives here. At least that's what it seems like when I look through his social media profiles."

"Yeah, well, maybe he doesn't keep it updated and *maybeeee* you should still get yourself a little taste of him." Paloma's voice takes on

59

a mischievous tone laced with a playfulness that I know will get us in trouble. Chaos, my best friend is chaos and I wouldn't have it any other way. I hip bump her and as I'm turning to help the customer who filled the stool behind me, I watch my best friend's eyes turn to saucers, and the scent of citrus and bourbon wraps around me.

"Taste of who?" The familiar voice is deep and sends a welcomed shiver down the center of my back, right to my core. When I fully face Jameson, his gaze is directly on me and I don't miss the sly grin that graces his lips. "Sounds like something I may enjoy, given that my girlfriend isn't much a fan of drinking in her old age."

Sinfully handsome and funny too, my kryptonite. "Hmm, maybe you would, but the verdict is still out on that." Cringing inwardly at myself, I can't, for the life of me, figure out why that is what I chose to say, but he only situates himself further, his eyes roaming over me. My body heats in response to his perusal which feels much more like a physical touch. "Anyway, what are you doing here?"

"I'm actually meeting a friend of mine about a project that I'm working on in town and I couldn't pass up an opportunity to see you," Jameson answers, pulling a stool out, he gets himself comfortable at the bar.

"Can I get you anything to drink while you wait, or maybe a book?" I wiggle my eyebrows at him as he huffs a laugh.

Forget the damn drink. Meeting his gaze again, I notice he is taking me in like I'm a cool beverage—the only one that can quench his real thirst. Without missing a beat he says, "Unfortunately, what I really want isn't on the menu." His voice lowers, causing me to lean further into his space to hear him. "So I'll settle for a whiskey and ginger ale."

I very much want to be on his menu.

Jesus, what is wrong with me? I read about instant love and lust all the time, but I never thought I would be standing here feeling some of those same feelings myself.

I turn, grabbing a tumbler and a whiskey from the top shelf, add a splash of ginger ale, and hand him the drink. Our fingers brush as he grips the glass, I don't miss his eyes connecting with my own as the heat from his fingertips warms my hand, traveling up my arm like an intimate touch. A touch that sends shockwaves of surprise through me, lighting up my entire body. Makes me wonder what his hands would feel like elsewhere. *Calm your nips.*

"You want to tell me how you managed to give me the wrong number?" His voice has an authoritative tone to it, his eyes still on me as if we are the only two people here.

I cough to hide the laugh at the thought of his elderly girlfriend before I answer, "Maybe you just misdialed." His eyebrows raise just a bit, a sardonic gesture that tells me even he knows better than that; he tips his head forward, urging me on. "Or...maybe I was a tad nervous and it was dark. Plus, all the strobe lights. It's a wonder my eyes don't twitch." Why am I rambling over a man I shared a few dances with? Maybe it's because, even though I'm nervous, he is every bit into me, and that is a power I am thrilled over.

Before I can say anything else, Paloma grabs my attention as she bumps into me. A quick apology is on her tongue, but I can tell she is quickly getting overwhelmed. Peering around this hulking man, I finally see things have picked up, significantly.

Though I'm enjoying Jameson's undivided attention and what it does to me, I turn to give him an apology of my own but a face belonging to a man I haven't seen in a while waltzes in. My eyebrows become quick friends with my hairline and my mouth drops slightly before I wave him over.

"Anderson? It's been too long, how are you? Are you stopping in for a drink?" I pepper him with questions as he claps a hand on Jameson's shoulder.

"Wait, you two know each other?" Jameson asks. This must be the person he is meeting with, what a small world.

"Hey, Cass," Anders greets me, pushing a closed fist my way. We do our handshake and I catch Jameson watching us, in awe as he chuckles in disbelief.

When I hired Triple C to remodel this place, there were days when things didn't go as planned. *With older buildings, it happens but we'll make it right* Anders would say, but for me, the constant shift in plans was always the first time. I never thought I would be buying my dream building, let alone remodeling it.

Remodel still feels like such an understatement when he ripped it down to its studs. On a particularly rough day, he walked up to me and grabbed my pinky with his own, before pressing our thumbs together and wiggling his fingers as he urged me to do the same. I remember huffing a laugh as the random act cut through the anxious fog I was suffocating in. Since that day, it has become a way to check-in with each other. He made the job easy because he was so trustworthy and did what he said he would. Moments like those blossomed into the friendship we have now; and even though it has been quite some time since he's stopped by, it doesn't matter. Some friends you talk with every single day and others, months or even years can pass.

"How do you have a handshake with Cassidy? We don't even have one! You've been holding out on me Anders!" Jameson's voice raises an octave, clearly in jest for his lack of a secret handshake.

"Don't be jealous, Jameson," I say, resting my palm on the bar. I lean into my hip before continuing, "We can have a handshake of our own."

Anders snorts at my comment and pays Jameson no mind, before answering my question about how they know each other. "This is the other owner of Crews, the one who does all the consulting and was out scouting new places when we were working here."

Anderson looks from side to side, taking in all the new updates since he's been in before he tilts his head in Jameson's direction. "He's also my best friend. It's been too long, Cass. The place looks great." He rests his forearm on the bar and I squint my eyes a bit, he is normally a man of very few words but maybe being with his best friend loosens his tongue.

It's been a few years since Anderson has been inside, well, since the grand opening come to think of it. When I bought the building, I hired Crews Construction and Consulting to separate the spaces and build out the bar of mine and Lo's dreams. Anderson became a quick friend with all the hours we spent together to get this place just the way we wanted. There was no way I could've known he was also Jameson's best friend, and now that I know, this information is blowing my mind. He has been so close to me this entire time.

I make my way around the bar, giving Anders a side hug before pointing at them both. "Anderson, it is so good to see you. We shouldn't allow another two years to go by, okay? I have to get back on drink duty but—" Knowing Anderson's no response, is in fact a response all on its own, I pull out my phone and turn to face Jameson. "What's your number?"

This somehow makes his grin deepen, it's beautiful and tugs at my heart, and on instinct I begin to raise my hand in my desire to touch him, but quickly change my mind, reminding myself that just because I read all about insta-love doesn't mean I want to jump the gun. His dimples peek through as he gives me a megawatt smile with perfectly straight teeth. He gives me his number and I make sure to send him a text, watching him as he leans his head down and peers at the screen. I can tell he has read it when his tongue peeks out a bit and he rubs his lips together. I nod with a smirk and turn to get a customer's order.

"Cassidy."

Hearing my name on his tongue with such an authoritative tone makes me stop in my tracks, a blush creeps up my neck to my cheeks, and I look at him from over my shoulder. Understanding he wants my eyes on him before he says anything else. "About that book recommendation?" My eyes almost dazzle, the thought of Jameson reading sends flutters low in my belly—but a recommendation from me? A book fiend's dream. "What about a book that fits the drink you were telling me about at the reunion, it's your favorite right? The one that started Shaken Tropes. I'd like to find out why."

One Bed.

He wants to find out why I love the one bed trope. And he remembered what I said, and fuck if it isn't sexy as hell. "Okay." My voice is husky as all the *one bed* scenes pop into the forefront of my mind, showing me what he is about to read. "Let me grab one for you."

The blue and black cover comes into view, the deep tones making it one of my favorites. Pulling it off the bookshelf, I tuck it under my arm as a customer approaches me about the upcoming tournament we've chatted about previously. He starts with the tournament and eventually asks for a sports romance focused on golf with a drink to match. "Let me just finish with this book rec and I'll be right over," I answer, making an internal note of where he sits down.

Last year we signed up to be a vendor at a professional golf tourna-ment, taking Shaken Tropes to the green. Paloma was actually the one to bring it up given she has experience with country clubs. She said it would be a great way to market us and invest in a charity event, it was an immediate *yes*.

I hustle my way back to Jameson, extending the book. "Here you go, it's one of my favorites. Treat it right." I glare at him, keeping my face stern as he takes the book, a soft smile gracing his face.

"Always." His answer feels like he is implying more than just the treatment of the book. I watch him for a moment as he makes his way over to where Anderson is now seated at a booth. I grab the towel off the countertop, toss it over my shoulder and get to work.

Shaken Tropes is packed tonight, whether it's regulars coming in for a spiked coffee and a book, or people walking in from downtown who are just intrigued with the space. Paloma distributed new flyers and has been pushing social media a lot lately. Clearly, it's paying off. When we first had the idea of the bar we were sure it would be a hit, there was no doubt in our minds. It was something we often saw in bigger cities or near popular tourist destinations, but there wasn't anything similar near us. We were certain, if we wanted it, then others must as well.

It has been four years since we opened the doors and I don't think I will ever regret it. We both took several bartending classes and made sure to hire a temporary bartender to help us learn in our own space. Brianna was amazing and pretty much taught us everything we know. She never left though, even after she finished training us she stayed on and became our lead bartender here. Though she did a bit of everything, from helping establish inventory, to connecting us with a chef who would make appetizers worthy of a book lovers' imagination, she also became a close friend. She told us sticking around Shaken Tropes allowed her time to work on her paintings, something she struggles to do when she is pressed behind a desk piled high with paperwork.

I can't help but continue to be grateful when I find more of my people.

Paloma and I work together to attend to all the new faces that are coming in tonight. Making quick work of drink orders and book recommendations as the afrobeats merge into a Lofi playlist that allows everyone to enjoy the music, but doesn't distract readers from their books.

As the night progresses there is one thing that is just as constant as the customers and book rec pairings—I can feel Jameson's eyes on me and it's taking everything in me not to meet his gaze. After depositing a book back in its rightful place on the shelf, I turn on my feet and head back towards the bar. My phone vibrates in my back pocket and a soft sigh escapes me as I look at the message.

Jameson

I could watch you do your thing all night, beautiful.

Am I melting right here and now? Maybe I should turn the air conditioner down just in case I turn into a puddle.

You're watching me?

Jameson

How could I not watch you?

A little creepy, no? *devil smile emoji*

Jameson

Not if you like it.

My mouth drops open and I involuntarily kegel... *Oh, I like it very much*. I snap my mouth shut and lean my back against the bar, replacing my shock with an insatiable grin, until I hear the two chatterboxes I'm sharing duties with tonight.

"What's got you smiling like that?" Brianna's voice perks up at the end of her question but I don't get the chance to answer before Paloma slides in next to us, pulling at one of my curls.

"MMmhm, maybe you should be asking her *who* has her smiling like that?" Her voice is teasing as they both wait for my response, wiggling their eyebrows.

"I think the who in question is that tall glass of hunk sitting in the booth with his friend," Brianna says before blowing a raspberry. "Who was clearly sculpted by the gods."

"You both are insufferable," I respond with a laugh. I swear these two will never let me live this down... I can imagine the teasing already.

"But seriously Cass, I've been working at the bar since the beginning and have never seen you glow the way you have been over the last week. What's up?" Brianna pipes in. I know she's right and I don't want to fight it.

"I haven't been able to stop thinking about him since the reunion. I'm either laughing or blushing from his compliments or by the way he looks at me." I look back over at Jameson talking with Anderson. Allowing my gaze to linger a bit longer before turning back to the girls, my phone chirps again. I know who it is which in turn makes my phone feel like it may burn straight through the back pocket of my jeans. I fold my lips into each other, holding back a tight smile while the girls stare into my very soul.

"He text you didn't he... just now?" Paloma asks. Her playful tone is serious with a need-to-know. "Bitch, don't keep him, or us, waiting. Open that text!"

"Could you be any louder?" I swat at her.

"Actually..." she says, leaning up on her tiptoes as I pull my phone out. She most definitely will yell it across the entire bar.

> Jameson
>
> **Now who's the creeper?**

> **You like it!**

> Jameson
>
> **Oh, I absolutely do.**

My cheeks darken and squeals sound around me, as the girls lean over my shoulder to see what he text.

"Okay enough out of you two, we've got to get back to work." I laugh at my instructions because I would much rather sit at the edge of this bar and text Jameson for the rest of the night.

"Fine!" they say in unison. Brianna goes back to the kitchen, I assume to check on a few appetizer orders, and Paloma heads towards the register where a group of customers are huddled nearby with our book pairing's menu. I send him a couple of blushing emojis and slide my phone in my pocket, where it's going to have to stay if I am going to get anything done tonight.

6

Jameson

shares song Usher: "You got it bad"

I know Anders is speaking because I can hear the hum of his voice but I can't bring myself to focus even though I know I should be listening. Coming to Shaken Tropes was supposed to kill two birds with one stone: meet Anders about the project we are going to be working on as well as see Cassidy.

What I wasn't expecting was finding out my best friend already knew her or that my eyes would follow her everywhere. Seeing her here, being in her element, makes me relive all those times I would see her in the hallways at Cypress Lake.

Janelle was one of my closest friends at school, she was almost like a sister. We kept up with one another as much as we could while she was overseas, but letters and calls were still few and far between. When we were in school, wherever Janelle was, so was her friend with the loud, boisterous laugh and bouncing curls—Cassidy—and my eyes found her often while she scanned the pages of a book or joked around with her friends.

I crack my knuckles, a bad habit I can't seem to be bothered with breaking, thinking of how those curls would feel wrapped around my

73

hand.

During all those years at Cypress Lake High, Janelle and I only shared a few classes, I was never lucky enough to share the same classes with Cassidy. Maybe sharing a class or two would have forced me to act on our seemingly mutual crush. We may not have had the chance to share a chemistry class but seeing her bounding down the halls, talking about anything at all with her friends, she was beautiful. Every single time I caught a glimpse of curls, I hoped one of her smiles would be aimed at me. I was the funny guy-friend to all my friends who were girls, and I didn't want the girl that I had the ultimate crush on to be the one to reject me, my ego was a struggle bus at best. Though it could be viewed as creep behavior, I admired her from afar.

Being funny granted me many female friends, just not the type that allowed me anything more than being friend-zoned. Being a teen, I often found myself with hurt feelings before I reasoned with logic. The girls in school didn't owe me anything. Which was fine, because the more I put myself aside and focused on the blossoming friendships, the more I realized that lifelong friends were all we were truly meant to be. Each of those friendships was missing that spark all those romance movies portray. That same spark that these now-women, who are still some of my closest friends, have found and built their beautiful families around. I want to believe it's that spark that I now feel flickering for Cassidy.

My eyes search the bar for Cassidy and I find her, walking towards a table of women with a stack of books in her hands. The joy on the women's faces as they welcome Cassidy to their table brings a warm smile to my own face.

I'm no saint, I have dated here and there, but no one has ever clicked and I'm not one to waste someone's time or string them along. I am in no rush unless it is the right woman. Maybe, the right woman is standing before me, passing around drinks and offering book recommendations like it is as easy as breathing. The one with bouncing curls and soft lush curves that I could grip my hands into.

"Man, how do you have it bad already?" Anders' question pulls me out of my thoughts. "Didn't Cassidy just give you her number?" His laugh makes me shake my head.

"I knew working with you was a bad idea," I joke. "I can't help it, she's all I can think about since the reunion. And why didn't you tell me you knew her?" I question my best friend

"You were out pulling in new clients. Then the team and I finished up here right before you came back, it just never crossed my mind to bring it up. You know how much I enjoy collaborating as much as possible with clients and building a friendship; I had no idea Cass had a connection with you.

"So, she's the one that gave you the wrong number?" Anders raises his brows, leaning into the table. "What has you so focused?"

"Cassidy makes it so easy to just be myself around her. From her welcoming demeanor to not letting me off easy with jokes. Man, she gives 'em right back." I bite the inside of my cheek to stop the laugh from escaping as I think about our texts. My hand itches to grab my phone and text her again, anything to keep her thoughts on me. When I turn my head back towards Anders he's looking right at my face and shaking his head. Yeah, I've got bad, but I couldn't care less.

"So, where do you want to start so we can get this house reno done?" Anders shifts gears and is all business. He's always been the type to need to know the plan so every detail is executed perfectly. During our college days, while I focused on my architecture degree, he honed in on engineering, which helped him when he went for his general contractors' license. He was always an all-or-nothing type of guy.

"I want to gut the entire place, make it so it has everything someone would want or need in this area. Luxury meets cozy night in... is that a thing? That has to be a thing," I respond and watch his face light up with ideas. I can already tell we are going to be here a while. This is why we've always worked so well together, I can give him the vaguest thought and he runs with it, ready to make my vision come to life.

Like magic, a server stops at our table, seeming to appear out of thin air. Her ash-blonde ponytail swings as she turns to Anders. She has on a loose, pink t-shirt with "Shaken Tropes" written across the front and a small, white name tag off to the side sporting a single letter, "B."

"How are you two doing?" She hands me their menu before continuing, "Can I get you anything, maybe a refill on your drinks and something to eat?"

"I didn't realize you all served food here," I say, looking up from the small menu. She smiles brightly and nods her head in response. Anders gives her our drink orders and she leaves us to browse the menu.

Sorting through his bag, Anders pulls out a notepad and pencil and unfolds a blueprint that shows the entire layout of the house of conversation. "Let's figure out what spaces you fully want to transform and I'll sketch out a rough plan. I find it helps the vision become more real, even if it is just paper and pencil," Anderson explains.

"Alright, let's do it." For the next hour or so, we discuss the plans for the house and how we plan to achieve them. We want to gut both bathrooms and put in a large tiled shower with a deep tub to nestle inside one of them, and the other, a large walk-in shower. Anders suggests an outdoor kitchen fitted with a large grill, fridge, and those twinkling lights everyone loves so much. He gives me a few ideas for the living room area that I wouldn't have thought of, like creating a sunken space. It will add to the coziness that I want to incorporate into the home.

After our second serving of loaded potato skins and garlic parmesan chicken wings, we call it a night. Anders lets me know he is going to send an email to our designer so they can decide how to move forward with colors and furniture for staging. I can already imagine inviting Cassidy over, having a movie night while we bundle up under a blanket on an oversized couch. I make a mental note to gather inspiration photos to provide to the designer. This all reminds me that eventually, I'll sell this house and buy another, continuing to build my portfolio, but I've got a while before I have to give my next move too much thought.

Vibrations pull me from thoughts and I pull out my phone while staring at Anders' sketches of the backyard landscaping. He wanted me to look them over and sleep on any new ideas or takeaways I may want to add.

Cassidy

> **You still watching me, creeper?**

I'm getting way too much pleasure out of knowing she enjoys my eyes on her. Really, she's the only thing I want to look at and I smirk as I start to type out another message to her.

> You're all I see.

And I intend to sit right here. I wave over B and place an order for another drink and one last round of potato skins. Leaving isn't an option for me, I haven't gotten my fill of Cassidy, not yet.

7

Cassidy

J-babe

Don't forget to spray perfume on your ankles.

Lo

IYKYK *devil smiley emoji*

Oh and I know! Can't forget the ankles. *laughing emoji*

B

When did I get added to this group chat? *eyes emoji* Fill me in about the ankles thing.

Lo

Are you complaining? Cause I can remove you.

B

No nooo. Don't get sassy!

You know. You spray perfume on your ankles just in case they'll be in the air later.

J-babe

YASSS!!! Put em up, put em up!

Last night was busy for us, which is surprising as it normally doesn't pick up until later in the week when ladies' night and book club events take place. I'm not going to complain, though. With wanting to build out the library area in the back and hire someone else full-time, we need the extra money for it all to be more than a concept. Anderson and I may be good friends, but I pay the same rate as everyone else. Crews is hardworking and always provides top-notch work, which means he is worth every penny. Rubbing circles with my thumbs into my temples, I take a deep breath because that process will be a whole thing. That's tomorrow's trouble.

Seeing Jameson last night was also something I didn't expect, but he was a welcome sight nonetheless. If I hadn't seen him at the bar I wouldn't have figured out why bourbon and citrus have been haunting my dreams. Haunt may not be the right word, considering I wake up with the sheets twisted between my thighs and hot with a need I can't fulfill.

Either way, after missing our chance during our teens, and apparently again when I remodeled Shaken Tropes, it was a mixed connection that I don't plan on losing out on again. I chuckle to myself at my play on words. Are you even funny if you don't find yourself hilarious? "I don't think so," I say out loud, as I point the hairbrush at the mirror and laugh at myself again.

Spraying my curls with a refresher, I work the product through. I switch on the diffuser and the soft hum starts, tuning out the afrobeats playing over the speakers. I make quick work of drying my curls before putting everything away and heading to the kitchen. Coffee is a must after the night I had.

Slight buzzing pulls my attention and I search the countertop, moving things out of the way or picking up papers. That's when I notice my cell phone is precariously perched halfway on the granite. Almost tripping over my own feet, I lunge for it and miss it completely as it slips through my fingers and my eyes widen at the thought of breaking yet another phone. Thank God it was plugged into its charger. I ball my fist as my phone slips through my fingers, gripping the charging cord before the device gets a chance to connect with the floor.

Plopping myself up onto the same counter, I finally open the notifications that almost ended the life of my *barely* dinged-up device. Rolling my eyes in frustration, I blow out a breath. I am on a mission to make this phone last. It's my second one since upgrading and I *refuse* to break another phone. I rub my thumb on the already cracked screen and click the message, ignoring the thought of maybe ordering myself a new phone.

Jameson

Wanted to be sure I texted you so you wouldn't think I ran off with my girl.

LOL. The jury is still out on that.

Jameson

Shaken Tropes was really great! I'm glad I got to see you.

Are you free Saturday?

I could be, what do you have in mind?

Jameson

I'd like to take you out.

Not a question, but a statement. Kicking my feet, I lean back and squeal at how direct he is. Finding a man who knows what he wants and isn't afraid to take the lead—an excited chill races over the surface of my skin—it's a characteristic I find sexy in every facet of the word. I was so used to being the pursuer and chasing after what or who I wanted, that at some point I stopped trying to date. I wasn't against going after the person I desired but I wanted it to be reciprocated, to be someone's first and only choice because they simply chose me.

Where are you thinking?

Maybe lunch?

Almost as though he was sitting waiting for my reply, his response comes instantly.

Jameson

If you want to do lunch, we can do that too. But the place I have in mind is dinner only. *winky face*

Even through text, this reads as if he wants me all to himself. I bite down gently on my thumbnail, a little pressure keeping me in this moment instead of imagining being alone with a man like Jameson.

Oh.

Oh. OH! That's all I could come up with. Jameson makes me feel like a schoolgirl again, getting tongue-tied and losing the ability to form true sentences.

Jameson

Yeah, oh. *devil smiley emoji* Can you be ready by 7pm?

I can! See you then. Can you pick me up at the bar?

My apartment is the upstairs loft.

Jameson

I'll see you there. *winky face*

Babes at Benny's Group Chat

Lo

Bitch you better send us a picture!

J-babe

Yeah, we want to see how hot you look too!
Jameson can't be stingy.

You guys are terrible! I promise I'll send you a
pic but I gotta finish getting ready.

Getting together with the girls soon is a top priority since we haven't gotten a chance to spend any time together since we had brunch almost a week ago. With Janelle leaving soon, we want to have a girls' night in, which is perfect, considering I'm going out with Jameson tonight and I want to share all the details with Janelle and Lo. I put my phone down, rolling my eyes playfully at Lo and Janelle.

"Fuck, I'm so glad this week is over," I sigh to no one but myself. Owning my own business can be incredible given I truly love what I do, my weeks never drag. I want to be at the bar, serving up mafia romance indulgences in cocktails to my customers, but this week was "as slow as molasses", as my grandma would say. All I could focus on was my date with Jameson, the excitement and anxiousness of being out with someone I'm getting to know.

That's a lie. It's him.

I've gone on plenty of dates, but I don't recall ever being this thrilled. Plucking a gold chunky hoop from my bathroom vanity, I take a cleansing breath and make an attempt to lessen the grin that's permanently plastered on my face. But as I watch myself put the other earring in, I give up the fight. This is such a full body feeling of intrigue, I don't want to let it go or hide it. And why should I? I pump myself up even more exclaiming, "Tonight's the night you see if your crush was everything you dreamt it was."

Butterflies in my stomach overwhelm my senses as I finish getting ready for our date. I expected to be nervous, but all I feel is excitement in seeing him tonight along with not knowing where we're going.

Smoothing my hands down my curves, the dark-red satin dress lays effortlessly against me. Two tiny straps hold the top up on hope alone, showcasing my ample cleavage, draping around my waist. I brace myself against the door frame and slide my feet into my open-toed, black strappy heels I set next to my mirror once I decided on my outfit. I wiggle my lilac-polished toes to get the right fit; I'm so glad to have gotten a pedicure this week.

I round the corner of my bathroom to fluff my hair and apply the matching red lipstick that has become my signature color over the last few years.

Red lipstick makes me feel powerful and feminine, it gives me that extra bit of confidence I searched for when I was younger, whether I needed it or not. I purse my lips, rub them together, and spray a fine mist of my favorite perfume. Warm vanilla and sandalwood fill the air around me.

No matter where this night ends, I'm ready for it. Just as I reach for my phone to check the time, I hear the doorbell signaling someone is at the front door of Shaken Tropes. Before I can see who it is, a notification appears on my phone screen.

I answer the incoming call and his deep voice comes through the line. "Hey, beautiful, I'm here. I thought I would walk to your door, but I'm not sure which one it is." He chuckles and I can tell he's smiling.

"I will be down in just a moment. Promise." Checking that my phone location is on, I text the girls to let them know I'm heading out on my date. I shake my hands, trying to breathe through the excited anxiousness that I'm feeling. I haven't been this excited for a date in a long time.

Turning, I lock my door and make my way down the stairs. Jameson is leaning against his SUV with a sly smile on his face as he watches me, before pushing himself off the side of the vehicle to meet me at the bottom of the stairs. Taking my hand in his, he extends our linked hands in the air and nods his head; I give him a quick twirl as the pink in my cheeks grows darker with how his eyes follow my curves.

"Hmm." It's the only audible noise he makes as he steps back to look me over once more and I preen under his gaze. Jameson's actions make me feel like the most beautiful woman in the world, like there couldn't possibly be anyone else in the room if we were standing in one. "You are absolutely stunning."

I step closer to him and drop my eyes to his feet and slowly raise them to his lips for a moment, before looking him in the eyes. His hair is down and pulled over to one side to hang down his back and over his shoulder. "You clean up very well yourself."

Taking in my blatant ogling he pulls me slightly, welcoming me into his space as a grin widens on his face. "Are you ready for our date?"

"So ready." So. Very. Ready.

He opens his car's front seat passenger door wide, offering me his arm as I slide into the soft, camel-colored leather seats. Leaning into me, his lips are but a breath away. I release a small gasp at his proximity, looking into his eyes that hold a glimmer of the same excitement that has me giddy. Without realizing it, I must have leaned in closer to him. My gaze dips down to his mouth and I watch him pull his bottom lip with his teeth, his tongue running over it before he sucks in a breath. His presence is intoxicating. I don't think I will ever get over how good this man smells. I'm so drawn into whatever this moment is I don't realize what he's doing until I hear the seatbelt click into place. He nods more to himself, before closing the door and getting in on the driver's side.

Soft music plays in the background as we make our way to our destination, one I'm still not privy to, but my focus is more on the man sitting next to me than on where we are going. He wears a pair of olive green, tailored dress pants that taper just above his ankle with an off-white button-up shirt which is folded at the widest part of his biceps. A brown leather belt matches his laced-up dress boots, completing his outfit; and it takes every bit of effort not to take a peek at his face after I have been ogling him. Before my eyes take their chance, I watch as his hand strains against his lap, it's not hard to imagine those hand necklaces I read so much about.

"So where are we heading?" I need to break this tension before I climb over the gear shifter, straight into his lap.

Turning his head toward me, his eyes peek over before returning back to the road. "There is this place, right outside of town, that I want to take you to, The Republic. Have you heard of it?"

Tucking my hair behind my ear to relieve a bit of nervous jitters, I ask, "How did you even get into that place with such short notice?" My surprise is more than evident.

The Republic isn't a place people are able to get into within a week. He'd either have to have a connection or have made the reservation months in advance. His knowing smile is one that tells me he isn't going to tell me, at least not yet, but if he wanted to impress me, it's definitely working.

Allowing the music playing through the car speakers to take the lead, I go silent for a beat and let the content feeling fill me as my shoulders relax. I twist my hands in my dress, quite literally twiddling my thumbs as I peer at the town from the window, appreciating the beauty of the place I've grown up in and have gotten so used to—I tend to forget how special it is. I peek at him from under my lashes, wanting to enjoy the view of the man who has stolen my breath away, and I suddenly let out a gasp as an ornate building comes into view.

He pulls his SUV to the front of our destination. A valet attendant opens his door, then Jameson makes his way around the front of the vehicle. Opening my door, he extends his hand and I intertwine my fingers with his as I step out. His hand is warmly wrapped around mine, and I can do nothing but bask in the closeness of him. I welcome the delicious shivers trailing up my arms from the contact of his skin on mine.

Holding my hand, Jameson leads me up the steps to the entrance of the restaurant where I finally notice the twinkling lights along the trees that frame the doors. The Republic is beautiful. Tall, white columns, with vines wrapped around each one, welcome us. My eyes follow the vines to the ceiling composed of low-hanging lanterns from different points all over the restaurant. Making an effort to close my mouth, I listen to my heels clicking against the floor. Pale wood planks stained a cool gray are set in a chevron pattern—even the floor is stunning.

The body of water the restaurant is situated by allows for the perfect scene for a romantic dinner. The inside is lit with wall sconces that flicker with a faux flame, giving off a warm and intimate vibe that I really appreciate. Small candles flicker at the center of each table, all the lighting working together to create a space for everyone to feel as though they are in a world of their own.

"Mr. Bennette, it has been some time." The hostess' smile is bright as she welcomes us inside and steps behind her stand to grab a couple of menus. Everyone Jameson interacts with seems to be just as welcoming as he is. Her eyes drift to my hand locked in his before looking back up at me—her gaze is a warm hug and she ushers us into the dining area.

Jameson gives my hand a small squeeze as we follow her deep into the restaurant where the walls are made of glass overlooking the sun setting on the lake. It is an incredible sight and reminds me of a serene backdrop I'd see in a nature documentary. The grounds just outside the window appear untouched and ripples appear on the surface of the lake from what I assume are fish swimming to the surface, along with a deer making its way to the water's edge to take a drink. The hostess leads us into a corner where we have ample privacy to enjoy our time together.

"Jenny, thank you," Jameson says, before she departs with a gentle nod after letting us know our waiter will be with us shortly. Jameson pulls out my chair, allowing me to sit and get adjusted before taking his own seat.

"Spill it, Mr. Bennette," I mock, shimmying in my seat with a matching, mischievous smirk.

"I think I kind of like you calling me by my last name, I may have to get used to that." A low chuckle leaves him and he leans on to the table, my body hums in appreciation of him. "I helped the owner close on this location and we have been friends since."

The waiter arrives and Jameson looks at me from across the table, "Do you trust me?" he asks, and I shrug my shoulders, feigning doubt.

"Hmm, well, that depends... but I guess we'll find out soon enough," I state, gazing up at him for a moment before my eyes return to the menu, smiling to myself at my playful indifference.

"Challenge accepted." He requests a bottle of sweet red wine I'm not familiar with and asks the waiter to give us a few more moments to look over the menu.

"Tell me, how did you go about helping the owner get into what is now, The Republic? Who are you, Jameson Bennette?" I ask him, as I prop my elbow up on the table and rest my chin on my hand.

The waiter is back in no time, bringing the deep-red, almost purple wine, and pouring each of us a glass before taking our orders, and then quickly disappearing to wherever he came from. Picking up his glass, Jameson takes a heavy drink of his wine. My eyes follow the path of his tongue, swiping at the corner of his mouth. I do the same and my eyes widen as the flavors of ripe blackberry, plum, and strawberry burst on my tongue. "Wow, okay, you can order me wine any day of the week!" I exclaim, taking another sip from my glass.

"I'm really glad you like it, it's one of my favorites here. Not many places have it, but any time I come to visit the owners, I make sure to order at least one glass." He beams at my clear love for my new favorite wine. I make a mental note to search for it through my vendor list.

"Please continue..." I urge him on, wanting to know as much about him as he will share.

"The Republic, or rather the building it's in now, just so happened to be a property I was looking into but it didn't feel right, at least not for me and not in that moment. The current owners are friends of previous clients, they were looking to open a restaurant and I simply connected the investors of the property with them. It's really done well here." He wets his lips in thought and continues, "I would have never been in the position to introduce them had it not been for working with my best friend, who you already know" —he smirks, raising one eyebrow up—"we grew up together."

"We've basically spent our entire lives together, from tots to university. His dad and grandfather worked on a lot of houses and I picked up a lot of renovation skills from spending the summers with him. I started flipping houses roughly six years ago, while Anders got everything in order for Crews Construction. We could have gone right into flipping houses but he was adamant about getting his general contractor's license so he could not just work on the projects, but be in charge of them as well, not needing someone to be an overseer is a privilege we both enjoy. Once the business was ready and he realized how profitable flipping was, he asked me to come on as his partner. It was a no-brainer for me to agree."

I huff a small laugh in disbelief. The man sitting in front of me right now can't possibly be real. He has to be a dream I created in my head. Everything about him seems to be what I truly want in a man. He's quick-witted and smart, his drive alone in creating something for himself is incredibly sexy. I don't think there has been a time where I laughed or smiled as much as I do with him, not to mention his confidence alone is sexy as hell. Jameson seems to be the kind of man who truly cares for those around him, he's not hard on the eyes either. Who am I kidding? He is easily one of the most handsome men I have ever seen. From his wide shoulders and trim waist, it's like I'm stuck in a movie from the eighties creating the perfect man, and if that's the case, I'm never leaving. I could have never dreamed that I would be sitting across from Jameson Bennette, my first major crush. I thought this entire situation would feel weird, and obviously new—but in reality, it feels normal and comfortable, like we just *click*.

His lips draw up in a crooked grin, tilting his head in my direction as if to tell me that it's my turn to entertain him with who I am now. High school felt like yesterday. I would see him in the hallways, and on occasion, with my own friends. It's not that I didn't want to be friends with him, it's just that somehow, our paths never had the chance to cross. But by the way he talks and looks at me I feel like he already knew who I was.

What in the Lifetime-movie is wrong with me right now?

High school was never a fun place for me, I was the fat girl, dealing with finding myself. Figuring out who I was, but without anyone to tell me that I was perfectly fine just the way I was. I've always had wide hips and a large chest which left me feeling hyper-sexualized my entire teen life, except I also felt incredibly withdrawn from it, trying my best to cover up a plus-size body I was learning to love. I was used to being spoken about, but not to. My body and my weight were picked apart or I was given back-handed compliments about how pretty my face was. A comment every fat girl has heard at least once in their lifetime, because how could they possibly consider complementing more than my face. I felt like more of an object for onlookers than a teen girl trying to find her footing in a sea of hormones and growing responsibilities.

When I did date, during high school and college, I was never the first choice. Always coming in second best or not being a choice at all. Only being good enough for quick touches and anticlimactic thrusts which left me feeling ashamed for even wanting that kind of contact with someone.

Cypress Lake High was a place I wanted to remove from my memory altogether, but out of that disappointment, I found true friends. I kept the loss of my parents and my body image struggles to myself. From everyone really, except Paloma and Janelle. They've always been the only ones who know the real me.

My chosen family.

Between laughs with the girls, terrible lunch food that somehow I still find myself craving—nostalgia at its finest, that breakfast pizza was so good—and boring classes, I remember seeing Jameson and thinking he was such a cutie. I'd find myself catching glances from him when I was trying to sneak away from crowds, but I allowed my insecurity to brush it off, thinking he couldn't be showing any interest in me. He was this bright spot among all his friend groups; I know this because where he seemed to be, laughter followed, and I so badly wanted to be a part of that. Our paths just never crossed at the right time.

"What's got that beautiful smile on your face?" His deep baritone pulls me from my thoughts.

"I'm having a really good time with you, that's all. Thinking about those passing glances I may have taken."

"Tell me more." His encouraging head nod keeps me going.

"It's funny that we were finally introduced at the reunion," I say, twisting the dainty gold band on my forefinger, a sudden thirst hits me with the small confession I'm about to give to him and I take a sip of water. "I may have seen you around school and I may have had a tiny crush on you."

The waiter arrives just as I finish my confession, placing a steak with fluffy chive potatoes and bacon-wrapped asparagus in front of Jameson. For just a moment, I'm jealous of his plate. The truffle garlic butter is puddled on the steak and smells incredible, that is until the waiter places my order on the table. I almost lose my composure from the sex-on-the-plate that's now set in front of me. Piled high in a twisted nest covered in a creamy white sauce, is my carbonara. The smell of browned butter and bacon creates a divinely delicious scent, and I twirl my fork into the pasta and take my first bite. The flavors burst on my tongue and I let out a moan of pure unadulterated pleasure. I almost forget that I've just confessed my crush to Jameson until he coughs slightly under his breath and I dart my gaze back up to him.

"I don't know what's sexier, hearing you confess that you had a crush on me too or hearing that moan after you said it." He looks down to my mouth and back up to my eyes.

Grabbing my napkin, I dab my mouth to gather myself, did he say what I think he said? "You had a crush on me too?" My question is hesitant, I want to be sure I heard him right.

"I did and I'm glad to know you felt the same, even if we didn't know it then." He brushes his fingers on the side of my wrist and then I feel his thumb rub the top of my wrist back and forth, before he pulls back to take another bite of steak. "Tell me how you and Paloma started Shaken Tropes."

"My inheritance became available after I turned twenty. I was fortunate to be left plenty to establish myself in a way that felt true to who I was, who I am. I realize an inheritance is a privilege not many get and I didn't want to squander it away, you know? I kept it in savings for a while, only using it for emergencies, or books while in college."

One night, my best friend and I were sitting together at her place, her business degree going nowhere and my marketing degree collecting dust. We were tipsy, having been sipping on a pitcher of our favorite sangria, when we came up with the idea of books and booze. We brainstormed and planned it out that very night. I don't think we slept a wink, pumped up on the excitement of creating something that was ours. The wine gave us the confidence to finally put ourselves out there, and my family's financial legacy made the pursuit of one of our dreams a lot easier." I grin, remembering that night like it was yesterday.

"I can understand that. Shaken Tropes is a great investment, and it's something you truly love. Having worked on as many remodels as I have, and owning a business of my own, I get it," he says, acknowledging the hard work I've put in. God, I love a man who listens.

"After early morning therapy sessions, I'd meet with Lo and we'd work towards our dream. We opened Shaken Tropes almost four years ago and it's been incredible!" I reply, excited to share with someone who understands how hard it is to be a business owner.

"The lights in your eyes are like fireworks when you talk about Shaken Tropes. Seeing you love what you do is attractive as hell, if I'm being honest with you," he says, as his eyes are fixed on me, listening to every single word I say. "What makes you say 'therapy?'"

"The inheritance I spoke of really helped me get on my feet, but it came with the loss of my parents. They passed when we were in high school and it left me with troubles that I really needed to work through, amongst other things. Therapy got me to a place where I could see my worth and that changed a lot for me," I explain, leaving out deeper bits of the story that wouldn't suit a romantic dinner.

Jameson's smile never leaves his face as I tell him more about our bar, in fact, it only grows bigger as I talk about my passion. I explain the concept we created and how we visited bars that were similar in other cities. Between Paloma and my love of cocktails and romance books, our dream was born.

I scoot closer to him as I talk more about the romance aspect of the bar and when my thigh presses against his leg, his grin turns downright mischievous. My pulse quickens, I chance a glance at him and am met with his lingering gaze while he sips his drink. A blush darkens my cheeks as heat travels up my spine. I dangerously want to be that wine.

As chatter around the restaurant begins to taper off from people coming and going, we stay nestled in our corner. I'm enjoying myself far too much to consider leaving just yet. Reaching my hand out to his, I brush my fingertips against the top of his hand. Hands like his need to be touched, and those thoughts pull me to the stories he shared about his childhood, and then university days with Anderson, culminating into Triple C.

I watch his features grow more animated as he speaks. Talking with his hands, smiling, or shaking his head at the foolishness that ensued when he and Anderson were around one another.

"One particularly exhausting summer, working with his grandad, we decided it was time to cool down. Anders and I had been working all day. Punishment for breaking a window while playing ball in the backyard when we were supposed to be getting ready for dinner." He shakes his head, looking lost in the memory. "We couldn't go inside because we weren't allowed in yet, so we headed down to the lake on his grandad's property. Wearing nothing but my boxers, I climb up the rope and give myself a good swing—we had to be fourteen or fifteen at this time. Anyway, I push myself off the hill, and just as I'm about to let go of the rope, my underwear gets caught on something. Don't ask me what." He looks at me then, urging me not to ask him the question. "My drawers get stuck and all but ripped from my body as I'm dangling for dear life on the rope before I eventually tumble into the water head first. I won't lie to you, I was screaming and I have never heard a scream so high-pitched leave my mouth since. Let's leave it to pre-puberty, and now Anders won't let me live it down."

He reaches his hand around mine that's leaving feather-light touches on his own and grabs his water with the other, taking a sip as he finishes his story. I try to hold in the bark of laughter, but at this point, my eyes brim with tears and as my smile grows further, my cheeks begin to hurt.

"Oh my God! So involuntary skinny dipping?" I say before snorting, bringing both my hands up to cover my mouth as my eyes widen.

"That was so damn cute." His lip twitches before he reaches over, grasping my hand back in his before sharing more bits of his life with me.

He continues telling me about his love of flipping houses, and his friendship with Anderson—the amount of trouble two teen boys can get into is insanity. Jameson and Ander's relationship seems so similar to mine with my girls and I love that for him.

Their friendship is reminiscent of the long weekends I spent at Janelle's house. We always stayed up too late dancing and singing around her room, gossiping, doing what teenage girls do when they get a chance to hang with their friends.

Any time her mom had her own girls' day by the pool she would make mango margaritas. She'd make them early to allow all the ingredients to meld together, at least that's what she told us. After staying up much too late and singing ourselves hoarse, we'd sneak down to the kitchen and sip the sweet nectar mixed drink.

I've never been more glad to have my group of girls back together. It was incredibly hard losing my parents and then, not even two years later, Janelle enlisted—it felt like I lost her too. Now that I have her back, however brief, it feels as though she never left.

"Your stories with Anders remind me so much of my own." I smile. "The weekends, especially during the summer, were always so much fun. Janelle, Paloma, and I would spend time at each other's houses, sometimes switching midway through the weekend. But during the summer, oh sweet sunshine, that was our favorite time. Janelle's mom would always make her famous mango margaritas."

"Famous huh?" he says.

"Don't ask me why they were famous but they were so damn good, I own a bar, that should tell you something about the glory of them. One night we found out what exactly she had mixed up in the fridge when we snuck downstairs and poured ourselves each a glass. We were drunkenly bumping into each other, dancing around the room, giggling like the fools we were. Her mom caught us red-handed and asked what was wrong with us? It was way too late to have the music up as loud as we did. I hiccuped. Paloma giggled and then burped like a full grown man, before Janelle ratted us all out. Too nervous about not telling her mom the truth."

"You guys must have been in so much trouble," he states, his eyebrows raised to his hairline.

"Oh yeah! She was pissed that we drank all the mango and lime concentrate." I chuff a laugh before I continue, recalling the most blasphemous part of the whole thing. "But get this? It was completely virgin, no alcohol at all. I think we were so excited to be drinking margaritas, we fed off each other's energy. She made us walk to the store to pick up more ingredients the next morning before the pool party."

"Virgins!" His deep laugh falls from his mouth as he throws his head back. "Ya'll weren't even drunk?"

"We certainly wanted to believe we were."

Jameson shakes his head right before the server comes back with our bill and wishes us a good night.

By the time we finish our last bites of dinner, we are both exhausted from laughing and very ready for dessert. One that we can't order from any menu.

The car ride is made up of easy conversation about tonight's dinner and the reunion. Some time between leaving the restaurant and pulling into the parking lot of my building, his warm hand found its way to my exposed leg and I find myself reveling in the feel of his calloused thumb rubbing the inner part of my thigh. We pull into the parking lot far too soon and I'm not ready for him to stop touching me.

Opening the door, he helps me step out of the SUV before pressing the door closed behind us. He is so close to me now that I can't help but be enveloped in the scent of him. My breathing picks up at his closeness as I lean my back against the door of the SUV, not wanting to go upstairs and end our night. But maybe I don't need to end it. Maybe just this once, I can let go of my rules and invite him up.

I walk my fingers up his corded arms and flick my gaze up through my lashes. Fucking hell, I want this man in more ways than one and I know without a doubt that he wants me too. Before I have the chance to invite him inside, he pulls me into him while threading one of his hands in my hair. Firmly he tilts my head back and watches me, his eyes asking for permission that I willingly give by pressing myself deeper into him. Jameson dips his head low, inhaling the perfume that I sprayed on my neck earlier.

"You smell heavenly." He all but groans before pressing a light kiss near the pulse point behind my ear, his beard is soft as it tickles my neck. I want to run my fingers through it, and I do. Jameson hums his appreciation from my touch and trails his tongue up the column of my neck, nibbling his way to my jaw, toying everywhere but where I want him. My skin heats as I fully give in to his grip on my hair and lean my head back, giving him better access.

I can feel his breath on my skin as his mouth leaves urgent kisses along my jaw. Every spot his lips touch sets my skin on fire, nothing could have prepared me for how delicious this moment feels and my body begs for more.

He licks the seam of my mouth and gently tugs my bottom lip between his teeth. I can't hold back the moan as he presses into me, opening my mouth for just a moment, he sweeps his tongue between my lips, and my skin flushes as a chill runs down my back. Giving into the urge, I trail my hands up his chest and nip at his lips, before resting my arms around his neck, needing to be closer.

I pull him closer, Jameson kisses me in a way that feels like he is making up for whatever lost time we missed out on. There's no rushed urgency, just full unobstructed desire, and it sets my body ablaze. Jameson makes me feel like I am the only air he needs to breathe and I want to drown in this sensation.

His grip on my hair grows more intense and I delight in being feasted on by this man. He continues his exploration, stroking his other hand down my curves, he slides it around my back and down to my ass, filling his hands as he grips it. Our breaths mingle in hot bursts as his fingers dig into my tender flesh and hope blooms, wanting to have a bruise in the morning. He breaks our connection with quick kisses down my neck and I try my best to slow my breathing down.

He presses his forehead to mine and says, "Let me walk you to the door." His voice holds a raspy quality to it that says he would much rather bend me over the backseat of his car and God, do I want to let him.

"Mm, yes, please." I let out a deep breath, looking up into his eyes as he lowers his head, giving me one soft, lingering kiss to end what we so quickly started, before brushing his lips against my forehead. Taking a grounding breath, a lust-filled laugh escapes me as I adjust my dress after being twisted about by Jameson's explorations.

I know if I invite him in he will say yes. We would grab another drink inside; one drink would turn into two, maybe three, and neither of us have the control over the chemistry we both feel. And I want that, I want all of it. I also know that I refuse to be a one night wonder. I want to be his choice for more than a good time. For him to pick me for who I am, what we could be together. There is something here, and I want to see more of it. Turning my key in the door to unlock it, I spin around to give him a quick kiss on the cheek. I turn back to face him, finding a shit-eating grin on his face; even with my racing heartbeat I'm breathless looking at him.

"Goodnight Jameson, thank you so much for tonight." He bends down slightly to meet me, even with heels, I'm nowhere near as tall as him.

"Goodnight, Cassidy." He leans into me and presses his lips to mine, pulling me to him as he grips my hips in a bruising hold, savoring the night within this lasting kiss. I can't imagine the night being over as we say our goodbyes, and though I know our evening needs to end, I need my fill of him more.

I wrap my arms around his neck, standing on my tiptoes to gain better purchase with his lips. I press my lips harder to his as his hands coasts around my waist and he holds me close. The lingering taste of plums is still on his tongue from the wine as I deepen the kiss. My core throbs from the feel of his hand running up the side of my thigh before pulling it up higher. His fingers against my bare skin sends tingles right where I want him. Here, in this moment, there is nothing but Jameson, and I breathe his name out in a wanton sigh.

Between quicker kisses he says, "You will have me on my knees woman, if you keep that up." My panties are liquid lava hearing him utter those words and I loosen another breathy moan. A giggle intermingles with my moan, because *fuck*, if I didn't just picture him on his knees in front of me. He breaks the kiss and leans his head down, pressing his forehead to mine as our heated breaths mingle together in the cool night air. The moon is our only witness to the feverish need we have for one another. He tucks a curl behind my ear before he inclines his head towards my door.

"I'm supposed to ensure you make it inside safely," he says, his voice is deep and raspy, the sound of desire coating every single word.

"Mm, yes, yes you are. I think I'm plenty safe." That pulls a chuckle from him and I press my hands to his chest. I give him a chaste kiss before turning the door handle behind me. "Goodnight, Bulldozer," I say, rubbing my lips together before stepping through the doorway.

"Goodnight, Beautiful," he all but whispers, glancing down once more. I give him a suggestive smirk before closing the door.

Resting my back against the door, I turn the lock and flick the light switch to turn on a lamp. If anyone were in here with me, they'd see exactly how flushed my skin is, but they'd also see the lazy smile that graces my face.

8

Jameson

Anders

You can't still be mad about the handshake?

How do you have a secret handshake with my girl but not me, your best friend since for too damn long.

Anders

Mannnn, we will come up with one. *eye roll emoji*

It's too late now… Your loss. *hands up emoji*

Walking down these damn stairs, away from her, is proving to be more difficult than I thought it would be. I would much rather be watching the chaos of her curls bounce as she throws her head back in that laugh I loved hearing during our date. Listening to her talk about her passions, watching her run around her bar all damn night—maybe… just maybe hear a few more of those lovely moans of hers—I can't get enough of her.

Images of her bent over the bar top with that dress pushed high up and around her waist flit through my mind. My hands tingle with heat as I imagine ripping her panties away and running my tongue up her pussy from the back. My hands holding her open for my tongue to fully explore, letting her juices moisten my beard. I'd untie the bow that kept her dress closed around her waist, pulling it off her and tossing it to the floor. It looks incredible on her but it would be so much better puddled in the corner. *Fuck*. The image of that dress is burned into my mind, the satin looked as though it was poured over her curves, like it was made only for her. A chuffed laugh leaves my chest as I breathe through my nose imagining what she would taste like. I bet she tastes as sweet as she smells, that vanilla scent clings to my clothes from having her in my arms.

The leftover blackberry and plum flavor of the wine was all I could taste when I kissed her and I knew I needed more. More of what I imagined and would now be replaying in my dreams. More of her than she would be willing to give me so soon. I won't pretend that I'm a selfless man... I fully plan on being selfish with her. But I know if I don't take my time with her, I'll live to regret it. She's more than something or someone to possess, but I want to; I want her in every way she'll allow me—heart, mind, and body. All of her. The crush may have started nearly fourteen years ago, during freshman year of highschool, but tonight it was clear it's even more present. She made me welcome the thought of what it could be like spending everyday together. Our conversation was easy and moved along without all the awkward newness which can sometimes abound during first dates. I want to explore all of what we are starting together.

Sliding into the driver's side of my SUV, I turn my key in the ignition and press my foot on the gas before I change my mind about leaving. I roll the window down, allowing the cool air to calm my racing heart.

This isn't another serial date. Spending time with Cassidy tonight was amazing and I almost feel foolish given my grin won't seem to leave my face. Hearing her speak about making her dreams a reality by opening Shaken Tropes reminds me of the same joy I felt when I opened the consulting division with Triple C. There was only a small moment when she mentioned her parents that I watched a sadness wash over her, but it was quickly removed by a soft smile lighting up her face as she talked about the plans she has with her best friend. She spoke about wanting to build a full library within Shaken Tropes, and one day turning her apartment into an event space once she buys her forever home. Her visions of her future only increase my excitement because I realize I can't wait to help her make her dreams come true.

My eyes search the cloudless sky for stars I know are out there, and I send a silent thank you into the universe. Love at first date is a thing, right?

Pulling into the driveway of the fixer almost dampens my mood, it's a reminder I'm not in Cypress Lake forever. We've already gotten a week and change under our belt with this project and I'm already finding myself wishing I had more to work on, maybe finding another project here in Cypress Lake is exactly what I need to do. Tonight was the reminder I needed to make a choice on what exactly I'm doing. I think it's time for me to find another house here in town. I need more time here. More time with Cassidy. My heart lurches in my chest at the mere thought of leaving here, of leaving her, and I decide right here in this moment that I'm not leaving unless she tells me to.

As if on cue, my phone chirps. The screen has a notification of my flight information and a goodnight text from Cassidy. Quickly I reply back, wishing her sweet dreams. I push my key into the deadbolt of the house and walk in, leaving my shoes at the door before locking it. A yawn works its way out but I make it to the shower anyway. I may have an early flight in the morning but after the kiss I shared with the most stunning woman I've laid eyes on, I have a cold shower calling my name.

Managing multiple job sites is difficult, but damn, having them this far apart was a fool's gamble. One that I hope pays off. I checked in with the property manager yesterday, letting him know I would be on-site today. He replied almost immediately and let on that everything was in line to finish on time, but it doesn't look like work has even started. I caught an early flight in, hoping I could be of assistance at least during the latter part of the demo. But as my eyes scan the shared kitchen and living room area, it looks like nothing has been done. There are two full garbage bags sitting in the corner of the room and the opposite corner of the carpet is pulled up, but just the corner and nothing more. As I make my way further into the house, I set down my duffle bag and squint my eyes in an attempt to peer into the backyard.

"You've got to be kidding me," I shout, assuming I'm alone and the manager is using the lack of progress as their final notice. The yard is terrible, worse even. "What in the *actual* fuck." I heave a sigh from somewhere deep in my lungs and I swear my eye is starting to twitch.

"Hey, boss. Did you pick up breakfast?" Loren, the soon-to-be fired property manager, asks from behind me, his voice happy and clearly unaffected by my soured mood. Slowly, I turn around to face him but my words are silenced as I take in his bare feet. My eye twitches again. It takes a lot to work me up but this is a red flag. Man feet. Not that I ever *need* to be around another man's feet. Come to think of it, I don't even remember the last time I saw Ander's. I've really lost it now, I'm having a full blown conversation with myself. Nope. He can't possibly have his naked ass feet out. On a job site. *My job site.* My eyes trail up from his hairy toes to the Christmas-themed plaid pajama pants. The sides of his torso are on display because his red shirt is cut open on the sides. I close my eyes and count backwards from five and against my will, my eyes snap back down to his feet. Hell no. Internally I feel like I'm being punked and tilt my head to look for a camera. Not finding any, I turn my attention back to Pajama Jo, while I silently thank my father for teaching me how to maintain a poker face.

"Loren. How are you? Please explain to me why you are standing in the middle of my property barefoot." I watch his eyes grow a bit wider as he takes a gulp. If there was any work being done in the house, his lack of footwear would be a serious hazard for his safety.

"Oh, I'm fine, boss. I just figured it was easier to stay overnight so I could get started early. I wasn't expecting you here so soon." He rubs the back of his head and my fingers twitch wanting to slap him up the side of it. He has clearly lost his marbles.

I watch him, waiting for him to continue with something that makes sense. Truly, I try to give everyone a chance to explain themselves but we've had issues with Loren in the past. He'd been making great progress and I foolishly thought he could handle this with a little oversight.

"The team I hired didn't show, so I've been trying to get it done on my own," he says, and I can tell that he's just as confused as I am.

"Why would you need to hire a team? Crews should have been here last week."

"When you gave me control of the project, I figured I would save the company some money and hire workers who were a bit cheaper." His nervous chuckle is even more frustrating. I can only focus on this man's toes wiggling into the carpet beneath our shoes. Well, *my* shoes.

At this point I am almost fuming. "Loren. Why would it make more sense to hire others when we are a construction and consulting company? Also, I never gave you the authority to do *that*." As I am speaking, I'm pulling out my phone and dialing Anderson's number. "I would like you to gather your things and meet me in the front of the house in ten minutes. Understood?"

"Yes, sir," he says and scuttles off.

The moment he is out of sight, I press send and wait for my call to connect. It rings three times before he answers.

"Hey J, how's the property?" His voice comes through the line.

"Bro. This fool has lost his rabbit-ass mind," I gruffly speak into the phone as Anders chuckles. I'm never going to hear the end of this, I can already tell.

"What did he do this time? I keep telling you to stop giving him chances. I'm taking this as you finally agree."

"He hasn't done a damn thing. I may have to stay here for a couple weeks and fuck man, I don't want to do that," I say, my frustration rising. My eye twitches again. "This man got his toes out, wiggling them in the carpet like we're at his home. *His toes!*" My voice raises an octave. I'm laying it on thick now, trying to hold back my own laugh.

"I can't tell if you're upset about needing to stay or about his bare feet more. Why the fuck are his feet out at a job site? That's a hazard." He laughs, though he sobers himself quickly as he realizes how bad this could be.

"He wasn't working. Loren was in his pajamas, Anders. He somehow forgot to do the one thing I told him to do, which was put the order in. He said he found a cheaper one... they didn't show."

There's no reason for me to have to see the hair on his toes. I'm calling the police." I chuckle. "We need to send out an email to everyone reminding them that they only take direct orders from you or me. This could have been a non-issue if he was even a little bit competent."

"I'll write it up and get it out. Good idea. Bigger question is, how did you and I miss this?" he says, agreeing with me but pushing back.

"This is my fault too. I shouldn't have believed he could take on a project this big solo. I didn't want to be out of Cypress Lake for longer than this weekend," I reply. I'm really enjoying getting to know Cassidy and spending time with her. I worry if I'm gone too long we will be over before we even get a chance to begin.

"You know what? Call Keya. She's just getting started but I have worked with her for multiple properties in the area and she just finished up her most recent project. She's a self-starter and quick, she knows what she's doing. I trust her. Actually, I will just call her and give her your location. Cool?" I was going to ask him why he didn't tell me about her sooner until he finished the last part of his thought.

"Yeah, it's cool. Thanks, Anders." We end the call and I already feel better, I'm hoping she's as great as he says because I would love to catch my confirmed flight tomorrow night.

Now to go fire someone I have indeed given too many chances to, and then wait for Keya to get here. I run my hands through my hair gathering it up; I wrap a single loc around the rest and knot it to tie my hair back in a low ponytail. Firing people is my least favorite thing of owning a business but as I make it outside I know it's the right choice.

During the past few hours, Keya has met me at the house and we've gone over plans to do a simple flip, one a new family could fall in love with.

"Thank you both for this opportunity. I worked on houses with my dad when I was a kid, this is a dream. I've really enjoyed all the projects Anderson has given me and this one will be the second flip I manage from start to finish." Her excitement for the project energizes me after what I walked into this morning. She reminds me a lot of Anders and me when we first started.

"I know you'll do great work. Anderson speaks highly of you and seeing your work on the last few remodels, I know you have the eye this house needs. I want to keep it simple and homey for new families. Think, just married, or one to two kids. Add in some modern touches like those pocket baby gates and a great backyard.

"Keep it simple with a few modern luxuries that young families need. Say less!" I already feel better about this project. After the lack of work that was done, I will need to add two more weeks to this house's timeline, but it'll get done.

I watch as Keya gives a debrief of the needs of the house to her small team. She then discusses design with the few folks who will go out to purchase materials.

I told Keya I will be here today and tomorrow to assist in getting the demo done inside the house. Landscaping the backyard is going to be easy, I want to design something really nice for a potential family. I am already envisioning a play space for kids: a rocking swing for parents to watch their littles play and maybe a few garden beds near the small patio, one I can see needs some tending to, now that I'm standing on it.

With the team busy working, I jump in with them and dream a little bit more about what this house will become for a family.

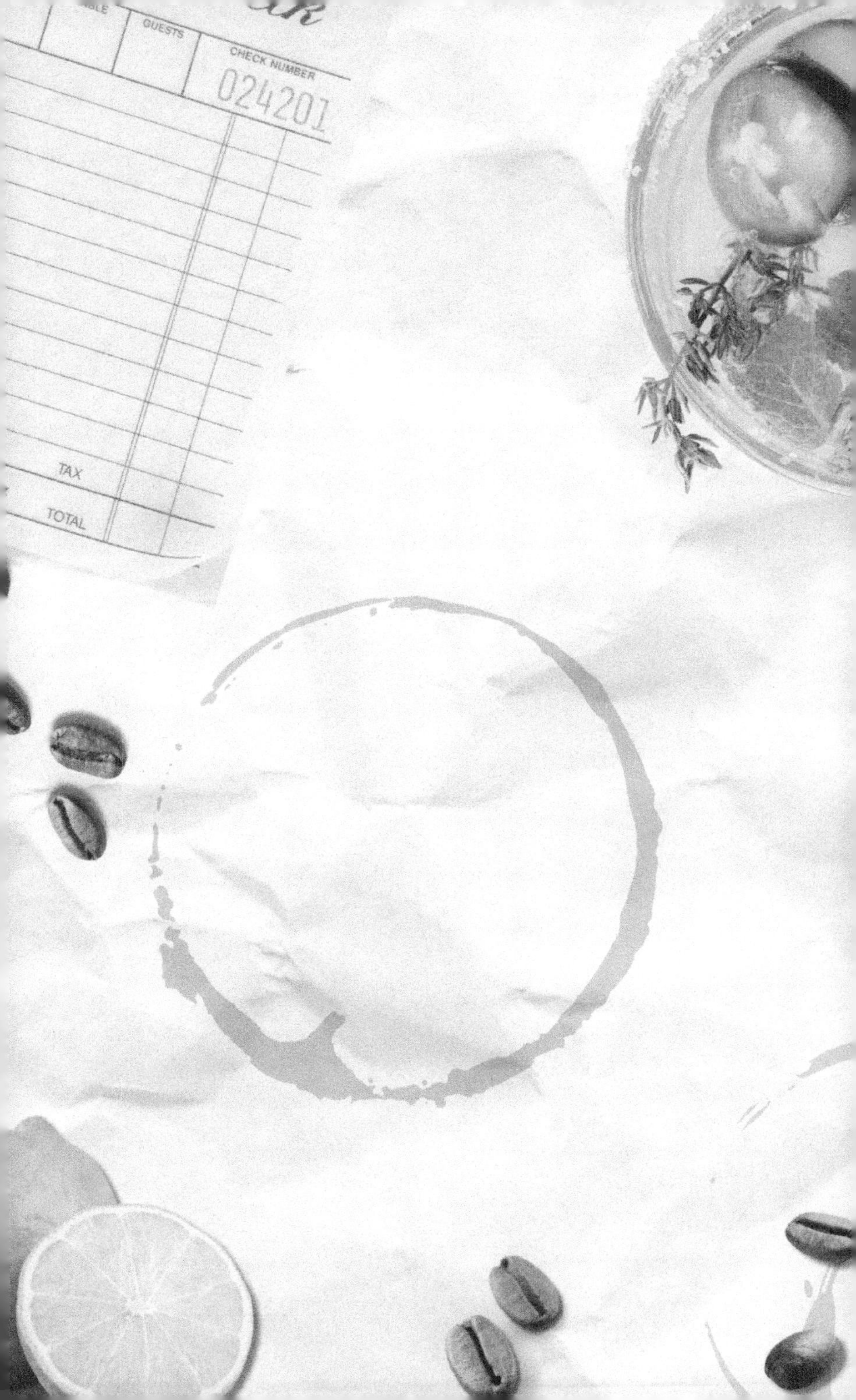
GUESTS
CHECK NUMBER
024201
TAX
TOTAL

9
Cassidy

J-babe

Get me General Tso's chicken and lo mein.

You've got no sense. *crying laughing emoji*

Lo, I want wings and fried rice.

B

LOL Holding down the fort, but order me something, send it down here.

Lo

I'll drop it off before I go up babe!

Tonight is Janelle's last in Cypress Lake before her leave is up. We opted to stay in and order Chinese as an easy, going away dinner, not that we need an excuse to be in our pajamas with lo mein and bourbon chicken.

Paloma placed the order and picked it up on her way to my place. We are waiting on Janelle as I grab a few drinks from the fridge before a knock echoes.

117

"I'll get it!" Paloma yells from the living room. "It's Janelle babe, grab an extra drink."

"I'm just going to bring out glasses and the pitcher."

Giving Janelle a side hug, I set everything down on the coffee table. "Sweet tea with lime, of course. We know you have an early flight tomorrow and don't want you sweating about alcohol."

Glancing over my shoulder with a smirk, I can see both the girls' gaping mouths at the thought of not having cocktails. Holding in my laughter, I toss an ice cube at them and make my way back to the kitchen. "Calm down you lushes, I'm grabbing the sangria from the fridge!" I yell as I dip into the fridge, grabbing what I need, along with a few extra orange slices for our glasses.

"That's what I thought," Janelle jokes before she continues. "I have an announcement! I have one more day, some things got shifted around and I leave the day after tomorrow." She looks at the both of us, hope filling her eyes.

"What I'm hearing is a pool day is in order?" Paloma dances, shimmying her shoulders as she makes her way closer to Janelle.

"Hell yes!" Janelle matches Lo's energy before they're both pelvic thrusting and dancing with finger guns. I join in with a few body rolls as I put on music that thumps loudly, before pulling them both into an embrace. "Fuck, I'm so glad you're here for another day!"

"Spill it, babe! We need to know how dinner went, you've kept us waiting all night." Janelle glances at me from under her lashes with a playfully judgmental look, one that she knows will get me talking.

I shrug at both of them. "We had dinner and caught up, then he walked me to my door."

"Bitch, please!" They holler in unison, I wave them off.

"Okay, okay!" Not wanting to keep them in suspense any longer, I fill them in about The Republic and our conversation. Both watch me intently as I continue on about how it felt like we had always known each other.

"Wait a minute," Janelle speaks up as I finally take a moment to sip my sangria. This recipe is totally going to be available in the bar, I can't stop drinking it and neither can the girls if the almost-empty pitcher tells me anything. "Did you say he buckled you in?"

"Yes?" I say, looking down at my fluffy bunny slipper-clad feet. Though it feels like we haven't missed out on several years, we have and I'm not completely sure what her response is about to be.

"That. Is. So. Fucking. Hot," Janelle yells, emphasizing every single word. The three of us all but melt into our spots. I rock my hips side to side to quell my jitters building at the memory. It was one of my favorite parts of the night. Did it surprise me? Absolutely it did, but I also felt so taken care of and it was sexy as hell.

Paloma purses her lips at me and I continue, filling them in on how breathless he left me before I got in the loft. "I can't believe he just left after a kiss like that."

"Honestly, I'm glad he did. I really like Jameson and want to see where this goes. I refuse to be a passing fling." I down the rest of my drink. Lifting the container of sangria in an attempt to pour myself another hefty glass. I shift my gaze to the empty pitcher realizing we've finished it. I let out a soft sigh and say quietly, "I just...I just can't be someone's backup or late-night romp in the sheets. I want more." I voice the one insecurity I have as it presses against my skin.

Not ready to lift my gaze to them, I watch my fingers as they grip the glass pitcher more tightly. This shame always seems to well up in me at the worst, and most unexpected moments. Until I met my best friend, I always felt like I was everyone's second choice—my so-called friends, family, hell, even my parents. Mom and Dad left me a gift I can never repay them for in my inheritance, but before they passed they were swamped with getting ahead in their career fields. Even when they were home, they weren't, they were too consumed with each other, or making their deadlines to be emotionally available for me.

I frequently found myself feeling as though I'd never be good enough to warrant their time or attention. I'd never be their top priority, they'd proven how little I mattered in the grand scheme of life over and over again. And like the melodramatic millennial I am, I resigned myself to not finding a man who would place me first. I just couldn't understand why choosing myself had to feel so fucking lonely. Tears sting my eyes, I refuse to cry another tear over something I've left in the past.

But when it comes to the possibility of what Jameson and I can be—the driving want rattles me. Of course, I've had a few really great boyfriends but the relationships fizzled out eventually.

Knocking me out of my thoughts, Janelle grips my elbow and pulls the pitcher away from me at the same moment Paloma comes to sit at my side.

"You are not alone anymore, Cass. We're here... and no, we will never ring you for a late-night romp, as you so eloquently put it." She smirks at me and I breathe out more of a groan than the laugh I was hoping for, letting my best friend's words ease me a bit.

Janelle picks up where she left off. "I know we aren't what you are longing for, but we choose you, the first time, and every single time thereafter."

Whatever floodgates I erected, collapse at their words. The dam for my tears finally breaks upon hearing their admission; healing the longing of belonging I always begged to find. Something I think we all need as we sob holding one another.

"Oh and bitch, it's called a booty call!" And just like that, Paloma has us all in a fit of laughter.

Getting up, Janelle refreshes our glasses with the sweet tea I originally brought out, and Paloma searches for a show to watch, while I make my way to the bathroom to wash my face.

Walking into my bedroom feels like the breath of fresh air I need, this part of my home is my true sanctuary and my lips twitch into a soft smile. The only lights that are on are the dim, motion-activated ones beneath my bed along with the glow from my phone on my nightstand. We promised to put our phones out of sight while we are together tonight and I took that seriously.

I gently shake my head, feeling my curls sway at the motion. Nope. I'm not going to answer the phone, or even look at it. I quickly relieve myself and then wash my hands and face. Snagging the towel I know is there, even in the dark, I pat my face dry.

Before I can make it out of the bedroom, my phone lights up again and this time I can't pass up temptation.

Jameson

I want to see you again.

It was really great catching up with you, and I would love to keep doing it.

Doing what?

Kissing me senseless…

I don't know why, but I can't help myself. I want to tell him how much I enjoy spending time with him too, but his little bubbles pop up, beating me to it.

Jameson

Senseless, hm?

I'm having a girls' night, lol. But yes, completely senseless.

Jameson

I'm free this week.

I would love to see you again this week.

Can we talk about it tomorrow?

The girls and I promised each other to put our phones away since it's the last weekend Janelle is here.

Jameson

Of course! Tell J-Dog I said hey.

I will, Bulldozer.

Jameson

winky face

I wait a couple of beats to see if he sends anything else, before placing my phone back down on my nightstand and rejoining the girls.

I wave my hand when I catch sight of the newly-filled pitcher of sangria set on the coffee table. Janelle is the one to speak up this time, "Babe, I love you, but you need more wine. Also, never say late-night romp again."

Paloma snickers in the corner of the couch and I snap my eyes at her before laughter tumbles out of my mouth. Why the hell did I call it a romp? It felt right at the time. "I'm never living this down, am I?"

"Absolutely not!" they both shout just as I plop down next to Paloma, pulling Janelle down with me. "I'm so glad to have you two. You're both staying the night," I state, not wanting either of them to leave. "Besides, tomorrow is a pool day, so there's no point in leaving."

"Sounds like the perfect night, just like old times," Janelle agrees.

Lo pushes herself to the edge of the couch, pouring each of us a refill of the deep-purple wine, and nods into a cheers.

"First choice."

"First choice," we echo back to her.

Three more glasses of wine later, the ending credits to one of my favorite nineties witchy movies plays in the background, and we pull ourselves off of the living room rug. The couch was putting us to sleep, so the genius that I am, figured we could all try to make one another levitate. Just like they do in the movie, except we were all tipsy and couldn't seem to get the saying right, no matter how many times we watched the film in our teens—the wine working against us. Paloma and I must have chanted "light as a feather, stiff as a whore" until our fingers cramped up and giggles echoed off the walls. By the time we caught our breaths, we couldn't feel our butts from sitting on the floor for so long. Things go numb!

"Okay babes, though it pains me"—Janelle clutches her hand to her heart in a false expression of agony—"I have got to get some sleep! Point me to my palace of slumber so I can pass the fuck out."

Pulling myself up from the couch, I grab Janelle's hand and lead her to the guest room. She halts her steps in the hallway, causing me to stop and look back at her, trying to see what made her stop.

Still holding my hand, she levels her eyes with mine, catching me off guard with her next words. "Take it from me, Cass. I know him a lot better than most after being friends for so long, you are never going to be second place or a fling for Jameson." I nod my head in understanding. I know she's right about that bulldozer of a man, but having been second choice so many times before rallies my thoughts. But I know it to be true, somehow; I can feel it in my bones, in the way he pays attention when I speak and how he looks at me.

We make it into the room and she throws herself on the bed. I make myself busy by grabbing her a t-shirt and shorts from the dresser. Once I turn around, clothing in hand, I notice she's already sound asleep. I swear, she and Lo can fall asleep anywhere. It blows my mind and pisses me off. I laugh at no one but myself, knowing that it takes an act of God himself, to help me fall asleep.

Silently I mouth the word *wow* and flick the light switch off, making my way back to the living room to check on Paloma. I find her in the kitchen, throwing away the empty boxes of takeout and putting our wine glasses in the dishwasher. I could waste time and tell her she doesn't have to clean up but this is how she shows love, and I appreciate her for it. Besides, if I were to say anything at all she would wave away my concerns. So instead, I squeeze her bicep a bit and say, "You're the best. Thank you, Lo."

"I'm going to crash out here." She smiles at me before walking to the couch and launching herself into the pillows. The guest room is technically her room on the rare occasion she stays over. She loves the couch more than the pillow top mattress that Janelle is currently snuggled up on.

"You know where everything is! Night, Lo."

Her goodnight is muffled by the pillow she's smothering herself with, and I pad my way back to my bedroom.

Maybe Janelle was right because when I pull the covers over me, popping one foot out to keep me cool, I have a goodnight message waiting for me from the bulldozer himself. He was definitely the hot topic of the night and seems to be within my dreams as well.

10

Cassidy

It's poooool day!

Your mom still making the sharkcoochie board, right?

How are you even awake right now?

UGHHH! Go back to bed!

No can do amiga! Get your asses up!

The next morning comes fast and loud, my head thumping to the rhythm of my heartbeat reminding me that maybe I shouldn't have made that last pitcher of Sunrise Sangria. Damn you, Benny! The recipe is his, after all. He should be the one to take the blame here. I certainly won't accept it, even if he did give me the recipe.

Walking down the hall, I stop at the guest room door and knock twice before popping my head in. Janelle is nowhere in sight until she pops her head out from the bathroom on the other side of the hallway.

"Morning, bird's nest." She giggles, toothpaste dripping down the side of her mouth, she points her toothbrush at my hair before tucking herself back into the bathroom. At that moment, a loose curl falls to the front of my face and I run my hand through my hair. Or I try to. Just as Janelle suggests, my hair is a bird's nest and it feels like there is a whole family chirping away up there. That's what I get for not changing my pillowcases back to satin, I'm going to pay for it when I try to detangle this monstrosity.

I continue down the hall and find Paloma dancing in the kitchen. She can't be a real person, she has to be a robot, because there is no way she isn't hung over. Bopping her head, she twirls in my direction before offering me a drink that looks much too thick to be anything I want near my lips right now.

"Oh, you are so drinking this. I promise it's worth it and it'll make you feel brand new before you strap your nips in a bathing suit," she says matter-of-factly, pushing the drink back in my hands and popping a straw in the dark-green sludge.

I toss the straw in the sink, eyeing her suspiciously and down the earthy-tasting smoothie. I stand there for a moment, caught in the thought of how I feel about the taste. "I guess it isn't that bad, but it isn't good either."

"You've drank worse. Go get your suit on babe! I want to catch the rays while they're out." She waves me away.

Heading back to my room to get ready, I pick up my phone and see a text from Jameson.

Jameson

Good morning, beautiful.

Hello, handsome.

I quickly get ready, loading my tote bag with sunscreen, a change of loungewear, and a few extra essentials before I hear Paloma yell from down the hallway. I pop my head out to see her tapping her foot. Janelle is already dressed in a pair of my joggers and a white tank.

"Come onnnnn bitches! It's time to get our tan on!" Paloma wiggles her ass, throwing her hands up in the air as she twirls to snatch up her towel and bag. She has on the cutest red bikini. The woman is blessed and bodied; I think about throwing a pillow at her head. But she's competitive and we don't have time for that. "I'm so glad I left this one here!" She tells me, the red strings of the bottom of her thong bikini dangle with gold charms, it's tied high up on her hips. Her top is made up of barely-there triangles tied at the neck and back. She reaches for a pair of jean shorts and pulls them up her legs before folding the corners flaps down, leaving it open, rather than buttoning them.

"Don't rush me, and watch it before one of your titties pops out." I point my finger at her before flicking my hair over my shoulder in a flourish. "I'm not throwing any dollars today babe," I joke as I pretend to rain down dollar bills.

I look down at the lavender polish on my toes, my favorite color, then back at my reflection in my floor-length mirror, smiling because I know it's going to be a great day. I can just feel it in my bones. I slide my feet into my mustard-colored sandals and toss my canvas bag over my shoulder. My swimsuit is lavender as well and is a deep v-neck top that wraps around my torso several times and ties at my side. My bottoms are high cut and rest at the highest point of my hips, giving me the illusion that my legs are longer and my waist more cinched. I blow a kiss and snap a picture of myself. Opening Jameson's text thread, I quickly change his name to something more suitable and send him the picture before making my way to Paloma and Janelle.

> Having a pool day with the girls. *devil face* What do you think of my sandals?

Bulldozer

> Girl, don't nobody care about them sandals. What sandals??? *crying laughing emoji*

I snicker and another text comes in.

Bulldozer

> You look sexy as hell. Have a good time, siren!

> You gonna get trapped by my song? What are you doing today?

Bulldozer

> Wrapping things up at the flip before I pack up and head to the airport.

> Already captured by your siren song. Got it on repeat, Babygirl. *winky face*

I send him a mermaid emoji and before I fully close our text thread, a link to the song "Addict" by Don Louis comes through from him and I click to listen. I am curious to know if it's my vibe before I respond. Immediately my head starts to bob in place, enjoying it immediately. The singer's voice is deep with a country drawl, reminiscent of Jameson's and tingles flutter across my skin. The song encourages me to sway my hips, and the sound of the door closing brings me back to reality.

I make my way to the living room, enjoying the song as the chorus comes back on, *and your skin, your hair upon my skin feels just like a drug to me*, the words that feel like they could have been written by the bulldozer himself. The girls have already made it downstairs by the time I lock up and I run down the stairs to meet them in the car.

We take Paloma's car when the weather is as nice as it is today, allowing the top to roll back so the wind can whip through our hair. She turns the radio on and blares Buckle Bunny loud enough to drown out our terrible singing, but that doesn't stop us from trying to sing louder.

The sun feels good against my skin as we lie out by the pool, warming me from the outside in and tanning my skin to a lovely cinnamon color I love so much. Keeping my eyes closed, I allow the sounds of my friends' chatter to keep me in the moment and not drift off to sleep. Lord knows I don't want to be a crispy piece of bacon by making the mistake of napping. As I open my mouth to say something, it's quickly forgotten when Lo sprays her sunscreen for the umpteenth time.

"My mouth was open!" I snatch the sunscreen out of her hand before I stand, hand on my hip I point it at her. "If you were going to be a lobster, you'd already be one."

"Yeah, but I am not reliving that burn again. I will never forget it and you two haven't let me live it down a single summer since." She laughs.

Janelle jumps into the pool and I watch the clear water lap up onto the heated pavement, almost making my mouth water, knowing the cool salt water will be as refreshing as it looks. "Girl please, let's play mermaids," I shout, jumping in after Janelle, listening to Paloma's laugh as my body hits the water.

Being at Janelle's childhood home brings back so many memories of my teenage years: the sleepovers, getting caught sneaking into the kitchen to eat her mom's snacks, sipping mango margaritas, crying over boys we thought we loved for all of a day. Anytime Lo and I came over, it was like the three musketeers were banded back together. Mrs. Paxton, Janelle's mom, would make a big lasagna with a garden salad and it felt more like family than a group of friends.

Resurfacing in the water, I prop my arms up on the edge of the pool, not wanting to get out from the cool salty oasis just yet. "So, where are we going? I vote someplace new." Getting together to have a pool day is amazing, but I don't want us to forget about planning this girls' trip that we mentioned during brunch at Eggs Benny.

"You mentioned Tulum at brunch," Janelle says, a mischievous smirk ghosting on her lips. "You could invite Jameson. I'm sure he'd be happy to blow—" She she isn't fast enough to avoid my splash and it catches her in the face, drowning out what she is about to say.

"Oop!" Is the only noise Paloma makes as she chokes on her soda.

"As I was saying, he could blow your back out under the moon, make it real romantic-like." She laughs, splashing back at me.

Paloma finally gains her composure, reaching toward the platter next to her. Mrs. Paxton had a busy day today and wouldn't be in the house while we enjoyed our pool day, but she did leave us a fully prepared charcuterie board and a pitcher of her famous mango margaritas. Janelle's mom always welcomed us with open arms and I've missed her.

After my parents passed, and we all lost touch, I didn't have the nerve to reach out, I didn't want to be a hassle or a burden. I realized many years later that I'm not a burden to those who love me. Paloma smears some creamed honey on a cracker before placing a piece of salted meat on top.

"Hm, maybe he'll spread me open like that char-coochie board right there." I dip my head back, allowing the cool water to dampen the heat rising in me anytime I think of Jameson's hands on me, feigning innocence. I pull myself out of the pool to get my own taste of the adult form of Lunchables.

"Bitch! No, you did not!" Lo says on a squeal as Janelle hoots at me from the pool, urging me on. I so did, and I meant it.

"But seriously, what are you girls thinking?" I ask, genuinely wanting to know.

"Well, I know we mentioned going to Tulum or on a cruise, but what if we did something more cozy?" Janelle pipes in from the avocado floaty she's lying on, tanning herself.

"Oh! Like a cabin?" Lo says, before stuffing more of the adult Lunch-able in her pie hole.

"A cabin would be dope! We could get a really luxurious one, with a hot tub, and maybe even have a chef come in and cook for us a couple of times. What are you thinking? A couple of weeks maybe? Oh, or is that too long?" I ask. Finding a cozy log cabin in the mountains would be such an amazing experience. We wouldn't be able to top that kind of girls' night.

"Not at all. I can get time off around wintertime! We can enjoy the snow, maybe Vermont?"

"Let's do it!" I yell, excitement coursing through me at the thought of going on a two-week vacation with my girls. I can't recall the last time I went on a vacation, it had to have been before Paloma and I opened the bar. "This is going to be amazing!"

Janelle and I both climb out of the pool, hovering over Paloma as she looks at cabins that look more like little mansions. We end up picking one that has a huge ten-person jacuzzi, a game room, and a decked-out kitchen so we can bring in a chef at least one night for dinner. Before I know it we have a chalet booked and the sun is beginning to set.

With tear-filled eyes we all say our goodbyes, knowing Janelle will have to be up before the crack of dawn to make it to the airport. It's almost harder to say goodbye now that we had an extra day together.

Pulling Janelle into a three-person hug, I squeeze her with all my might, not wanting to let her go, but knowing I have to.

"You'll text before you take off right?" Paloma asks Janelle, tears lining her eyes.

"I promise," she whispers, her voice cracking as tears flow freely down her cheeks.

"Love you so much," I whisper back to her, pulling her in for a deeper hug.

Paloma and I get into the car before we can act out our plan of kidnapping Janelle and becoming fugitives of the country. It's just not something I want attached to my resume right now, but that doesn't mean I don't seriously consider it.

For my girls, I would do just about anything.

11

Jameson

Why do I have one of those smutty books on my audiobook account?

My bad Mama, I was logged into yours by accident.

That doesn't answer the question.

Is it any good? *eyes emoji*

I'm reminded why Anders wears those flashlights strapped to his forehead. He looks absolutely ridiculous, but my phone flashlight isn't cutting it as I squint, and angle my neck, in a way I'm sure can't be good for my vision or my spine. I twist the tubing tightly with the wrench before my eyes cut over to the pinging noise from my phone.

It's been a couple weeks since my visit to Shaken Tropes and I haven't been able to get Cassidy, all curves and chaos, off my mind. It could also be that we've ramped up our texting game, bantering back and forth late into the night. I adjust the pipe again, catching the grooves as I twist and a yawn slips out. Maybe I've been staying up later than I should be, but I'm getting to know the world through Cassidy's eyes.

Getting to my feet, I pick up my phone and check my notifications, running my tongue against my teeth.

Babygirl

Hey, handsome.

What are the chances that you're all sweaty right now?

Eyes Emoji

I stifle a laugh before texting her back.

I'm definitely sweaty.

What are you reading right now?

Babygirl

Maybe a western romance with a little bit of spice.

How do you feel about cowboy hats?

I have a feeling I should buy one right now. lol

I open up my reminders app and make a note to look up western romances the next time I'm in Shaken Tropes. I'll know which one it is the moment she locks eyes with the cover. The image of her shy smile and slightly tinted cheeks cross my mind before I pocket my phone. It's an image that may have crossed my mind everyday since I asked her for a book recommendation. I rub my lips together before pushing myself off the counter I'm leaning against.

Anders made a lunch run, since we've both been here since early this morning; we needed to put a dent in the work for this house, and I for one, cannot wait for his ass to get back. I still haven't come up with a name for the place. Each house we flip, we name, but this one evades me. I stand and look around at the progress we've made so far, I'm not going to push the name, it'll come to me. Swiping the back of my hand against my forehead, I brush aside the sweat that's gathered and has begun to drip, before getting back under the sink.

The primary bathroom in the house is in shambles after taking down the walls and pulling up the flooring, there is dust and insulation every-where. Demo is easy but the mess is my least favorite part of the job; I would rather be conceptualizing a new add-on or the framework for a feature wall. The Crews team will be here tomorrow, but Anders and I wanted to get an early start on things, simultaneously giving us a chance to hang together in our old element, something we haven't done in quite some time.

Speak of the devil, Ander's voice echoes through the empty house but I can't really tell what he's saying, not over the afrobeats playing through the space. Water sprays in my face from under the sink in the kitchen and I hold up my hands to stop it from drowning me. I wrap my hand on the wrench from inside the work bag next to me and give the pipe a hard twist before a shadow covers me.

"What's up, man?" Anders laughs under his breath at the rookie mistake I just made by not turning the water off first. With all the years working with his grandfather, I know better. My mind is focused elsewhere, on a particular someone. He throws a towel to me and I wipe my face, drying off my hands before I take his outreached one to stand. "I'm not even going to say it." He holds his hands up in defense from the pointed look I'm giving him.

We started focusing on our own houses in college when we did odd jobs for his dad and grandfather, Anders being naturally handy with an eye for seeing the end goal before the walls are even up, he simply had a calling for it. Besides, he's always had a way with hearing my ideas and turning them into the vision I pictured in my own mind, even if I was unable to fully explain everything. He may be a general contractor, but I think design is his true passion. I'm just waiting for him to admit it or open up a new division in our company. Working together is seamless and that's the way I like it. Since joining forces and co-owning Crews, we haven't often had the chance to work side by side with each other. He is the ying to my yang when it comes to business. Having the chance to work on this project together feels like old times. But fuck if I am not tired of working and it is barely past two in the afternoon.

"I'll say it. It was a rookie mistake that I wouldn't have made if I wasn't living on the property. I'll start looking into hotels. I even considered my parents' place." The tension in my voice is apparent but not aimed at Anderson.

"I don't know why you aren't there anyway, the place is fully renovated and I didn't think anyone was living in it," he says.

"Before I came into town, there was a family using it as a short-term rental but they just requested an extension. I don't have the heart to tell them no," I respond to a flighty Anders, who's already shouting his response back to me.

"Shit, forgot something in the truck. Be right back." He rushes out to the car, leaving the front door open in his wake.

Glancing at the doorway, I pile some of the old flooring in my arms before making my way to the backyard where the dumpster was delivered at the crack of God's ass this morning. Nothing in my body would make me a morning person. Did I still get up early as hell and get things done? Yeah, but I am still going to hate it when I do. Shrugging to no one but myself as I toss the old tile. Just as I'm about to turn back into the house, my phone chirps with a notification from my girl. I don't quite know when I decided she was mine but she is, whether she knows it or not.

Anders walks in before I get a real chance to respond to Cassidy and he's right back into work mode. He has no off switch unless there is food involved. Dude is a foodie!

"I'm glad you are finally seeing it my way, brother. There's always space on my couch if you want it." He claps me on the back and points his thumb over his shoulder at a bag on the counter.

Walking over to it, the plastic crinkles as he pulls out a couple of brown paper bags that have darkened in some areas. Grease. My stomach chooses that moment to express just how hungry I am.

Still holding my phone in one hand, another notification pops up on the screen. "You got that goofy-ass grin on your face again, fool. Let's take a break." Anders walks out of the room with his hands full, his arms holding multiple brown paper bags.

"You are the man!" I exclaim and I follow, grabbing one of the bags from his extended hand.

He laughs before biting into one of the Cuban sandwiches he picked up for us. Simple pleasures are my favorite. Nothing is better than good food, no matter if it's a five-star meal or a toasted Cuban from a corner sandwich shop.

I quickly unwrap mine, diving in and taking a bite far too big for my mouth, but enjoying it regardless. That's until I feel something cold drip down the side of my face and just know it's mustard.

"You gonna tell me about that goofy grin or what man? It's Cassidy who's got you acting all gooey isn't it?" He asks, exaggerating the oo sound in gooey. Anders and I have always been really close and I'm surprised that he held out this long. This fool can't even keep gifts a secret, at most he rolls the bag up before handing it to you, way before the day it's meant for.

I shake my head, holding back a laugh from the memory of him handing me my birthday gift early, a few years back. My birthday was months away but he couldn't stop himself. I was picking him up for lunch before we had to go into work; he got in the truck and tossed the gift bag at me with a big-ass smile on his face. He had just bought it and still had the receipt in the bag and everything. He's not just a friend but a brother to me.

Swiping the napkin across my mouth, I swallow and finally answer his question, "Yeah, it's her. I can't get her out of my head and I don't want to. I don't know man, we just click together like puzzle pieces." The grin makes its way back to my face as I think of her. She makes me feel a lightness in my body, and a calm that can remove any worry plaguing me, things I've not experienced before.

"There is just something about her that makes it easy to be who I am, even in the small interactions we've had. It's" —nodding my head side to side, I attempt to find a word about her that fits—"effortless man, she is just the right amount of everything, and somehow it's effortless. Cassidy isn't a woman I want to ever forget about. I've always wanted a woman who's sure of herself, strong in her beliefs, and knows what she wants in her life. I want to build a life with someone who can ebb and flow with me, where we can laugh until we grow old and senile. She's funny as hell bro, and beautiful. I've had a crush on her since seeing her in the halls in high school. It's crazy how the universe brings people back together."

"It sounds like you might have found your girl," he replies, not quite a question as he shoves a piece of the honey-toasted Cuban sandwich into his mouth.

I nod my head, taking another bite of mine.

"When Crews worked on Shaken Tropes, Cass and I built an easy friendship. She has a way about her that makes you feel like family, like you belong in her circle. If she's the one for you J, how are you going to make a relationship work being a nomad?"

"It's a concern I've been trying to figure out."

"You know the answer is as easy as moving, right?" Anders squints his eyes at me as he stuffs the last bite of his sandwich in his mouth.

"Isn't it too soon for that? She would think I was crazy if I just up and moved here," I reply. But even saying that out loud doesn't seem quite right.

"Look bro, I'm gonna be real with you, okay?" He pauses briefly to make sure I'm listening. "Cassidy isn't someone who is going to give a rat's ass about 'too soon' if it's right and if what you say is true, then it is. Figure out your shit and make a choice." He's right and I know it. There is only one choice I have to make but I want to be sure, I won't flip flop around with her heart.

141

"Guess I have some figuring out to do. I can't imagine not having her in my life. I've got it bad." I huff a laugh through my nose thinking about her book suggestion and make a mental note to start reading one of them tonight if I'm not too tired from the day's work.

I've never bothered with dating around. Have I dated? Of course, I've dated women but I never let it get too deep. I know what I want and maybe I was just waiting for the curls and hips to show me the way.

Grabbing my phone from the counter, I open the text thread, unable to hold back any longer. After our date, I switched her name in my contacts to the nickname I call her by, even more than her own name.

Babygirl

Do you want to come over to the bar tonight?

Is 9pm too late?

Babygirl

Not at all.

When I look up from my phone, Anders is shaking his head and barks a laugh at the lovesick grin I'm sure I'm sporting.

"I'd put money on it—she's it for you, Big Dog!" His laugh echoes down the hall, aiming for the bathroom. He has no idea just how right he is.

Dropping my head back into the hot spray of the shower, I feel the weight of my exhaustion hit me. We finished demoing as much of the house as we could before the construction team starts on it tomorrow morning. Normally, I wouldn't be washing my hair this late into the night, it takes forever to dry, but no matter how tired I am, I won't be skipping Shaken Tropes tonight, I gotta look my best for my woman.

I knew I wouldn't be able to sit down and read the book tonight, so I decided to buy the audiobook. I programmed my Alexa device to play it while I was getting ready to hop in the shower. It's been playing for a while and I can't lie, I'm into it. I grab the shampoo bottle, squeeze just enough into my hands, and begin to work it into my scalp, allowing the rich lather to run down my hair as I rinse it out. The story started right off with some action between wolves. They were surrounded by others like them. The narrators are on point with the scene, adding in growls and rips for when the lead character bites into the other's neck.

With a speed I was unprepared for, he presses himself against me. Pushing me until the back of my knees hit the bed, forcing me to fall back. My submission is what he is after... but I'm not entirely sure I'm ready to give it to him so easily.

The water rains down on my head, washing away the shampoo that seems to be never-ending. What is going on in this book? I make an attempt to open my eyes, squinting in the direction of my Alexa device, wiping away the lingering suds from the shampoo before it burns my eyes.

His wolf all but growls at me while grinding his length against me. "If you think for one second that I'm sleeping on that floor and not in this bed with my cock sunk deep into your dripping c—"

"Alexa, pause the damn book," I yell from the shower. Alexa continues playing as if she didn't hear my command. "Fucking AI!"

He drops between my thighs like a beast ready to devour his prey; the gleam in his eyes tells me that he isn't ever letting me go after this. Not when he calls me his mate. My eyes drop for just a moment. The width of him makes my mouth water and my sex clench in anticipation.

"ALEXA!" I wait, listening for the quiet that follows when it awaits my next command, but it doesn't come. The only one coming is the she-wolf playing on the speakers from my audiobook.

I finish my shower as it continues to play. I went in blind to the book and I'm kinda glad I did, I wasn't expecting the spice and I was a bit nervous for Anders to walk in given it's also our current flip. I can already imagine the shit talking. It may not have been a book I picked up on my own, but I'm really enjoying it. The sex scenes are out of this world and the action doesn't let up. I see exactly why she loves this story so much and I hope to hear which parts are her favorite so I can commit them to memory. Wrapping the towel around my center, I walk into the room to get ready.

Pulling on my light-tan, cloth joggers, I snatch a fresh long-sleeved, white shirt and pull it over my head before slipping the matching tan hoodie on. The audiobook plays in the background, an epic fight scene is being read that I don't want to pause in the middle of, but I have to if I'm going to make it on time.

I lace up my sneakers on my sock-clad feet, grabbing my essentials before making my way to the door to see my Babygirl.

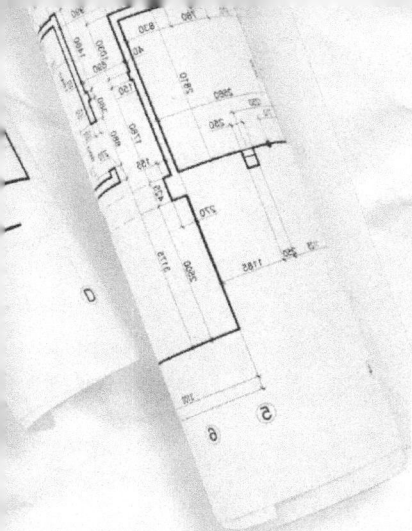

12

Cassidy

> I invited Jameson to the bar tonight.

> I really like him guys.

J-babe

Legs Up, Perfume On

This makes my heart so happy

Fuck my fucking life. Of course, the night I think Shaken Tropes is going to be easy, it just isn't. B would normally be here a bit early stocking the bar, but she caught a terrible stomach bug and is out.

Paloma is never late, never. And yet here I am, without anyone else to help me on a surprisingly busy night as I scramble around trying to not look like I'm chasing squirrels.

I wasn't technically on the schedule tonight, but I just had a feeling after B called, that I may want to jump in. Boy, am I glad that I did. Sending a quick "Are you okay?" text to Paloma, I stuff the phone in my pocket before handing a sweet older woman her drink. Not forgetting at all to grab the book suggestion that I think she just might love.

"Thank you so much! My granddaughter says she loves this place and that you lovely girls would give me the perfect—" She stops, almost pressing the book to her lips in a forgotten thought. "Oh! The perfect book boyfriend." She wiggles her eyebrows at me, taking with her the BDA martini and the small-town billionaire romance.

BDA is short for Big Daddy Apple, it's a spin on a spiced apple martini and tastes just like an elevated apple tart. The flavors make me think of all those small-town characters and the billionaire ready to make their dreams come true. This particular book follows characters in their forties, as they realize they have a second chance at the love they missed out on. There's an apple picking scene I think she's going to melt over. Whew! Even just thinking about it makes me want to fan myself.

My nerves get the best of me and I pull out my phone again, hoping for a notification from Paloma, but there is nothing. Worrying myself won't help either one of us, I'm just going to believe she is okay unless I hear otherwise. But if she doesn't text me back before the end of the shift... then I am going to hunt her down.

A frustrated sigh escapes me before turning around and making eye contact with the most devilishly handsome man—it has to be a sin to look that damn good. I'm almost positive there is a law against it somewhere.

The stress from my face begins to melt away as a small smile curves my lips. Sliding my phone into my back pocket, I exhale a short breath and snap my eyes back up to the bar. I shift my eyes back and forth, assessing if anyone is in need of me before I see Jameson making his way to me in long, purposeful strides. He is eating up the distance between us with a look on his face that says he's ready for duty. I almost salute him but think better of it.

"Hey Babygirl, where do you need me?" He waves his hand at the surprised expression that I know is on my face before pulling the deep-green towel off my shoulder. "You've got it written all over your face. Let me help you."

"Really? I couldn't ask you to do that. You came here to hang out, I didn't realize it would be a night like tonight." I sweep my hand out showcasing the blissful chaos of the night. His gaze meets mine, giving me a slight once-over as if to say, *girl please.*

"I came here to be with you and that's exactly what I plan on doing, in any capacity you need me. Besides, you didn't ask, I offered. So let me." He rubs his lips together before shaking his head, and breathing out a laugh.

I stare at the man in front of me for just a moment before nodding my head and pulling him around the bar, a spark lighting up through my fingertips from our contact.

"Tell me if I need to slow down!" He nods his head in understanding. Pulling the sweatshirt up and over his head, he stores it away behind the counter and my eyes track the movement of him rolling the sleeve of his long-sleeved shirt up. Watching the muscles strain as he turns his arm just right. Why is that so fucking hot? Taking a deep inhale I give him a run-through on the register, instructing him on the ins and outs.

The night moves along as I mix drinks and tend to the tables that we set up in the dimmer areas of our bar. The only problem is, I keep catching myself stealing glances at Jameson when I should be focused on matchmaking customers to books. Though he got the barest of bones of training, that doesn't seem to dissuade customers, he's great with them, making them laugh with his jokes to ease the longer wait time. I'm not completely sure if it's because he is a people person or if they just like the eye candy. One customer in particular is a bit more bold as she leans over the counter, closing the distance between them, batting her lashes.

Heat rushes up my neck causing me to loosen my shoulders from the tension of—dare I say, jealousy? Before I can take a moment to clear my head of that thought, that same customer runs her fingers lazily against his on the counter; he pulls his hand away quickly, but I'm already making my way over from the other side of the bar.

Running my hand up the side of his back, I twist myself just slightly so I'm but a breath away from being pressed against him.

There's no moment of apprehension, no wonder of what's going on or pause. He simply wraps his arm around my waist, closing the distance between the two of us and lowering his chin slightly to look me directly in my eyes and my breath hitches.

Recognizing her dismissal, she thanks him and walks away. I would look to see if she left but I can't manage to tear my gaze away from Jameson. Especially not when he dips his mouth close to my ear. "You plan on explaining to me why I keep getting referred to as 'Book Boyfriend?'" Jameson's warm whisper of a question lingers between us as I fight the tremble coursing through my body from the feel of his heated words so close to the underside of my ear, so near my neck.

Instead of waiting for my reply, he continues on without missing a single beat, "Maybe after we finish up, we can grab a quick bite to eat and I can share my thoughts on the book you recommended to me."

"You read it?" My core clenches at the thought of what he's read. I didn't think he would actually read it. Maybe he'd hold on to it or possibly lose it—I inwardly cringe at the thought of one of my books being lost. I also considered that he'd give it back to me and pretend he read it. My cheeks blaze at knowing what's within its pages having read it myself—a few times if I'm going to be honest.

"Yes. No..." He pauses, tossing the green towel over his shoulder. "I bought the audiobook before I jumped in the shower. The narrators are very *expressive*." His gaze darkens slightly as he finishes.

"Audiobooks totally count as reading," I find myself saying as warmth spreads over my chest and down my belly. The smile on his face doesn't hide the desire behind his eyes and I can only imagine the part he ended on. He squeezes my waist a bit before releasing me.

Taking another towel tucked beneath the bar, I wipe the counter down after the last drink I made and look out into the bar. Customers are starting to slow and the ones who are settled have their heads tucked into a book or are sipping away on their drink. My contentment is suddenly interrupted when Paloma rushes through the front door.

"I'm so sorry!" Lo says, eyeing Jameson behind the counter. She wraps her arms around me as she exclaims, "Promise I will make it up to you and will explain everything."

"I was worried sick. What's going on?" Side by side we make our way to an empty booth.

"I know, and I swear I will tell you what's going on... just not right now." If it wasn't for the look of pure exhaustion on her face, I would be pressing her for more information.

"Shaken is about to close. Why don't you take the rest of the night off and go do something with the finest barkeep in Cypress Lake," she adds.

I take that moment to look around the bar. The night has dwindled to the last few lingering customers and our part-time worker came in about an hour ago.

Can I talk myself out of her offer and work for the rest of the night? Yeah, I totally could. But this is another *yes* that I'm going to give myself. Paloma knows if she absolutely needs me, I'll drop everything to be here. I'm literally a knock away and in her case, she has the keys.

"Okay, but you'll let me know if you need me?" She purses her lips. "Cool, but also, if you don't need me that would be fucking incredible and don't forget we've got to go pick out our *girl* tomorrow!"

Pulling myself from the booth I give her a quick side hug, I really am so relieved she's okay. But I have a man who I would really like to scale like the mountain he is.

Toeing off my sneakers at the door, I take a step to the side to allow Jameson entry into my sanctuary. It may seem silly, but this is far more than just my home, this is the place where I can turn off the world and just be.

The walls in my living room are painted a green so deep that on most days it looks like a velvet black. Overlapping commissioned works by B, along with pieces by other artists, hang on the walls with gallery lights above them. A do-it-yourself installation I saw on Pinterest one day that turned out amazing.

Plants can be seen throughout the entire space—hanging, or occupying multiple surfaces—but what really livens up the room is the window seat. It's my favorite space at night. A small stack of books is set on the side where plush pillows don't overtake the area.

This home is my getaway, only my gran and the girls have been up here. Why invite someone into my peace if all they will do is bring havoc?

Reaching past Jameson, I brush against him as I flick the light switch that turns on the two small lamps placed on either side of the television. I watch his eyes take in my space and I wish I could say that I'm not nervous, but I am. Everything here is an extension of me, and I want him to enjoy what he sees.

A soft smile lights up his face, his mouth tugging to one side a bit like he has an inside joke. "Smells just as good as you do." He continues to take in small areas I created in different spots of the room as he lifts his foot, slowly untying his sneakers and setting them to the side. "It looks like you. It's perfect."

"Thank you. Would you like something to drink or something to eat? We could order in." Walking into the open kitchen, I pull out two glasses and try to keep my distance for a moment, in an attempt to calm myself. "And thank you for helping me tonight."

"You thought I was going to turn down a night with you? I would rather be scrubbing down the bar than not seeing you at all, Babygirl. We can order out if you want..." His voice is right behind me lingering on the last couple words, allowing me to choose. But he's so close that I pause, not missing him calling me "Babygirl" again. And why do I like it so much?

As if on autopilot, I pour us both a glass of tea. Before I opened the bar, I sat a pitcher of water and several tea bags out on the porch, with the sun shining bright it made the perfect pitcher of sun tea. It's my favorite way to make sweet tea, it's less bitter and smoother this way, it tastes like sunshine. Along with the glasses, I grab the container of lime wedges I keep in the fridge and honey from the cabinet. Squeezing two lime wedges into each glass, I blush realizing I didn't ask what he wanted as I hand him his tea before sipping mine.

He takes a deep gulp and I watch his Adam's apple bob as I take a swallow of my own. There has to be a hole in my lip, swiping my tongue out I lick at the drop escaping and see his gaze follow my movement.

I watch him appear almost larger, as he stops leaning against the counter, coming to his full height before he takes the few steps that are between us. Staring down at me as I keep myself rooted to the floor trying to convince myself not to climb up his body.

Biting at my bottom lip, I return the same heated gaze.

"If you don't stop worrying that lip of yours, I'm going to have to find some other way to keep it busy."

"Mm, really, like what?" The challenge is clear in my tone. One that he takes full advantage of as he grips the fullness of my waist, anchoring me to him.

His tongue slowly licks up the center of my lips and I gasp at the feel of it, then his mouth is on mine. His free hand wraps into my hair, pulling it slightly to give him more access to my neck. Hungry lips graze my collarbone, teeth skim over the skin of my neck where his tongue blazes a trail up to my ear and goosebumps cover my skin. Having him this close to me in my kitchen leaves me breathless. He peppers kisses to that one spot behind my ear that has heat curling low in my stomach. I run my hands up his arms, feeling every bit of thick muscle, and gently rake my nails down the back of his shoulders. A breathy moan escapes me as a tremble quakes up my back and down to my sex at the feeling of his strength. The smoky bourbon and citrus of his cologne flow through my senses at an intoxicating speed. I would drink him in if I could.

This man is in tune with the reactions my body freely gives to him because when he lifts me on to the island, he leans into my neck and bites down near my shoulder while his hand connects sharply against my ass. Pain and pleasure mix together, leaving me shuddering through a deep moan.

"Fuck me."

"Not yet Cassidy, I'm just getting started and I've been dreaming about this since dropping you off after our first date. May I?" Looping a finger into my belt loop he tugs me into him and rubs his thumb over the button. Consent has never been so sexy and I nod my head. His voice is a low rasp as he says, "Need to hear you say the word."

"Yes." The only word I can say, caught up in his bourbon warmth and it's the only word that matters.

He unbuttons my jeans, unzipping them and slowly pulling them down my thighs. If I had any insecurities about my body, they'd be thrown into the fire with the hunger in Jameson's gaze.

His eyes dip low and I watch them go molten, taking in the triangle of bright red mesh between my thighs. We need to have this talk right now and get it out of the way. Running my hands up his arms—they seem to be my new obsession—I let the heat of the moment meld with every word that leaves my mouth. "I haven't been with anyone since before my annual checkup a year ago, my results came back negative."

Jameson's big hands knead my ass as he lifts his eyes to mine before he responds, "My last physical was about six months ago, all negative, Babygirl." He runs his hands up my thighs, his thumbnail grazing the soaked material and I purr my response. I fucking purr.

"Lean back Cassidy and bend your elbows for me." His grip tightens almost painfully around my thighs and his hunger is evident as he licks his lips, staring down at my red mesh panties. God, I'm so fucking glad I wore these. Obeying his command, I lean back.

The translucent red mesh must surely show the wetness at this angle. His thumbnail runs up my slit, over the mesh, creating a delicious feeling that has a breathy moan falling from my lips. Jameson slips a finger through the side of my panties and rubs his thumb into my wet folds before circling the bundle of nerves with a soft pressure. "Is this all for me, Cass?" His hands ghost up the outside of thighs and grasp my panties, gently pulling them from my legs and pocketing them.

The devilish grin he gives me tells me I'm never getting those back and fuck if I care. I watch him spread my thighs wide before he takes in a deep inhale and looks back up at me.

"Eyes on me, Cassidy."

My brain very well may have short-circuited hearing those words. The same words I've read in books until the sun was threatening to rise. The same words I've come to in my shower.

Now those words have me dripping at the sound of his deep, velvety voice speaking them as he spreads my legs. The concrete countertop is smooth and cool in contrast to how hot his palms are on the fleshy part where my ass and thighs meet.

Before I can consider his next move, his mouth is on me. Licking up my center, he dips his tongue into my wet heat as he presses my thighs further back. Leaving me open and completely at his mercy.

"Fuck," he growls, sucking on the lips of my pussy, he kisses each side before devouring me completely. Driving sounds out of me that I'm unfamiliar with. "You taste as sweet as I imagined." I become increasingly aware of my own heartbeat, the need to touch and explore him is overwhelming as he tongue fucks me.

I can feel his teeth graze against my clit as he softly bites down before sucking my sensitive bud into his mouth... hard.

"Oh, oh my God! Yes." My body shudders beneath his ministrations. This is another yes—another *yes* to myself—and fuck if it doesn't feel incredible to be worshipped with abandon.

"That's it, Baby, give me those beautiful sounds." He presses his tongue flat against my center while sliding two fingers deep inside of me, fucking me with them slowly at first.

Picking up speed, he curls his fingers nudging against the spot that will send me over the edge and my back bows off the counter. His other hand leaves a trail of heat behind as it travels up the side of my thigh, gripping on the thicker areas.

"Jameson, I'm so close." Guttural moans pour out of me. Screaming his name feels like the puzzle pieces are connecting and shattering all at once.

"Not yet, Cassidy. Don't you dare come yet." His calloused hands pinches and pulls at my nipple as his tongue laps up my juices. My toes curl, holding my breath as I attempt to hold off my oncoming orgasm. As if he knows what I need, his hand slowly glides between my breasts. Higher and higher it climbs until it braces my neck before he grips it. Not tight enough to cause panic but enough to bring my attention to him. "Leaving you breathless is my job. Need you to breathe for me, Baby."

He squeezes my neck once more before I beg him for more, "Please."

Still between my thighs, he looks up at me. "Please what? Use those beautiful words of yours." I gulp, pushing down any hesitation I have.

"Tighter. Please." My voice is barely audible given my need for release. His hand tightens around my throat and I plead with my eyes that he will stop edging toward a cliff that I want to free fall over. Feeling the weight of his hand against my neck sends shivers over my sweat-soaked skin.

My eyes are still watching him, taking the command he gave me seriously. Never being ordered around before I have nothing to compare his request to, but it heats my skin and makes me giddy all at once. Lingering, he slowly runs his tongue through my folds, pumping his fingers at an agonizingly slow pace. Once. Twice. My orgasm is so close that I can feel the tingle starting in my toes.

"Give it to me, Cassidy." My head drops back, chest heaving, and I let it take me completely over in a silent scream, my walls clenching around his fingers before my body turns to jello.

"You're so fucking beautiful coming around my fingers." His entire focus is on me, but mine, no mine is on his glistening fingers. The same ones he is currently licking. "But I need to feel you around my cock now." My chest rises and falls from my uneven breaths, from both the incredible orgasm Jameson just gave me and also from his naughty words.

"Yes, please." I sit up, my voice needy and heavy with lust. This man is created of pure sin and I say a quick thank you, barely stopping myself before I say it out loud.

Holding his hand out to me, I take it and pull him back to my bedroom. I don't know if I've ever been spread open quite like that—on my counter no less—but I am far from done and I need him to know that.

13

Jameson

My cock strains beneath my sweats as she pulls me through the hallway towards her bedroom. I want nothing more than to sink myself deep into her. Her splayed on that countertop was the best meal a man could ask for and it would be foolish to try convincing myself that I don't want—*no*. This is more than a *want*. I need another taste of her.

Shaking my head slightly, I attempt to remind myself what tonight is about. Tonight is about hanging with my Babygirl and getting to see her just as she is, which is perfect from this view. Her t-shirt hugs her curves, stretching over her hips, barely covering her ass that's peeking beneath the hem.

Her panties are burning a hole in my pocket. I don't know what made me take them, it's not something I have ever done before, but I have also never been so consumed with someone before either. I'm not going to question my gut reaction too deeply.

Seeing how she turns back to look at me, her gaze filled with wanton desire tells me everything I need to know. She needs to be fully taken care of. I take a long stride right up behind her and wrap my arm around her middle as we enter her bedroom.

"Do you need to feel my cock, Cassidy?" I know she does, but I want to hear her say it.

"Yes." Coated in need, her voice is all moan. I grind myself against her ass, needing her to feel exactly what she does to me. I lean down, nipping at her neck before my tongue travels up to her ear. She tips her head back against my chest, a soft smile playing at her lips as she sways her hips into the hardness beneath the fabric of my joggers and I steal a kiss, unable to hold myself back. I gently stroke my tongue against hers and I cup her breasts, massaging them as she deepens the kiss, her flavor still on my tongue. Cassidy spins in my arms, pressing her half-naked form against my body. Running her fingers along the top of my pants, she slips them beneath the waistband and strokes my dick through my boxers and I groan.

"You going to give me what I need, Bulldozer?" she questions playfully, her fingers sliding over the waistband of my pants, and I press my hand to hers, stopping her teasing touch. Her voice may as well be a siren's song because I nod my head in response, but I'm also conveying a request I hope she sees as I crowd her, backing her against the end of her bed.

I watch the way her thighs move as she makes her way up the bed, hunger in her eyes that I'm sure is matched in mine. I hook my fingers under the waistband of my joggers and tug them lower in one smooth motion. I watch her eyes widen, her mouth dropping slightly open as my dick springs free, curved, and standing at attention for her. I wrap my hand around my shaft, pumping once, twice, until she pokes out her tongue, ghosting it across her lips. Seeing her eyes widen with satisfaction sends a shiver up down my spine.

My mouth draws up to one side, the way she looks at me makes me want to puff out my chest, instead I grab one of her ankles, pulling her to me, a yelp escaping her as I do. "You're so fucking beautiful. Come here, Cassidy." Pulling her onto my lap, I sit back on her bed, guiding her lush body onto my own. "Come take what you need."

Without any hesitation, she fully straddles my thighs, and slowly, so slowly she lowers herself. "Oh. My. God." She enunciates every word like a prayer, puffing out a breath on each word, her skin is covered in goosebumps as she rests her palms on my chest. "You're so thick."

"You take me so well." I groan, gripping her hips as I help lower her down until her clit is pressed against me and I press my hips into her. Watching as her mouth gapes open and her head drops back takes my fucking breath away.

Then she's moving, moving her hips in circular motions as she adjusts to my size. She presses her weight into her palms as she rides me, taking what she needs from me and I fucking love it. The feel of her hot sex as she clamps her walls around me. She feels so tight, better than any of the sorry-ass daydreams I've been having.

Her curls are like a closing curtain to my view of her on top of me as she drops her head. "Fucking hell Cassidy, you feel so good. So *fucking* good. But I need to see your beautiful face while you ride my cock." Smoothing her curls to the side, I palm the side of her face, until I see her brown eyes meet mine. I find myself daydreaming about her wild strands; her curls are silky and right now, the feel of them is like a drop of dopamine. Once her eyes are back on mine, I can't stop myself as I thrust into her from underneath.

Her cheeks are a deep pink, her mouth hung open in an O shape. There is nothing more sexy in this moment than her, and I need for her to see what I see while she takes every inch of me. "Turn around for me,

Baby."

"What? How?" She questions, but does as I ask with a slight whimper as she pulls herself from me. I press my back against her headboard and grab her waist, pulling her back on me in a reverse cowgirl. Slowly, inch by inch, I press into her warmth and groan as she contracts around my length. If I come right now, I'd be a damn fool.

"Look up."

"You're kinda bossy." She huffs a laugh.

"Oh, you think so."

"Yeah." Turning her body slightly, she angles back to look at me with a smile tugging at her lips.

I reply with a squeeze to her side. "You gonna listen?" I ask, adding a bit of snark. I watch her eyes catch our reflection in the mirror that's situated in front of her bed. When she does, her gaze widens. "I think you like that I am. Now watch." Not giving her another second to think, I lift her hips slightly and grind into her.

Her moans fill the room, sweat covers her skin and the light reflects off her, giving her a glow like the fucking goddess she is. She bounces on top of me and I meet her thrust for thrust, pumping into her with such force she almost topples over me. Anchoring her to me, I wrap my hand around her as I grab a handful of her belly. She's so soft and I want to feel every single inch of her, like she is me. Lowering my hand, I rub circles on her clit as she rocks herself closer to her climax. "More, I-I need more."

Her pleas don't go unheard as I lift her from my cock, soaked from her wet slick. "Get to the edge of the bed Cassidy, one leg on the bed." I don't ask, seeing how much she enjoyed my instructions earlier, bossy or not. Rounding behind her, in a slow lick I run my tongue up the back of her cunt and push my tongue deep inside of her as I grip my aching cock.

"Fuck." She tastes so fucking good. I pull back and blow cool air against her tender flesh and watch as she shivers. "Such a pretty pink pussy." Spreading her wide open, I thrust into her to the hilt, knowing that I'm hitting the spot that is going to send her over. I pump into her, my balls slapping her pussy before I pull her up and against me. Wrapping my arm over her shoulder and around her chest, I grab one of her breasts as my other hand dips low, stroking her clit. The sounds of skin slapping echoes off the walls of the room. "Soak this dick Baby, let me have it," I almost beg her, before giving her pussy one quick slap.

"Jameson!" she screams my name and does exactly like I ask. The pain and pleasure mingling together is evident in the whimper of her voice. If I could have this moment on repeat for the rest of my life I would be a happy man. I find my own release quickly as her walls squeeze around me and we both fall to the bed, catching our breaths.

"Let's get you cleaned up, Babygirl," I say to her, getting up from the bed as I go to her bathroom. I wouldn't have known it was there if it wasn't for a tiny night light illuminating the room.

"There are hand towels underneath the cabinet, to the right," she shouts from the bed, her voice pleasurably exhausted and I follow her instructions. Turning on the water, I allow it to heat before wetting the white towel. Slipping in and out quickly, I meet her back on the bed, cleaning up our mess that feels more like a masterpiece. We lie in each other's arms for a while, enjoying the moment as our breaths mingle together. Every single missed interaction leading us to this moment leaves me feeling drunk off Cassidy. I run my hand up and down her side, her body is lush as I give soft squeezes here and there as she nuzzles deeper into my side.

"I'm starving and I need to pee." She laughs, untangling herself from my arms and rushing to the bathroom. I think about the night we've had together and I don't want it to be over yet.

Her moans are my new favorite sounds and I will do everything in my power to continue to hear them. Kneading my thumb deeper into the arch of her bare foot, I watch as her head drops back against a satin covered pillow on her bed.

"If you keep making faces like that, I'm going to have to do more to you than rub your feet."

She smirks at me before snatching another dumpling from the container of takeout we ordered after she came out of the bathroom. When I walked in with the food, she slid her laptop into the drawer of her nightstand and put a bed tray on the top of her duvet so we could enjoy our food bundled up together in the blankets.

This is the kind of woman I enjoy seeing. One comfortable in who she is, in her home. She came out of the bathroom in an oversized t-shirt and shorts so small, I was sure they were really panties but she refused to confirm. Feigning innocence we both know she doesn't have, or need for that matter. I love it, it's cute as hell.

"There is no way they based this off reality. My firemen don't go to these type of lengths!" Her head drops back in laughter at my thoughts on her favorite television fire drama. Neither of us wanted the night to be over, and why should it be. There is no place I would rather be than here, getting to know another piece of my girl. We agreed I would order take out while she picked a show for us to watch. And now I'm sitting wondering how I am going to catch up on eight seasons. "And look at him! He has slept with several women and somehow still has the energy to scale a building. No."

"I'll have you know this is the number one show on right now. It won an Emmy! Or some award..." she says in mock anger.

"This can't be real." Throwing my hands in the air, I point at the television. "He's the one who started the fire in the first place."

She wiggles her toes at me and I continue massaging her foot before Captain Save-a-Hoe rescues another damsel in distress. As a commercial comes on, she turns to look at me.

"Why is it we never spent time together in high school? With you and Janelle being so close it's wild that we weren't friends." Her question would have surprised me if I hadn't been thinking it myself over the last couple weeks.

I remember seeing her often while in school but I never got the nerve to introduce myself. Teen hormones will do that to a guy. She was beautiful, but there always seemed to be this underlying pain resting just behind her eyes. I've seen it every so often since the reunion and I want to find out what it is, so I can remove it. Even when I joked with Janelle in high school, the moment I spotted Cassidy heading towards us, my nerves would get the best of me and I'd find a reason to excuse myself. By the end of high school it seemed like whatever opportunity I may have dreamt up...was long gone. At least in my mind. But it's easy to talk myself out of something great when I am not confident.

"Honestly, I was nervous as hell." Rubbing the back of my neck, I allow myself to be vulnerable with her, it's not something I share often with others. But I don't want to hold back with her. "I was always the funny friend and you were this sight to behold, and I very much didn't want to be just your friend. I also think it had a lot to do with timing. It never felt like I had the opportunity to approach you on my terms."

"Oh please, you could have come up to me whenever you wanted!" She wiggles her eyebrows, lightly swatting at my arm before I tickle the bottom of her foot.

"I wish I could say that was true, but I was nervous. I had no experience with girls back then. Honestly, my game was weak and I wasn't the type who focused on impressing girls. I really just wanted someone to like me for me." I rub the back of my neck again as my nerves get to me. "Why didn't you ever approach me?"

"I guess you're right about the timing thing. I had a lot going on and even more so after high school." She takes a deep breath then and I know whatever she is about to say next is going to be hard for her, so I take the chance to pull her into me. Wrapping my arms around her, she eases herself between my legs and rests her head on my chest. "After my parents passed, I was lost to grief and the only thing holding me together was my anger." Her voice breaks on the last word and I give her a moment to gather herself before she continues.

"My parents worked a lot, so when I was sixteen I decided to move in with my grandmother. It was better than being alone all the time and it was easier to get to school. Besides, I was sixteen, so it wasn't like they were missing out on anything but teen angst, you know?" She releases a breath that sounds more like a breathless sigh than a laugh. "Anyway, they left for a weekend business trip, which was normal for their line of work. They were both executives at a large healthcare company, so it wasn't anything that I felt like I needed to get back home for." She snuggles in a bit deeper. "When they didn't call me later that night, I just...I just knew something awful had happened. I'm sorry, this is not how I planned on this night going." She wipes at her eyes while turning to face me.

"Never apologize for sharing with me. I want to know who you are, all of you. And that includes knowing them." Her chestnut curls bounce as she shakes her head. "If you want to continue, I'm here to listen."

"Okay." She leans over and grabs the lavender-colored, glass carafe from her nightstand, pouring herself some water. "When I got home from school that day, my grandmother and the police were waiting for me. My parents were involved in a car accident, someone had hit them. The driver was a young guy, he apparently had too much to drink and wasn't paying attention. The police also confirmed he was texting and dropped his phone in his drunken foolishness. He reached down to grab his phone and in that moment the light turned red and he careened into them."

"Oh Babygirl, I'm so sorry."

"Yeah, they...they never made it to the hospital. They died on the scene. The officers said it was quick and they were lucky, but what's fucking lucky about that?" Her sniffles call me to action, lifting her into my lap fully so I can hold her properly. "I don't really understand why I was so angry to begin with. They were never home. I guess, I just wished I had had more time with them. More time with them being alive."

For a long while I sit there and rub her back, allowing her to get it all out and give her space to share. We sit like this for minutes or hours, until eventually she cries herself to sleep. It's clear her parents were more focused on work than spending time with their daughter—I imagine it's hard to balance life. Once a child enters this world, they should feel loved, welcomed—whole. But it seems like Cassidy's parents had forgotten about her all together, allowing her to just exist in their lives rather than living it with her. I want to be angry with them, to rip them a new one and let them know how much this beautiful woman should have always been their top priority. That doesn't matter, not really, they're gone and she has had to be the one to pick up the pieces—to figure out how to become a whole person on her own.

As gently as I can, I lie her down in her bed, tucking her in beneath the soft duvet and make my way towards the bathroom.

"Are you leaving?" Her voice is a soft whisper.

"I wouldn't leave without telling you first. I was heading to the bathroom."

"Will you stay?"

"Of course. I'll be right back."

After relieving myself, I wash my hands and look at my reflection in the mirror. My locs lay down my back, I bend forward and toss my hair over the top so it hangs low, before gathering it up into a high bun at the top of my head. It's too much to sleep with when it's down and if I am staying, then I may as well be comfortable. I step out of the bathroom, pulling off my t-shirt and folding it, setting it on top of the chair where I placed my sweatshirt earlier. I curl myself around her, tucking the covers around the both of us. It's not long before I'm pulling her into me, reveling in the feel of her, loving how perfect she fits against me, and drift off to sleep.

14

Cassidy

I am so ready to get on the course!

Our carriage awaits. Posthaste!

On another regency romance kick, huh?

I wake slowly, enjoying the warm comfort of my plush blankets. Stretching my legs and wiggling my toes, I feel the wonderful soreness between my thighs from the night before. Bringing my arms up above my head, I stretch them in an attempt to fully wake my body up. The heat is becoming almost too much, to the point that I'm beginning to sweat. Did I forget to turn the air conditioner down last night? I always sleep better when I notch the air conditioner down. I'd much rather bundle up than to be a sweaty mess... like I am, right now.

Maybe I was too caught up with Jameson, the memory of him feasting on me comes to the forefront of my mind; if I wasn't so warm I'd be snuggling deeper into this oven I call a bed. I'm toasty, way warmer than I normally would be.

Throwing the covers back, I attempt to roll out of bed, but corded muscles flex around my abdomen as they pull me tighter. A different type of warmth constricts me. Flashes of the night before flicker through my head, reminding me of Jameson stretching me in ways I had only imagined during hot showers, and then he stayed with me after I shared about my parents, holding me for the rest of the night. The memories make my eyes misty. When did I become such a sap? Jameson's strong arms are wrapped tightly around me, my shirt is bunched up around my waist and his hand rests low on the softer and thicker area of my belly. His other wraps around the front of my shoulders in a possessive hold that causes butterflies to swarm within my stomach. If I could wake up this way every morning, I most definitely would.

"Where do you think you're going?" His voice is deep and raspy from sleep. Hearing his morning voice short circuits my brain and I consider never leaving this spot.

"Just going to the bathroom. I need to cool down a bit." Why am I blushing in my own damn bed?

He smirks at me then. "Hurry back, I'm sure your day is just as busy as mine and I want to hold you for as long as I can." Fuck that's sexy, and I quicken my pace to do just that.

Since he is going to wait for me, I may as well stick to my normal morning routine—we can leave my place together. I turn on the faucet to heat the water so I can wash my face. It's the only way I'm able to fully wake up before splashing cold water on my skin to cool it down. The cold water is a shock to my system but it is also incredibly refreshing. I finally take a moment to look at my reflection and realize just how puffy my face is from crying all night.

I never share about my parents, the only people I've ever talked about them with are Paloma and Janelle. I was not planning on sharing so much with Jameson last night. My parents just weren't around, and though I love them and think they were trying their best, they weren't there for me. Their work was always their first choice. I know they loved me, deep down, I know they did, but I needed more than that. I needed their physical presence in my life more than their money. I don't fail to recognize how well their financial prowess helped me out in the end, but the fact remains, they weren't there.

Walking in the door to my grandmother's house feels wrong today, but I can't continue to stare at the door like a fool. I need to cross the threshold and just go inside. Rooted to the front steps, I eye the police cruisers parked in the driveway. I hope she's okay and whatever this is is some kind of misunderstanding. I take a deep inhale, allowing the exhale to relieve some of the tension I built up in my body from simply standing at the door. Finally putting my key in the lock, I turn the knob to see my grandmother in one piece and I feel relieved that all seems well. Maybe all the worry was just in my head.

"Gran, you're okay. I was worried something happened when I saw the cruisers out front." Setting my backpack down, I squat to untie my shoes before toeing them off at the shoe rack. "What's that all about?"

When I take a moment to look into her eyes, I can tell she's been crying. "Oh honey, we need to talk. Will you come sit down?" She pats the couch before standing, my gaze following her movements as she turns her head towards the kitchen, her hand outstretched to me.

"Thank you ma'am for the water." The officers come out of the kitchen and notice me. "You've arrived."

"What is going on?" It's the only question I can get out before my grandmother embraces me in a side hug.

"There's been an accident. Your parents...they didn't make it." The

female officer approaches me, her voice sounds like she's speaking to a wounded animal, unsure of how I will respond.

The officers' voices begin to sound muffled and muted as I fold into my mind, searching for someplace safe to hide from the terrible news. Taking in the information, I realize I'm upset and the burning knot in my throat urges me to scream or cry, anything really, but I just stand there.

My parents have been ghosts to me for a long time and I'm not sure how to say goodbye to people I was never given the opportunity to truly know. I feel my grandmother walk me towards the couch, sitting me down before thanking the officers and escorting them to the door.

"It's pretty much a closed case ma'am. Once we have a trial date, we will be in contact," the deep voice of the male officer says, as he stretches his hand to shake my grandmother's, before they both leave. I hear the door closing and the lock turning but that's all I can focus on.

"Baby, I'm going to make you something to eat and some ginger tea, okay?" I shake my head in response to her before getting up to go change. By the time I come back in my oversized, gray sweats and tank, the tea is waiting for me and so is my gran. She tells me what happened and that the person driving will most likely go to prison, but all I can focus on is the fact that my parents are gone.

"I thought I had more time, Gran. I-I thought...I thought I would have time to get them to love me more than they loved their work." My voice is a croak as she pats my head.

"It's not your job to get them to love you, honey, it's not your job to get anyone to love you."

I swipe a lone tear from my cheek taking another long look at myself in the mirror. After so many years of receiving less than the bare minimum from my parents, I learned I was also accepting the same from relationships. So I closed myself off—from relationships and also from life.

When I made the pact with my therapist and Paloma, it was because I didn't want to just coast through life, I wanted to experience all it had for me. I didn't want to just accept the bare minimum anymore, and expecting more began with saying *yes* to myself. Therapy allowed me to build myself up and to dream of what I want in a partner. I want to be first thing on their mind. To be loved after spending so many years feeling unlovable—I want to be loved for being me.

I close my eyes for just a moment, take a breath, and pull my hair up into a high ponytail. I'll wash it, but it's not happening today.

Before I open the door I hear a bit of commotion from the bedroom and then hear Jameson curse. Wanting to make sure he is okay, but not wanting to intrude on possible bad news, I slowly open the bathroom door. He hasn't noticed me just yet as he checks his phone.

His posture is still relaxed as he sits at the edge of the bed, the duvet is wrapped around his waist leaving his chest on full display. He is all hard muscle and my eyes track down to his trim waist and the V cutting so deeply, it may as well be an arrow pointing to exactly where I want to be.

I blow out a quick breath as I shudder, then walk out and ask him, "Are you good in here? I thought I was coming out to more snuggles." I place my hands on my hips, playfully upset as I quirk my eyebrows at him.

"I would do just about anything to stay in this bed with you, as promised, but Anders just called me. He's running late to the house." He unties his locs as he stands, his hair drops to the middle of his back and I hold in my sigh. "Which means I need to get to the house before the designer gets there."

He looks up at me then and his smile builds slowly. I'm standing in the doorway of the bathroom, still in my tiny shorts and oversized t-shirt from last night. His eyes start from my bare feet, moving slowly up my body before he's on his feet and moving, eating up the small distance between the two of us. Coming to stand in front of me he grips the top of the door frame and leans into me, and I tip my head back to look up at him. With lazy fingers, he twirls a loose curl around one of his fingers. "I promise you, Babygirl, that if it wasn't for an emergency, I would be cussing him out. But he's at the vet with my niece."

"Your niece—wait. You said the vet?" The confusion at those two words war within me a bit, my eyebrows furrow and my confusion is clear to him as well.

His laugh brings a smile to my face before he answers me, "Yeah, um, my dog-niece. I keep telling him to stop treating her like a child, but she's his baby." He pulls out his phone from his pocket and shows me a picture of the mammoth man himself, holding a long-haired dachshund. She's spattered with blonde, brown, and caramel hair, sporting light-blue eyes. A smile stretches my face so much that my cheeks hurt. His niece.

"She is absolutely the cutest thing." And she is but I can't hold back the giggle at the clear size difference. "I would have expected something...*bigger*."

His head falls back with laughter. "Yeah, when he told me what he wanted I laughed too, but he's a teddy bear really...Well, for her he is anyway. I thought he would cry when I surprised him with her almost three years ago."

"You bought her?" It's endearing, hearing him talk about his best friend and buying him such a thoughtful gift.

"Sure did," He puffs his chest out a bit. "I'm her emergency contact at doggy daycare."

"Stop it right now!" It's my turn to throw my head back in laughter, holding my stomach. I can't help the howl that escapes me.

When I catch my breath, I see him watching me with a dimpled smile on his face before he pulls me to him. "You are so beautiful."

I rest my palm on his chest, running my fingers over his shoulder and into his hair, rubbing his scalp with my nails. He relaxes his body, dropping his head further into my waiting hands as he leans down to kiss me gently, pulling me flush against him, one hand resting on the small of my back. This kiss is slow and deep, he takes his time exploring my mouth with his tongue. He pulls away slowly, but not before giving me one more soft kiss on the lips and takes a small step back, before letting me go.

He walks into the bathroom and splashes some water on his face, using a spare towel to dry off. Tugging on his t-shirt, he pulls his locs to lay on his back and fuck, if that doesn't send heat right to my core. Walking over, he leans in and gives me a small kiss. "I promise I'll call you later, to check in." The only thing I can do is nod my head like a damn fool before walking him to the door.

After locking up when Jameson leaves, I jump into the shower, making quick work of the hot water that soothes the lovely soreness of the night before. Not only did he make me feel incredible, he stayed to watch Fire Zone with me. Picking up my shampoo, I lather my scalp before rinsing and repeating the process with my conditioner. My thoughts about our time together warm my skin. I turn off the shower and wrap a towel around me and brush through my curls quickly.

I put on a fitted white blouse and wrap the skirt on next, tying a bow at my hip. Swiping on some red lipstick, I rub my lips together and smooth down my hair that is now braided at the nape of my neck.

Lifting my eyes to the clock, I release a breath of relief—I am not running late, for once. I still have plenty of time to get to the golf course to meet Lo. Today we are officially buying our cart for the charity tournament.

I take a peek at the vendor pin board Paloma made and see the cart she added. I've got a good feeling about today, I smile to myself. "Let's buy a golf cart."

Paloma and I have been at the course for a while now, double-checking we have all the documentation we need to ensure our part as a vendor runs smoothly. She was on a roll, every now and then I would see her space out a bit, almost as if she had seen a ghost, but she shrugged it off quickly.

"This place is huge!" I exclaim, taking in the ranch-style clubhouse. My eyes focus on the large screens near the bar area first. Anytime there's a bar, I immediately size it up. They all mostly look the same, but occasionally one will surprise me with something new. The walls are painted in a cream color while warm wooden beams stretch along the ceiling. Twin off-white pillars line the walkway of the ritzy golf club, making it feel more extravagant than needed.

"How did you line this up so perfectly?" I ask Lo, fully believing that if she put her mind to it, she could move mountains. "The clubhouse is hosting a gold fest this weekend, so they have all their best carts out to choose from. The salesman assured me they would have multiple selections so we can get the best bang for our buck," she answers.

I am still learning all the ins and outs of golf life—let's say I much prefer my books and cocktails to being on a hot and humid golf course. It is beautiful though, I'll give them that. The course is miles of hills and valleys covered in lush green grass that looks soft enough to roll or tan in for hours.

"Come this way," Lo ushers me around the clubhouse as though this is a second home to her, guiding us near tables where patrons are enjoying lunch.

Walking down the sage green carpet, we finally make it to the other side of the country club where a set of see-through double doors frame a picturesque view. Even inside I find myself squinting from the sun reflecting off a man-made body of water, small waves ripple along the surface from the breeze, like something out of a magazine. I understand exactly why the club has the doors situated in this spot.

A heated gust of wind presses against the door as Paloma makes an attempt to open it; I give it a firm press of my palm to stop it from pushing her over. I take in a deep inhale, enjoying the smell of fresh-cut grass, still dewy from what I assume would be the sprinkler system. A

A hum of voices from the golf cart sales staff and potential customers have me turning my attention to men in polos and joggers. My eyes widen and I snap my neck back in horror at the amount of colors and patterns covering the salesmen's bodies. *This cannot be real,* I think to myself as I shift my gaze to Lo, sending her a message with my eyes only. One that says, *Girl, why the hell are these men dressed like a pack of Skittles... that exploded?*

She rolls her eyes at me, sending a message back that says, *Don't start!*

She nods her head for me to follow. I sidle up next to her and give her a small nudge.

"Did I miss the memo," I whisper, "Why does that man have on neon green flamingo-printed pants with an equally disturbing shirt?"

I watch her cheek hollow out, denting in from her biting back a laugh. She has to know I am not mature enough for this, a giggle slips out before she pinches me. "This is what golf clothes look like. I mean, some options are more neutral but—" She chuckles, noticing my wide eyes along with my eyebrows that are sure to be melding with my hairline. "Some golfers are more flamboyant in their appearance. It's a good time all in all. Come on!" She squeals with excitement, tugging my arm like she's back in her element. She drags me straight to the greens, where several golf carts are parked for purchase. Peacocks—I mean, the salesmen—walk buyers around, some with serious expressions, while others joke and laugh with those they're hoping to make a commission on.

"We need to be sure to find one with a bar that's attached to the back of it, we can always get it painted—" I begin to say, but Lo interrupts me.

"Purple? Yeah, babe." She chuckles. "I know, you love purple. Besides, it will pop against the fringe."

"Be honest, Lo, do you think this is too much? To buy a cart for this tournament?" I ask, knowing she's been spearheading this idea but also has some reservations about expanding.

"I think it's a great idea! This tournament is going to bring in a lot of business. Besides, this course is one of the busiest around and has exclusive memberships." Her voice is animated as she responds.

That's when I see it.

I never thought I would fall in love with a golf cart, but it's perfect! The two-seater cart is deep purple with a white and purple striped canopy top to shade us from the sun while we drive from hole to hole. The beverage area on the back is expansive and has multiple areas to store all the ingredients to a great cocktail along with a cooler at the bottom for ice.

When my eyes land on the price tag, my mouth drops slightly open as my feet stop moving. Paloma is chatting away until she realizes I am no longer standing next to her. "I know, babe, but we have it saved. This is an investment that will pay for itself. I promise."

We've been saving and technically, I don't need to worry about money. I've invested my inheritance and have been equally as smart throughout the year. Still.

"It's a lot to spend on a cart. Is this what they go for?" I pause, listening to myself worry. "You know what, ignore me. I know you got this. You've never led me astray, babe."

Lo lightly bumps her shoulder into mine before nudging us both to keep moving. "And never will. Come on, let's go take a look. Besides, we get a discount."

This piques my interest further. We speak to the salesman and decide to make the purchase, we get a steep discount since this is the course we will primarily be vendors at, and because it's the first day of the Golf Fest. I feel a bit better about the final price, the salesman made sure to let us know they would drive our new cart to the detailer to get our logo and the last few adjustments made.

By the time we are done and sitting in the clubhouse restaurant, I'm excited all over again. Watching my best friend closely as she finishes her BLT sandwich, I notice her eyes widen and she seems to hold her breath. Her leg shakes underneath the table and it reminds me how on edge she's been lately. "I don't know if I can do this." Her words are just slightly above a whisper but I hear them nonetheless. After the afternoon we just had, I'm surprised by her sudden change of heart.

"Hey, are you okay?" I ask her, waiting a moment but her gaze is still on the screen of her phone. "Paloma?" Her lashes flick up towards my face as she realizes she zoned out. "Listen babe, if you don't want to be the one to manage the cart then I will see if Brianna wants to take over. It's fine. But are *you* okay?" I couldn't care less about her bowing out, that's not the problem—B and I got this. But Lo's nervousness and secrecy are starting to get to me; I'm concerned and I don't know how to help her if she won't let me in.

"No, I'll do it," she states firmly.

"Then what is going on? You don't ever flip flop like this and it's really starting to worry me."

Releasing a deep sigh, she starts, "Honestly, I have a few things on my mind. I'm working through them. Would you be upset with me if I said I wasn't ready to talk about it?"

"Of course not!" I reach across the table, clasping her hand in mine and give it a squeeze. "You're my best friend Lo, I just want *you* to know I am here when, or if, you need me."

"I promise, the moment I feel like I'm in too deep." She chuckles. "I promise I will talk to you." We clean up the table, stacking the plates, before we get up to leave when both of our phones chime.

J-babe

Hey babes!

Lo

I miss you so damn much! When are you coming home again?

How are you?

I watch as Janelle's bubbles populate but disappear several times before she finally replies.

J-babe

I'm doing okay. I miss you guys too

We finally bought the golf cart!

Tapping on the camera button, I go into my photos and send Janelle a picture of Paloma and me standing in front of our new wheels. I wish she was here with us—this will have to be the next best thing.

Lo

I'm gonna name her Penelope...

J-babe

PENELOPE! She's a babe!

Oh, I gotta get back but I love you both.

Lo

Love you more.

Love youuuu.

J-babe

> Oh! Can you guys send me something spicy to read? Do your worst.

Lo's phone chimes once more but it's not from our group text thread, and I can tell her attention is split with whomever it is texting her. I know she is aware I'm here for her, but it doesn't stop my concern. I have to trust in knowing that if she needs me, she will tell me. When she's ready. As soon as she pops her head back up, we finish our drinks, chatting about our new cart, Penelope, and how we can't wait for the charity tournament. It may be seven months away, but we are officially ready.

15

Jameson

Are we still on for our Criminal Minds marathon?

And miss out on what Gideon is gonna do next?

Wiping my hands on my pants, I grab a cold bottle of water from the fridge and chug it. We've done nothing but work on this house and watch the days fly by. We've finally got the entire house painted in a range of moody colors, my favorite being the first bedroom that has been color drenched from ceiling to baseboards in a deep green. I wipe my brow and double check that the paint cans are all closed up.

The flooring team should be arriving in the next day or two and the install is going to make a world of difference, along with freeing up my schedule for a couple days.

I haven't been able to see Cassidy as much as I want because of all the work. We've been texting and video calling, but it's not enough, it's never enough, not when it comes to her. The last time I saw her was when we spent the night together, talking about her parents, and enjoying each other's company. Throwing the tools in my bag, I snatch the towel off my shoulder and wipe my face. Maybe I can find a way to see her tonight, even if just briefly.

"I think I might be calling it a night. The doctor said I need to get Pepper in for a checkup to make sure everything is healing well after being spayed. I don't want to be a dog grandpa... *ever*," Anders yells from the only working bathroom in the house. "And your cheap ass needs to get a hotel because this room is next! No more air mattress!" he says.

"Yeah, I know!" I laugh off his instructions, but he's right. "Go ahead and head out, I got a few more things I want to finish up."

"Alright man." Knocking his fist with mine, he pounds his fist with my outstretched one before heading towards the front door. "Pizza and wings tonight?"

"Hell yeah!" I nod my goodbye and walk through the house, admiring all the work we've put in. It's starting to look more like a house again and all I can think about is showing it to my Babygirl.

Taking what is probably one of my last showers here, I yell to Alexa to play my last audiobook and laugh a bit to myself. It wasn't that long ago when I first listened to the naughty werewolf book Cassidy lent me. Now I'm stuck on this series of shifters. The action in it is wild, and I can't lie, knowing exactly what turns her on does it for me. Does she want an angry wolf-shifter man throwing her over his shoulder? Probably not. But I love knowing what she enjoys. A smile starts to creep up my face and if I were to look in the mirror, I know I look like I'm up to something.

And I am. I know exactly what I need to do.

Toweling off from the much needed inferno of a shower, I rub oil onto my scalp and let my hair air dry before pulling on a pair of gray joggers, a deep-green t-shirt, and a flannel. Unplugging my phone from the charger, I can see I have just enough time to grab what I need before meeting Anders at the pizza joint downtown. I clasp the gold watch around my wrist, slide on a few of my favorite rings and I'm toeing my shoes on before making it out of the door. I press the key fob to my truck twice to unlock the doors, hop into the SUV, and my bluetooth speaker connects to resume the second book of the shifter romance I was listening to in the shower.

Is this what it's like to be a book lover? I've listened to plenty of books on business, self-help, and finance, all things that would give me knowledge to better myself, or work on growing Crews. The content in those is enjoyable, but not like this. Not in the way I can completely escape with these stories.

My phone rings and Alma's name shows on the screen, along with a picture of her smiling. Thumbing the "answer" key on the steering wheel, I greet her, "Alma, what's up?"

"Jameson, honey, how are you? How's that pretty young lady doing?" If we were on a video call I know she would be leaning way too close to the phone, giving me that willful look she has.

"She's incredible. I'm falling hard." I speak the truth, noting how well Alma and I have gotten to know each other since the night of the reunion. Mixed with her years of life experience and just being one of those people who can see right through others, she reads me like a book. We've kept in touch since Babygirl accidentally gave me the wrong number.

I have since learned Alma's husband passed away several years ago and they never had children. It's just her unless she visits Europe where her only sibling and their children live. I kind of adopted her in a way. I make the next right on Ridge Street and pull into the parking lot of the farmer's market.

"So you're staying then?" she asks, though it sounds more like a statement than a question. "You can't be travelin' around if you're going to settle down."

"I can't imagine being anywhere else." And it's the truth, but if I am going to make that a reality then I need to make a permanent decision. Traveling to meet new clients is something I enjoy. I love it. But I love— the thought stops me. Do people fall in love this quickly? Am I nuts? I shake the thought away, blinking a few times as my chest fills with a warmth that feels all-encompassing.

"You are a treasure, Alma, I don't know what I would do without you," I say, truly appreciating the friendship we've grown. The senior-only neighborhood she lives in reminds me of high school but with walkers.

"I can't wait to rip them a new one. I've been working out, using those two-pound weights. I'm going to slaughter them!" Her war voice is scary, even with the quiver of old age. "Are you still coming up for my surgery?"

"Alma, you gotta lay off the true crime shows." I chuckle. "Heck yes, I'm coming. I'm not letting you go through surgery by yourself. The next time we talk, I'll be up there and you can tell me how you took down Janice and her team. They never stood a chance!"

"Well, alright." I can hear the joy in her voice, she's going to give them hell. "I love ya," I say my goodbyes and shut the truck door, having arrived at my destination.

This is one of the few places that carries the wine I love so much; I want to get a bottle for Cassidy. She loved the taste of it and I'm addicted to how she tastes when she drinks it—she's my new favorite flavor.

Walking quickly to the pick-up counter line, I wait for the attendant to finish up with the person ahead of me when I feel a small thump at my side.

"Oh my God, I'm so sorry." She looks at me for a moment before she starts to squint. I'm not sure if she can't see or if she's stuck in a memory. "You're Jameson, right?"

"I am. We've met before." Not quite a question, not quite a statement. I recognize this woman, but placing her is a fog to me. She can't be any taller than five feet, her deep-magenta hair falls in loose waves, cut sharply just above her shoulders. That's when it hits me. "You're Paloma. Cassidy's best friend."

She laughs off my aha moment which I'm thankful for and asks, "So where have you been? I haven't seen you around Shaken Tropes lately?"

"You both have a great thing going at the bar, I planned on stopping by later tonight. I've actually been working on the flip I bought prior to the reunion," I reply.

"You flip houses?" Paloma's voice perks up at that. Anytime someone is interested in flipping I get excited.

"I do. Actually, my buddy did the remodel for Shaken Tropes. I'm part owner of Crews Construction and Consult. It's a small world," I explain. Her eyes widen in surprise and I continue, "Truthfully, I'm kinda in love with this house I'm working on. I'm considering listing it as a short-term rental since there's that golf tournament happening, I think it'll bring in good, short-term tenants."

"That's a really great idea but, um, you know mentioning the tournament reminds me I need to go check on our golf cart." She seems to clam up just a bit, and her eyes snap away to look at anything but me.

"You know what, I'm running late to meet a friend, so I'll see you around?" I say, the syllables falling around me lamely as I give her an easy out. She nods her head and scurries away like she can't move fast enough. I never really know what someone is going through and I don't know her well enough to ask.

I move towards the back of the truck so I can stash my goods. Pulling open the lower level compartment, the floor of the trunk slides open to reveal a secret opening. Sometimes I'm too busy between errands to run home to drop off things, but this truck has this secret stash area. It is completely hidden and puts my mind at ease that I don't have to worry about anything going missing. Watching the rear lights blink as I click the lock button on my key fob, I turn and begin jogging towards Wings'n Tings, the pizza and wings spot where I'm meeting Anders.

The door swings open as I grab the knob, and a few guys walk out clapping each other on the back.I make my way in and spot Anders in the back booth. He throws his hand up in a wave, ushering me over.

"Hey man, how's my niece?" I ask, squeezing his shoulder before sitting down across from him.

"She's great, bro." He huffs a small laugh. "I almost didn't leave her."

I smile at the thought of Anders and Pepper snuggled up at his house in that oversized couch of his. Maybe I need to order Pepper a dog bed and a few new toys. What kind of dog uncle would I be if I didn't? She is the greatest gift I have ever given him. I remember he told me he was thinking of getting a dog but he was holding back, not sure he wanted to take on that level of responsibility while running a company.

I got Pepper for him a few weeks later, knowing if I took some things off his plate he'd have more time for a pet; I'm glad I did. He takes her everywhere, including projects, when she's not at doggy daycare.

"My niece needs a mama, Big Dog," I jest.

"Yeah, I just don't see the point J. I don't want to be bothered with a relationship." He smirks then, peering over his shoulder at what I assume is his next victim. "Not yet anyway."

I shake my head at his thinking. "One day the perfect woman is going to spring up on you, then what will you do?"

"I'll believe it when I see it. How are you feeling about the design plans for the house?"

"I like it a lot, man! You really helped me create the vision I wanted. Moving on to the remaining rooms in the house makes more sense now from an aesthetic perspective, then we can get the backyard fixed up."

Since my side of Crews is spanned across three different states, I travel a lot. Between connecting clients with potential properties or paying subcontractors to complete remodels, I'm always on the go. It's great to be in Cypress Lake for an extended period of time working on this project together. It makes me realize that I wouldn't be moving here just for Cassidy, for Anders too.

My eyebrows raise nearly to my hairline as I tilt my head to the side in a joking manner. "I don't know if I want to give it up though. Maybe I should just keep it for myself."

"You can have another house, J. Not one this good! This one is in a prime area where we could really make a lot of money." He stops for a minute, shaking his head before taking a sip of his water. "What do you mean keep it for yourself? Are you thinking of moving back home?"

"*Back home.*" I know he meant it as being back in our childhood home town, but it does feels like home again, not just a place for a quick visit. Cassidy is here and she is what makes this place feel like home for me. I didn't realize it until this very moment, how much more Cypress Lake feels like home, more than any other place I've lived in the last ten years, even more than when I was a kid.

That's not because it was terrible living here either. My parents are amazing. From game nights with aunts and uncles, who later on in life I found out weren't blood related, but were my mom and dad's closest friends. Sleepovers where my friends and I stayed up way too fucking late playing Donkey Kong. Or the last weekend of every summer break when we would have the family over. Every single time my dad would burn the burgers on the grill, before he awakened into the grill master he is now. He would complain his way into the kitchen for the back-up burger patties Mama made him buy, *just in case*. There were two too many times for him to burn the burgers before Mama decided enough was enough.

I felt like a stranger coming back to Cypress Lake after being gone, basically, since graduation. Once I went to college my parents wanted to travel, they were still pretty young then and wanted to see the world once they were empty nesters. When they decided they wanted to travel the world, they gifted me the house.

Which is exactly why I have short-term tenants in it now. It helps with keeping up on the costs that come with homeownership. Having people live in the house, who truly care, helps me out too. I don't have to worry about looking after it as much because someone already is. It was my first official flip, and the first one I couldn't sell. I don't think I ever will, I want the option to pass on my parents' house to their grandchildren one day.

But being back here now, with Cassidy—what I'm starting to hopefully build with her—makes this whole placet feel like home.

"I know man. You know I get attached easy." His head drops back as he wraps his arm around his stomach, laughing at the truth in my statement. His hand waves frantically, silently begging me to stop. Anders knows me well enough to anticipate I'll crack a joke, and where it's going. Before I can get another word in, my phone chimes and "Babygirl" flashes on the screen.

"Hey babe, what's—" Cass' panicked whispers stop me from finishing my greeting.

"No, no, no this isn't happening!" Her voice is filled with fear and silent sobs come through the line. "Jameson, please, please, please."

"Baby, talk to me. What's going on?" I force my chair back and stand up, moving towards the exit. I can't sit still waiting for her to tell me what's wrong. I can hear panic in her voice and I need to get to her now. "Cassidy."

"Someone is in my apartment, th-they kicked the door in. Please. Oh my God. Please, before he finds me."

I don't bother explaining anything to Anders but I know he's right behind me, without question following me out of the bar. I jump into the driver's seat, the phone automatically connects to bluetooth and we peel out of the parking lot the moment Anders shuts his door.

"Baby?!" The phone is quiet, I can hear her heavy breaths and muffled sobs. "I'm on the way. Fuck!"

I can get to Cassidy's house with my eyes closed and we arrive in less than five minutes. Throwing my door open, I look back at my best friend, nodding my head before I rush to the stairs. I take two steps at a time to get to her apartment when I notice the door is slightly open, and I quiet my steps. The pounding in my chest is unrelenting, it's beating so loudly I can hear it muffled within my ears. Easing the door open, I take my first step inside.

Anders is only a few paces behind me, pulling his phone out to make sure the police have been called the moment we see the vase from the counter, now shattered on the floor. My call with Cassidy is still connected, which gives me the faintest amount of hope that she's still here and safe, somehow. I make my way deeper into her space.

A heavy *thunk* from the back of her home urges me into a sprint as I make my way to her bedroom and see the bathroom door wide open. Broad shoulders that aren't my Babygirl's hover in the door frame. The person must hear me behind them as they turn, quickly barreling towards me. I have about a second to think, but I'm not concerned, I have at least sixty pounds of muscle on this guy. Nothing is going to keep me from getting to her.

My fist connects with his face and I hear the crunch of his nose breaking beneath my fingers. I lean into my next swing, connecting with his jaw, knocking him off his feet before my best friend is behind me, his hand gripping my shoulder. "I got him, J. Go find your girl."

I nod at him, not looking back before picking the phone up and putting it to my ear. "Cass, Baby, can you hear me? Are you still there?" I say, loud enough for her to hopefully hear me on the phone as well as in the house. She must have put the phone down because she's not responding, a faint sob catches my attention from down the hall towards the spare bedroom. I force myself to slow my steps, not wanting to scare her, but also wanting to get to her as quickly as possible.

Pulling the door open, I see her curled into a tight ball, her knees pressed into her chest in the corner of the room. It's dark in here but I can't take my eyes off her.

"Jameson. Y-you came!" Her voice trembles with adrenaline that I'm certain is leaving her body as she reaches for me.

"Of course I came, Babygirl." I wrap her in my arms, pulling her onto my lap as I sit on the edge of the bed. "I will always come for you."

16

Cassidy

J-babe

Is Jameson taking good care of you?

Always.

I'm faintly aware of Jameson and Anders talking with officers who arrived moments after they found me in my guest room. Their eyes linger on me a bit longer as they answer questions from tonight. I've already given the officers my statement and watched them arrest the guy that broke into my home. Any energy I had is long gone as I sit here on my couch, staring at the very uninteresting wall behind my television.

I'm too deep in the recesses of my mind to notice the officer making his way to me. His worn leather boots step in my line of sight, close enough for me to know he is here to talk to me but far enough away to give me the space I need after the events of tonight.

"Ma'am, we are getting ready to get out of your hair." I peer up at him, noting that Jameson is standing nearby. "We don't think he initially planned to break into your home. Not that it gives you much more relief. We believe he was attempting to get into your bar downstairs but wasn't quite smart enough to realize someone lived up here. It doesn't appear

195

he was looking for anything once he made it inside."

I nod my head, frustrated that my privacy and home have been violated by some idiot who couldn't tell I live here. There is an entire porch decorated with a welcome mat, plants, and other frills I have out on my landing.

Pulling in a deep breath, I thank the officer for his work, not bothering to get up. I simply don't have it in me to move from the spot on the couch I'm currently marinating in.

"Since the suspect was caught and apprehended by your—uh..." He pauses to look at me, maybe looking to find an answer to his question floating in the air, but I don't have the energy to speak. He nods and continues, "...by your boyfriend, on your property, along with your statement, we have enough to press charges—whether you choose to or not. He meets the description of multiple break-ins that have been happening to businesses lately. There were notices left on all the doors of businesses on this street almost a month ago. It could have been missed." He gives me a gruff head nod and makes his way to the front door before he takes a quick step back so he isn't pummeled by whomever is running up the stairs.

"Where is she?" I hear Paloma's voice before I see her. Her face is frantic, her eyes meet my red-rimmed ones the moment she makes it to the doorway. The officer juts his arm out in a feeble attempt to stop her but thinks better of it when she gives him her full attention. Daring him to stop her as she continues her hurried steps before wrapping me in her arms. "Cass."

Hearing my name from my best friend gives way to the emotion that has been climbing up my throat all night, and I finally let go. My shoulders slump and I fall into her embrace, allowing the sobs to wrack through my body and I cry into my Lo's shoulder.

She cries too; we've been friends since high school and I can't imagine how she felt getting a phone call about the break in. I would have lost my mind if I were in her shoes. We hold each other on the couch for, I don't know how long, until she gets up to grab tissues. She comes back and wipes my face before heading towards the kitchen.

"I'm going to make you some hot tea and something to snack on, okay?" She doesn't wait for my response, she knows me well enough to know that I need some quiet and my internal battery is dead at this point.

Anderson left earlier to check on Shaken Tropes and to get a temporary lock set up for the front door. I've never been more glad that my boyfriend owns a construction business. *My boyfriend.* Where the hell did that come from?

Twisting myself around on the couch, I refuse to acknowledge my own previous thought and I wiggle my toes in the plush rug that's centered in my living room, appreciating the feel of normalcy before padding to the bedroom.

The sight in front of me stops me in my tracks, I can't move as I let the scene in front of me play out. Jameson is on his knees, pulling the rug back into place. There is a small trash pail off to the side that must be holding broken items. My eyes shift to my dresser and note the missing items, ones I know I will miss tomorrow, but tonight, tonight I'm spent and focused on this man who couldn't possibly be any more perfect than he already is.

"Hey, Babygirl." His voice is like a balm, smooth and deep, coating me in comfort that I didn't know I needed.

"Hey." It's all I can muster, but with him I don't think I need to say anymore. He opens his arms wide and I press myself against his chest, letting the feeling of his body wrap around me and soothe the last bits of worry.

I know I wasn't harmed during the break-in, but there is something about the vulnerability that comes with having someone in your home who isn't supposed to be there, it was a traumatic experience no matter how my brain wants to spin it. I won't pretend to be okay because I'm not. "He broke into my home."

Jameson runs his hand up and down my back, before pulling back slightly and dipping his hand beneath my chin to lift my head. He leans down, kissing both cheeks that are now wet from silent tears. "He did, Babygirl, and you're okay. I promise you, I'm not going anywhere until you tell me to." He brushes a soft kiss to my hair and continues, "You may have to kick me out." That earns him a small laugh. His lips are warm and soft as he presses a quick kiss to my forehead before folding me into his chest once more. "What do you need?"

What do I need? Sleep, I need to sleep this day away and start fresh tomorrow. I need to feel safe again. That's when I realize that I'm safe, he is here with me. As if knowing, Paloma pops her head in.

"Oh, I didn't mean to interrupt." She looks at Jameson then. "Are you staying with her tonight?"

He gives her a quick nod.

"Okay, then. I'm going to head home unless you want me to stay, babes?"

"You head home, I'll be okay." She waits a moment before coming into my room and giving me a kiss on the cheek and then she heads out, leaving me in Jameson's embrace. I'm glad to have him here, my eyes lock on him as he stands, outstretching his hand for me to grab.

"Come on, Babygirl, let's get you to bed." Grabbing his hand, he pulls me into his side and walks over to the side of the bed I always sleep on, near my nightstand. "Get in the bed, Baby."

This man tucks me in and looks at me with, not a look of pity, but one of care. Like he sees my needs and just wants to attend to them, the softness in his eyes wells tears in my own. I watch his hand reach out, his thumb wiping away the tears from my cheeks before they can drip onto my pillow. His calloused fingers send shivers down my back, goosebumps erupting all over my body as he tucks my hair behind my ear. Leaning down, he kisses me with such tenderness that if I was standing, my knees would have buckled. No matter how much I want the kiss to continue he backs up just a bit and a yawn creeps out of my lips.

Crawling in behind me, he pulls me against his hard chest and that's all the safety I need before I let sleep take me.

My arms shoot out to my sides, my chest rising and falling at such quick bursts as the fire alarm blares from the kitchen.

"What the fuck?" I grab my phone, my panicked gaze scans the screen for the time. It's seven in the morning and the spot where Jameson was sleeping is empty, that's when I smell it. Something is definitely burning, but it's not my apartment.

I throw the covers back and rush down the hallway towards my kitchen to find Jameson frantically waving a towel at the fire alarm. "Shit, shit, shit, shit. Why me, Lord?" His deep voice is a murmur. Whispering is useless because the whole neighborhood can probably hear the alarm.

The counters may be clean, but bowls and a few pans fill the sink from what I think may be an attempt at making me breakfast. I cover my mouth, holding in the laugh I want to let go of so badly, but I have to see how this plays out. Holding my phone up, I snap a picture. There looks to be pancakes still in the pan that are so burnt and crispy, they could be used as frisbees.

The alarm finally stops blaring and he throws a towel over his shoulder before he turns around, catching me leaning against the wall watching the chaos ensue. My eyes go straight for my lavender fuzzy bunny slippers that are several sizes too small for his feet and his black boxer briefs, that would be incredibly sexy if not for the slippers. Though, if I'm being honest with myself... it's still pretty hot.

"After the night you had, I wanted to make you breakfast, so I got up a little early, but I'm no chef. Clearly my talents lie elsewhere." He laughs. "I promise I'll clean up the kitchen while you're getting ready. I need to get you fed."

That's when I let it out. The *guffaw* falls from my mouth as I bend over, clutching my stomach in an attempt to breathe.

"Oh, you think it's funny huh?" He teases, rounding the counter he scoops me up in his arms and places me on the kitchen island before wiggling his fingers and tickling my sides.

"No, God, please." I laugh even harder, tears pricking at my eyes from the laughter pains.

Wrapping my legs around his middle to ground myself, I grab his hands as he slowly releases me. Placing both hands on the countertop, one on each side of me, caging me in.

"I don't know what's funnier. You setting off the fire alarm and almost burning my kitchen down with pancake mix or you in my too-small slippers." I take another peek at them, he has on the bunny ones that have floppy ears attached to the front and there is a fluffy ball at the back. Which is supposed to be a tail somewhere beneath the rest of his foot. "I can't take you seriously with those on," I say through a snort.

"They were all I could find, my socks have been eaten by the rug because they are nowhere to be found." Even over the burnt pancake smell, his warm bourbon cologne pulls me in as I run my fingers up his forearm.

"And what might have happened to your clothes? No apron?" I jut my thumb back to where my canvas apron hangs. He moves to the apron then, sliding it over his head before he looks down and reads SLUT FOR BACON in all caps with bacon slices surrounding the words.

Crossing my legs, I say, "It suits you. But isn't the surprise breakfast supposed to come with a naked man... or is that just in the movies?"

Swiftly he pulls his feet free from the slippers, but only long enough to remove his boxers. He tosses them at me as I scream, unable to hold back my surprise and excitement. He slips the bunny slippers back on his feet and walks over to me. I allow myself to be bold and slip my hands around his middle, opening my legs and pulling him closer to me.

Wrapping his arms around me, he grabs two handfuls of my ass before pulling me up against him. I inhale a quick gasp, feeling his thick length pressed against my center. Fuck me.

"Is this better for you, Cassidy?" His voice is dripping with desire, warming my insides as I curl my toes and clear my throat. He doesn't wait for my answer before pressing his lips softly to mine. His lips are like soft pillows as his tongue licks, seeking entrance as he presses himself further against my core and I whimper at the contact, enjoying the feel of him.

Taking the moment as a welcomed invitation, his tongue explores my mouth and the kiss grows hungry. He wraps one of his strong arms around my middle and urges me closer as I rock against him. The feeling of him between my legs, even with clothes on, feels dangerously intimate and I want it all.

"Ooh, yes, Jameson," I moan his name as his dick rocks against my pussy. I'm soaked and hating that my panties are in the way right now.

"Let me hear those beautiful sounds, Cassidy. Take what you need from me." He pulls my thighs tighter around him, tapping on my feet from behind his back, and I cross them instinctively. "Grind your pussy against this dick."

I swirl my hips against his length, dropping my head back at the sensations of him and how good he feels. His warm palm climbs up the sides of my body, squeezing at the fullness of my belly and up higher to my breasts that hang slightly to the sides from the heaviness of them. My whole body feels hot as I work myself towards a climax still in my panties.

Jameson grabs my shirt, an old purple Shaken Tropes t-shirt I still have on from the mess of yesterday, pulling it up and over my chest so it's puddled at my neck, giving him better access.

"Fuck," he growls. Leaning over me he palms a handful of my breast before sucking my nipple into his mouth. Tugging the sensitive flesh with his teeth, I arch my back allowing him to pull me deeper into him.

"Oh my God. Fuck me." It's all I can muster, all I can say. Then he's reaching down, rubbing my clit in circular motions through my soaking wet panties.

"I'd love to, Cassidy, but not yet. Let me take care of you." His voice is more growl, more manly than I've ever heard. "Now give me what I want, Baby."

He pulls the fabric of my panties up creating a new type of friction. He drags his tongue down the center of my breasts and blows a cool breath across the moistened area. Goosebumps cover my skin and I pull in a sharp gasp at the new sensation. This man and what he does to me, focusing only on my needs is something I've never experienced before. My breathing picks up, growing faster as uncontrolled moans spill from my mouth. He pinches my clit and I feel the heat climb from my curled toes up through my body until it's all I can do to hold it together.

"Give it to me, Baby," he demands as he slips two fingers inside, curling them ever so slightly as he rubs his thumb back and forth across my clit. "You're so pretty when you come." His dirty words are the final nail in the coffin before I'm falling over the edge of my climax. But that doesn't stop him, no. He continues his pursuit at a punishing speed and I drop my head back too lost in the sensations.

He tuts at me, before saying, "Eyes on me, Cassidy." Jameson's voice is a deep command that works its way through my body, I follow easily, loving that I can completely let go as he works me over. "One more."

"I-I don't think I can." My eyes are already on him, focusing on his beautiful face. Sweat coats my skin and he dips his head between my thighs, dragging his tongue over my sensitive flesh. "Jameson, please."

"I like hearing you beg." He looks at me through hooded lashes as he works me over with his tongue, angling me in such a way that allows him to fuck me deeper with his tongue, dipping in and out of me. My body shudders from seeing how he looks at me, drinking me in as my release coats his beard.

Taking both his hands, he lifts my large thighs and presses my legs back against me, opening me wider as his tongue explores me deeper. His thumb finds my clit again and he circles before light explodes behind my vision and pleasure floods my system, overwhelming me all at once and I clamp my thighs around his head, he doesn't move, does not try to escape them. No, his hands only massage my legs more firmly, adding to the sensations that have my second orgasm holding my breath hostage. Dropping back on to the counter, my breathing erratic, I finally close my eyes from exhaustion.

Jameson untangles himself from my legs, easing them down gently as he moves through the apartment. When I finally regain composure, I open my eyes and watch him make his way back to me, words aren't needed at this moment as he begins cleaning me himself. Fuck, that's hot.

"You want some coffee?" His question is so normal and so not, given what we just experienced.

"Fuck coffee," I say, pulling him in for a kiss, tasting myself on his tongue after the orgasms he just gave me, he is all the caffeine I could want.

Pulling the apron up and over his head, I wrap one arm around his neck and stroke his thick cock with my other hand. There is absolutely nothing I want more than to feel him fill me, my sex squeezing at the anticipation. "I need you," I say, as I guide him to my wet heat.

"I'll always give you what you want, Cassidy." Easing me back onto the counter, he spreads my thighs apart again and I watch his length slowly slide into me.

My eyes snap up to him, watching as well, transfixed on us as he pushes into me again and again. My nipples harden, becoming more erect than they already were, almost painfully so. His hands have a bruising grip on my waist and I fucking love it, the feeling of his fingers gripping me this way as he takes me has me feral. I release a shuddering breath.

"Oh my God." My words bring him back to me, his mouth dropping open slightly as he reaches one of his hands up, wrapping it on the back of my neck, anchoring me to him.

"You feel so good. So fucking wet." His words are a low groan. I whimper at the feel of his thick member and his dirty words, watching him unravel has to be the hottest fucking thing I have ever witnessed.

Then he fucks me. Thrusting into me as he pulls almost all the way out before driving himself back, sinking into my pussy.

I throw my head back, meeting him thrust for thrust. He swirls his skilled fingers in circles on my clit with an intense pressure. The only sounds in the room are our heavy breaths and skins slapping together. His brutal pace adjusts to slow, deep strokes, hitting the top inner spot that has my toes curling.

"You're always beautiful. But like *this*, wrapped around my cock, you're magnificent." His words choke me and it feels like the very air around us changes within this moment. There are no words to fully express what I want to say, too drunk on how Jameson makes me feel. Our bodies are slick with sweat as we hold each other's gaze. Electric heat burns from my toes, up my calves and thighs.

"I—Please, Jameson." I'm not sure what I'm begging for, but I need it, whatever he will give me, I need. I roll my nipples with my fingers and massage my breasts, imagining my hands are his.

"Mm. Come with me, Baby." He gyrates his hips, driving circles into me before he leans down. He gives me a kiss, swirling his tongue into my mouth as he ravishes me.

Thrusting one final time, my back arches into him as he roars his release and I writhe beneath him in a silent scream. If I had neighbors, they would all be awake now.

He leans over me, pressing his weight into me and it feels incredible. That wasn't just sex, that was making love, and I want to tell him exactly how I feel at this moment, but I can't. I can't even think of speaking, my body and mind too exhausted.

Standing to his full height, he pulls me with him. He grabs my ass in his hands and pulls me up onto his waist and my eyes widen, not having realized he could lift me. *Holy fuck.* I wrap my hands around the back of his neck and he tosses me up against him for a better hold. I suck in a gasp at the feel of his dick slapping against me from beneath, still hard and ready.

A smile plays on his face as he takes in my surprise. "I'm going to have to wear these for round two." His words don't compute and I blink a few times before I respond.

"Round two. Wasn't that round two?" I pant. "Wait—Wear what?"

"Your slippers," he says, before kissing me quickly and I look down at his feet, seeing he just made love to me in my damn bunny slippers. "They've got good traction."

I can't stop the laugh before he tosses me on my bed, a mischievous grin on his face as he climbs in after me.

17

Jameson

Hey Bulldozer, what are you up to right now?

Bulldozer

I'm actually at Sweet Bean.

That's right up the street from me.

Maybe I'll come share a coffee with you…

Bulldozer

Turn that maybe into a yes, Babygirl.

A smile graces my lips and I grab my woven tote bag and slide my feet into a pair of strappy sandals to share a coffee with Jameson. I walk down the street with an almost imperceptible pep in my step, knowing he's so close makes me happier than it probably should.

Pulling the handle of the door, the fragrant scent of buttery pastries and the strong bitter aroma of coffee wafts into my face. I groan at the delicious smell and set my gaze on the man sitting in a corner booth, my desire for him matches my greed for my favorite coffee. I don't think he has seen me yet as he hasn't made any move to get up.

Going to the front counter I order my favorite: cafe con leche and a honey glazed croissant. The barista at the counter hands me a ticket and lets me know they'll bring it over to the table once it's ready. Thanking her, I make my way to Jameson.

He is looking down at his computer, focused on whatever he's working on. As soon as I get close to the table, his eyes snap up and he attempts to stand, always the gentleman. I place my hand on his shoulder and squeeze, bumping my hip into his arm. "Let me scoot in next to you."

He moves over on the bench and places his warm palm on my thigh as soon as I'm settled. "It's good to see you, beautiful."

"You too. What are you working on?" I ask him, purposely invading his space as I take a look at his laptop. I would crawl into his lap if the older woman next to us wouldn't give me the eye. Different backyards are on the screen, a design mood board looks to be in the corner, and he has maybe twenty tabs open on his browser.

He moves his hand from my thigh and wraps it around the small of my back, squeezing my side gently as he allows me to click on his open browser tabs. Somehow this feels incredibly intimate and I catch myself smiling. One tab has architectural design software loaded, the next, an article on said software's pros and cons, the others are mainly different features of backyards and different layouts.

"I'm gathering inspiration for the backyard of my second property," he says and I dip my head to the side as I look over what he has so far. "This home is hopefully going to have a young family in it. The inside is going to be pretty simple and I want the backyard to be a fun space they can enjoy with one another." I watch his face light up as he talks about the family he has created in his head that equally matches his vision for this home he is working on.

"You really love this," I say, more of an observation than a question.

"I've always loved the design of buildings and the inner workings to make them practical, yet also beautiful. I blame it on the building blocks I used to play with when I was a kid. I also enjoy digging into my imagination and creating something for a family or person to thrive in."

When he clicks on the mood board it expands and I realize, "mood board" is an understatement. It has a three-dimensional layout of the house and backyard, with the landscaping mapped out in multiple ways. "I haven't really decided how I want it. Design is frustrating as hell, but it's also one of my favorite aspects of the construction process."

"Number seventeen? Seventeen." I hear a voice moving away and I look down at my ticket and wave my hand at the server. Placing my large cafe con leche and pastry in front of me, they walk back to the kitchen area and I sip my heaven-in-a-cup, unable to hold back the soft sigh.

"Let me get a taste, Babygirl," Jameson requests, and I hand him my cup. Except when he grabs it, he leans into me. The hand he has wrapped around my waist pulls me in close and he presses a firm, yet gentle kiss on my lips. He softly drags my lower lip into his mouth, tasting the sweet coffee from my tongue. Warmth pours through me as he presses his lips against mine once more, his words a grizzly whisper, "I think I'll have one more taste." He brings the white cup to his mouth and takes a sip. His every move has my attention after he kissed me into utter silence. "It's damn good but the first taste was better."

"I'm glad you enjoyed it." I try to smirk at him but I'm too stunned by my want for him. "You're real smooth, Bulldozer."

"It's the truth, Babygirl, everything tastes better with you, you're my favorite flavor." Fuck me twice on a Tuesday, this man. "You did say you'd share a coffee with me."

"I definitely said 'maybe,'" I counter. "Sweet Bean is my favorite coffee spot, it's unmatched. Paloma turned me onto it a few years ago and now no one can make my coffee like they can."

"I've never been a coffee person but you might have changed my mind," he responds and takes another sip.

"Listen now, when I said 'share a coffee' I didn't think you'd be guzzling it down." I snicker as he blows a breath from the heated liquid he just consumed.

Before he can take another sip, I grab it and take one of my own as I lean over and click on the pin board he is looking at. "What about this?" The picture has a tree house that's maybe only four or five feet above the ground. There are hexagon-shaped concrete pavers that create a pathway to a little deck that leads to the front door of the treehouse. I pin it to his board and click on another image that has string lights hung around the perimeter of the house as well as in the middle of the yard.

"I love that! I was also thinking this would be a great addition. I like how everything is set up to be a place of conversation. How the swings are wide and comfortable with garden beds assembled around it," he explains, pointing at the areas he is envisioning in this backyard for a family that doesn't own it yet. He truly cares for people and I see that in the way he is planning this space. No matter if he is going to keep a property or flip it, he wants to ensure everyone is satisfied. Cared for.

He rubs my thigh, gripping it a bit as he says, "Mm. Damn girl, I want a bite of that." My cheeks instantly flush with color from his words, but also because the little old lady who's sitting at the table next to us is now looking at me. My neck heats further. "Oh, you can share your coffee but not your croissant." When I look at him, his smile is mischievous and

I can tell he knows exactly what he is doing. Well, two can play at this game. But not with my croissant.

"Nope," I say, popping the "P" hard. "I'll share my coffee, but that glazed beauty is all mine." He scoffs.

"Is that so?" His grin is still there, but now it looks like he's holding on to a secret. Just as I'm about to answer him, he grips my sides and wiggles his fingers. A laugh falls out of my mouth instantly.

"Oh my God, Jameson!" I exclaim, breathless giggles are all I can afford as I swat at his hands. "Please. Anything but the croissant."

"Anything?" His torture stops quickly as his hands reach for my coffee, taking a big gulp of it. "Shit, it's still hot." He holds his hands to his mouth and we both crack up at our flirty antics. Wrapping his arm around my waist, he brings me in closer. "So, you want to help me plan this backyard?"

And we do just that for the remainder of the morning. At the end of the afternoon, and one planned backyard later, we exit the Sweet Bean with our hands intertwined. Without any questions I follow him to his truck, not wanting to separate from him yet. He opens the passenger door and clicks my seatbelt into place before rounding the truck and getting in. The drive is only a few minutes but he fills the time by talking about the place and the new property manager.

"Keya reminds me of Anders and I when we were young. Except when we were her age we were still fumbling over projects we were working on. She is far ahead of that. She does an incredible job, not a single issue, especially with keeping me in the loop. I thought I would need to extend the remodel an additional two weeks after Toes mess—."

"Who is Toes?" I question, cutting him off, surprised by the word so out of the blue.

He chuckles and eases into a parking space behind my building before he responds. "Toes..." He shudders. "No grown man should bear witness to another man's toes without warning. He was my former property manager," he tells me.

"I remember you telling me about that, but I do not remember the toes," I say, wiggling my own toes in my sandals in response, and I almost giggle at my internal joke. Anderson's name pops up on the truck's display.

"Hey bro, I'm dropping off Cassidy right now then heading your way," Jameson says as he answers the call.

"Dope. Tell Cass I said hey and get your ass over here." He disconnects the call as Jameson parks and exits his door, already on his way to open mine. He walks me to my apartment and gives me a quick kiss before heading back to the truck. Not driving off until my door is closed.

Though the break-in has been in the back of my mind, work has required a lot of my focus, it's kept me busy, which I'm glad for. I glance over our checklist for the golf tournament once more and realize it's almost done.

After the very delicious breakfast, and I am *not* talking about the burnt pancakes, Jameson left only to grab a few things he needed from his job site and his extra toolbag from his truck to fix my door. Making sure the door frame was like-new, he added in longer screws to make it harder to break down. He also grabbed an extra security camera, measure with smart features, to affix to the front of my door, one I can monitor from my phone if I choose to. Hopefully, adding these new, minute improvements will deter anyone from considering my home as their next big break.

Though that's a great thought in theory *and reality*, I can't help the sudden gasp or dropping of the very expensive bottle of alcohol that is now broken on the floor, when I hear the front door slam shut and I jump. I know I'm safe, but the break-in really did a number on me.

I've had a few scenarios playing on loop in my head of what could have happened if Jameson hadn't gotten to my place when he did. Was it stupid to not call the police first? In hindsight, probably, but I am not going to focus on that. I freaked out when I heard the door busted through and my first instinct was to call Jameson. I was digging through the guest bedroom's closet to refresh the sheets on the bed when I heard the door slam and splinter.

I can't pinpoint the exact flight response that came over me, but all I could think was, *this cannot possibly be happening to me*. People never truly know how they'll react when things happen, but I don't regret my decision for a second.

My I've-read-one-too-many-romance-books heart is telling me that I need to let go and fall all in with Jameson, that clearly I am his first choice. But my brain, my stupid, fucking cock-blocking brain, is reminding me of what happened before: that my parents didn't even choose me, so how could this incredible bulldozer of a man, want to prioritize me in his life? Why would he want to choose me when no one else has before? No one but my Lo and Janelle, but still...my sheets have been frosty and my girls aren't warming them. Which feels ridiculous to think about since Jameson has been here: present tense.

Maybe a call to my therapist is due. I want to overcome the hurt of my parents not being there for me. I'm ready to move on but this feeling, deep down inside of me, is getting in the way. I am getting in my own way of my own happiness and it's time I get on board with giving myself this *yes*. Jameson is a yes that I don't believe I will ever regret giving into—living without him... just thinking about it, is painful.

When I look up, I see Paloma struggling with the front door. Her frustration bubbles over with a scream, one that sounds more like a roar, as she yanks the door back. Her reaction pulls me out of my thoughts of Jameson and the break-in. She slaps her palm against the door frame, catching herself from almost falling on her ass in the process. She pulls the door open with so much force that I'm actually nervous she might rip the door off its hinges. Small but mighty. She leans her body halfway out of the door and snatches her bag free from the traitorous handle it was caught on.

"Puñeta!" It's the only intelligible word I hear, but I know she is cursing under her breath. Who pissed in her Cheerios this morning? She adjusts her shirt, needing something to do with her hands after such an outburst, a nervous habit of hers that she doesn't let many see. Her gaze suddenly pops up to me as she realizes I'm watching her.

I still have my hand pressed firmly into my chest as I try to calm my ragged breaths from hearing the door slam open. Paloma slowly blinks before she doubles over in laughter, dropping my hand I follow after her. Howling at the clear annoyance that we've all been through.

"Girl! You want to tell me what made you so pissed off at the door?" The words leave my mouth before I can stop them as we continue laughing for another few minutes.

"Carajo! Fucking door, I swear its always something." She snorts, her frustration still brimming at the surface. "One slightly minor inconvenience and I am going to lose my shit. One. More. That's all it's gonna take."

We both attempt to gather ourselves, calming the fit of giggles that plague us. We are still resisting the urge to giggle or snort, we have a way of feeding off one another's energy. We both start at the mess, her with the broom while I grab the mop.

"Oh my God! My cheeks hurt," I say to her, cleaning around the bartop. I pull her into a quick hug and kiss her cheek.

"So you tell me what's wrong and I will make us both a drink." I watch her body sink, her shoulders rounding as she closes herself off and I'm not having it.

"I'm totally fine." She's a terrible liar and she knows it.

I start the espresso before I reach under the bar and open the mini fridge, grabbing the white chocolate creme liqueur and the vodka from the top shelf. Shaking the ingredients with espresso ice cubes, I pour us each a glass and top them with a salted caramel infused cold foam. "You're a terrible liar." I tip my glass in her direction then allow myself a small sip.

"If you don't want to tell me, that's okay babe. But don't lie. You don't need to lie to me, I'm your best friend and I'm never going to judge you. I hope you know that." Before I can set my drink down, she takes a deep breath.

"You remember that guy I dated years ago and had that fling with?" She sighs deeply, a shuddering breath leaving her. "Well, I didn't tell you the whole story. I've seen him a few times recently at the course, apparently he is raffling off lessons as a vendor, and I-I was a fucking idiot, Cass. I was such a fool. Seeing him again brought all those feelings back that I tried my damnedest to stuff down." This time when Paloma looks at me, her normal joy-filled gaze is one of deep sorrow.

"Lo." Rounding the bar once again, I pull my best friend into a crushing hug and hold her there until she calms down long enough to sit back. We finish our drinks and talk about everything since their breakup.

Finding out he's in town explains why she's been so funky lately. We both catch each other up on what's been happening in our respective lives until it's time to open the doors to Shaken Tropes.

18

Cassidy

> We need another Benny's date.

> I need waffles.

> You're obsessed, and YES.

"And now that your home is reinforced, how are you feeling about being in the space now?" Donna's calm voice comes through the speaker of my laptop.

We've been on video for a while now, over the years I've grown to enjoy the support of having a therapist like her in my life. Her home office is a lovely sage green with white sheer curtains swaying on either side of her open window.

After Paloma and I shared a drink, I decided to text my therapist. I need a chance to sort through my emotions and talk to her about my insecurity of being "emotionally abandoned," as she calls it.

I so badly want to drop my head against my desk, frustrated with feeling like I took a step back, which is why talking with her is so important. Even though I no longer need weekly or even monthly sessions, I like to reach out when I am feeling a bit on edge. Like when I decided to finally make the pact with Lo. I appreciate the security I feel expressing my thoughts and concerns with Donna.

"I feel okay, I guess. I mean, the worry that it will happen again is still there, given that it's still so fresh. But I feel better. Jameson has stayed the last few nights since it happened."

"It sounds like Jameson makes you feel safe. Tell me more about him," she prods.

"He does. For once, I feel taken care of and—" I swallow before saying the next word—"seen. He makes me feel seen." I take a moment to breathe in and I anticipate her next question, having been with her long enough that I know she is going to refer right back to me, to have me dig a little deeper.

"That's a wonderful thing to hear." She watches my facial expressions change, my confusion clear on my face, a gentle smirk graces her aging features.

"I was expecting—" I mimic her calm demeanor— "dig into that feeling a bit more. Or have me talk about the pact I made with Paloma. You sound pleased, happy even."

"Well, of course... But more importantly, are you happy?"

I nod my head. "I am. When I walked into Cypress Lake High, he was the last person I expected to see. He wasn't even on my radar, but now that he is, I feel like I was missing a piece of myself before." I chuckle at how cliche I sound. "Not that he completes me, but that he adds to me."

"You should be incredibly proud of allowing yourself to experience the happiness you've created by saying *yes*. One small word that can change or open so many avenues in life. And you're doing it." Her encouraging words feel like a hug and I sit with them, thinking about what she just said. Saying yes used to feel impossible but now, it is starting to feel like second nature. Like, why wouldn't I invite new adventures into my life, no matter how big or small? Could a *yes* lead me to frustrations or heart break, of course it could.

"Jameson is the kindest, funniest, sexiest man I have ever met, and Donna, I want him to make me his first choice so damn bad. I won't lie to you," I admit.

Am I attaching an insecurity a bit? Yeah, maybe, I'm human. But it's truly because I see a future with Jameson. One that I want. Saying *yes* to Jameson leaves me open to the risk of heartbreak, but it's one I am willing to take. No matter how confident I am in him, in us, the little voice from years of wanting my parents to choose me rears its ugly head.

"There is nothing wrong with wanting to be his first choice."

"And what if I'm not?" I question her, knowing that she won't give me the answer but wishing she would all the same. "What if this one thing that I want is just—" My thoughts stop because what *if* I'm not enough.

"I can't answer that question for you. What I can say is that your intuition won't steer you wrong. You've worked so hard on yourself the last few years, bettering your coping skills to handle whatever life throws at you. And this is no different," she reassures me with a gentle smile.

"But what if—" No, fuck that. Fuck the what-ifs. I need to claim why I'm so consumed with not being an option. "This feels scarier. It feels different."

"Cassidy, it *is* different. And different is okay. I have every confidence in you being able to navigate this. Treat this like any other relationship—not one with a hot man," she says chuckling lightly. "What would you do?"

I sigh before responding, "I would look at the relationship objectively and trust the foundation we've started to build. If this is meant to be, it will be, and I will have faith that we will both make the right decisions for ourselves."

"See, you have those natural instincts within you. Don't let fear hold you back from what you want because of what-ifs or else you'll be stuck in the same place."

"You're right." I smile at her, feeling a twinge of confidence build in my chest. "Thanks, Donna. I don't know what I'd do without you."

"I think we both just witnessed how far you've come from our first sessions. You figured it out on your own. I just nudged you a little bit," she says. "Our session is up for the day, but I'm so glad you called me for a check in. It was lovely to hear from you, Cassidy."

"Thank you as always, Donna. Have a good rest of your day." We end the call and I take a deep breath.

Jameson has done nothing but show me he is trustworthy and honest. The questions that linger in my head are more of my own insecurities, and not anything he has or hasn't done. I trust him and I think it's time for us to have a conversation about what we are doing.

"Phone for you, Cass. They say it's important!" Brianna yells from the back storage closet. I shake my head, pulling myself out of my thoughts before standing to pop my head out, looking at her as she covers the mouthpiece of the phone and shout-whispers at me, "They sound panicked and asked to speak to the owner." She shrugs, her eyebrows climbing to her hairline.

I normally have all my calls routed to my cell phone during the day but I've been trying to delegate a bit more now that we've brought on Brianna full-time. Initially, she wanted to stay part-time but when she started talking about an art showcase she was going to miss out on, I may have mentioned we needed someone here to assist during the day, which we do. I didn't want her to feel pressured to say yes, having shared her work boundaries early on. B came in the morning one day and asked me if I would consider giving her a few more hours a week so she could save for the showcase. It felt natural to give her a permanent position, now she can make more money and have benefits. I told her by the time the showcase comes around, she would have accrued enough time to take the week and half off, paid. She leapt out of her chair and into my lap. I would have given her the time off regardless.

I wave a hand back at her and quicken my pace to the office. "Shaken Tropes, where your next steamy chapter is a sip away. What's your pleasure?" I say, not really knowing who to expect.

"Hello, are you the owner of-of Shaken Tropes?" Her voice is tight but pleasant, and B was right, she does sound panicked. The line goes quiet, or as quiet as it can given the heavy breathing on the other side.

"Yes, one of them, I'm Cassidy. How can I help you?" We don't often get complaints. Honestly, I have never had to take a call like this. Or at least what I'm assuming this is. A muffled cough comes through before they continue speaking.

"I, um. Well…Fucking hell." The last two words are more of an angry whisper to herself. "Okay, well. I'm not sure if this is something you even offer, but my sister is getting married in a little over a month and I'm sorta-kinda planning her bachelorette weekend. I've got all these really fucking great literary events happening during her weekend, but one drunken night she yelled about wanting to go dancing in a library and your bar is the closest thing I could find to it. Please tell me this is something you can accommodate… pleeeease tell me you have a library we can dance in."

Gobsmacked. I think she said all that in one single sentence, I don't remember hearing her take a single breath as she stammered through her request. We normally like to keep the music low and vibey but I can't bring myself to tell this girl no. She clearly wants to give her sister the best bachelorette party she could ask for and somehow I don't think any of our customers would mind. If this takes off and our customers love it, we could make Dancing in the Library a monthly thing. Imagining music jamming in the background as people dance, drinks in hand, while others joke and talk with their friends over our loaded potato wedges. I pull my bottom lip into my mouth, holding on to it with my teeth as I grin. "Actually, yes, I do have a library you can dance in."

"I knew it was a longshot but I—wait...You do!" The anxiety and panic from her voice are in the rear view. Replaced now, with a giant sigh of relief and joy. "Thank, fuck. Oh, my God. I am so sorry. I hate calling people. It makes me so nervous. You saying yes wasn't a part of my script." She laughs.

I've never been a fan of calling people either, if I can find a way to send an email, I will. I give her all the details and let her know not to worry about the deposit she was begging to pay me. She isn't renting out the whole space and this feels like a small gift I can give to someone. It sounds like she could use a pick-me-up and I'm glad to be the one to deliver.

I learned her name is Candice. Her sister, Jennifer, is getting married in the next couple of months to the love of her life. Both her and her sister have always loved romance novels and Jennifer's soon-to-be husband works in publishing. It sounded like Candice has a wonderful brother-in-law-to-be who could have been "written by a woman"—her words, not mine. But we both laughed nonetheless.

She apologized multiple times at her last minute request but again, they planned to come and enjoy what we already have. Which is exactly why, as soon as I ended the call with Candice, I dialed Lo's number. I gushed about throwing the bachelorette party here. The library that I promised we had, now needs to get done as soon as possible. We have to turn Shaken Tropes into something those girls can really get down in.

I make my way back into the office to get all the details into the calendar so I don't forget. I scribble a note for Lo on the desk calendar, she is going to get in touch with Crew Construction and Consult. I make it a point to emphasize that we all need to have a sit-down meeting to get it done, and if need be have Anderson call me directly. All hands on deck as they say.

I'm so glad I'm not working tonight, I'm exhausted from this week. My delicious bulldozer has been staying over at night, fawning over me until he devours me later in the evening. My skin warms thinking of the things he said to me this morning. I've come to think of him more and more as mine. Even though the commitment absolutely scares the shit out of me and we haven't spoken about what we mean to one another, it pops up unbidden in my mind. I'm falling head over heels for him and I don't want these feelings to end. I make my final notes in the calendar and close the office door, before making my way upstairs.

Loosening up my shoulders, I feel lighter already. This bachelorette party is exactly what I need after the break-in. Something I can throw my creative brain into and get back to normalcy. I'm not one of those people who can stay still when life throws punches, I need to be busy. My parents' passing forced me to focus on finishing school and get Shaken Tropes off the ground. Keeping my mind focused on the future is how I find my sunshine.

Just as I'm slipping my feet into a pair of my fluffy slippers, my pocket chirps. I've never been so glad to be home alone when I see who text me because the goofy grin has become a permanent fixture on my face. Maybe he isn't as much of a bulldozer as he is sunshine.

Bulldozer

> Hey Babygirl, I'm jumping in the shower and heading over to you afterwards!

Before I can reply another text from him comes through.

Bulldozer

> How do you feel about a change of plans?

> What kind of change are you thinking?

Bulldozer

> If I said it was a surprise and to dress comfortably, would you be down?

> Oh! A surprise?

Bulldozer

> You'll love it and I promise to feed you…

> I get to be with my man and he's going to feed me? I'm down! *kissy face* I'll be ready when you get here.

I press send and then realize what I sent and I think about editing the text but he's already read it. Shit. Though I may have jumped the gun, it feels completely right and a soft smile washes across my face when I see his three little bubbles turn into a reply.

Bulldozer

I like being yours. See you in a bit, Babygirl.

Unconsciously my lips part and I read his text again. He likes being mine. The thought of a surprise date, mixed with his words, gives me a bounce to my step.

I've never been a spontaneous person, but Jameson makes me want to try new things. He makes me want to put myself out there and I truly don't even care what we are doing as long as I'm doing it with him.

Without a second thought I punch in Paloma's number and video call her.

"Hola, you beautiful bitch! What's up?" Her voice comes through the line and it matches her smile.

"Jameson just told me he likes being mine and switched plans up on me! And I need help choosing something comfortable, but an outfit that will keep his eyes on me." I bite my bottom lip with excitement.

"Babe, you are worried about his eyes being on you and he just told you he likes being yours?" she shouts through the phone, shimmying her shoulders. "I don't think you will have any issue with him keeping his eyes on you. Have you seen how he looks at you?"

I know she's right, so I tell her so. "I don't know where we are going.

He told me to dress comfortably."

I rummage through my closet, grabbing a few different options that we can pick from. We both settle on a pair of textured, light-purple shorts; there is a small ruffle around the opening of each leg, giving it a fun flair to the comfort they offer. I give the drawstring a quick tie before pulling on the white, cropped graphic t-shirt. It's a thrifted tee I bought years ago and decided to cut a few inches off the bottom to give it a bit more shape and style.

"What do you think?" I sing-song as I slide on my ruffled socks and sneakers.

"Those shorts make your ass look incredible." She bites at the air and I stifle a laugh.

She's not wrong, taking a longer look at myself in the mirror I take in the simple outfit I have on. The cropped tee is just long enough to end right at the top of my waistline, showing the faintest amount of skin. I add on a few layering necklaces and bracelets.

"Seriously, you look hot. Spray on some perfume and get lotion on those thighs. Ow. Ow!" She mimics howling noises before she snickers.

"I love you, Lo."

"Love you more."

Ending the call I go to do just that. Walking into the bathroom, I unscrew the top of my vanilla bean whipped body butter and slather it on my legs. The soft shimmer in the lotion makes my skin glow under the lights; I feel comfortable and sexy as fuck. I spray on my favorite perfume to all my pulse points, including my ankles and behind my knees. If there is even a small possibility that they'll be wrapped around his head, I want him to experience just how good I smell.

Before turning off the bathroom light I adjust my hair, it's been a good hair day for me. My curls are still wild and sticking out wherever they choose but it's a low frizz day, a win is a win.

I curl my lashes and use my fingers to rub a peachy-coral blush on my cheeks before applying dark-brown mascara and my chapstick. I'm keeping things simple. I don't want to fuss over myself while I'm with him. As soon as I get my chapstick in my bag, I hear a knock at my door and the smile is right back on my face.

"Coming!" I shout to the door, knowing it's Jameson.

Pulling open the door, the first thing I notice is his megawatt smile and how he has his locs tied up in a low bun, lengthy pieces hanging over his shoulder. I all but throw myself into his arms and he takes the opportunity to kiss me. My body molds into him as he deepens the kiss, wrapping his arms around my waist. His tongue licks at the seam of my lips and I open easily, taking him in as much as I can.

He slows the kiss and plants one more soft kiss on my forehead before he's lowering me so my feet are fully on the ground. "Hey to you too, Babygirl!" His voice alone makes me melt.

Jameson looks so damn good. I love that he can pull off the clean and buttoned-up look like he did for the reunion, but I think his casual and laid back vibe is my favorite. His wide shoulders fill out the black graphic t-shirt which has large red letters across the front of his strong chest. Smiling up at him, I slide my finger into the buckle of his black belt. His brown Dickies land just above his ankle with a distressed hem meeting his white socks and black vans.

"So where are we going?" I ask as he walks ahead of me. Hand in hand we make our way down the stairs.

"If I told you, then it wouldn't be a surprise." He follows that comment up with a panty-dropping smile.

"Oh, confident, I like it." Pulling my bottom lip into my mouth on a grin I can still taste the strawberry flavor of my chapstick he all but kissed off, and I smile back at him. I will be climbing up this man's body tonight.

He takes the few back roads like a pro, turning the music on quietly to give us something to listen to. Within a few minutes he is slowing down near where the Night Market is held, pulling into a parking garage nearby. He's at my door, unbuckling my seatbelt before I get the chance to even consider it.

"Oh my God! The Night Market." My cheeks perk up, I love this place. They've always got something interesting going on and I never really know until I'm here or had the chance to scope out the scene on social media...but by then it's packed.

He must have checked into this earlier and found something happening that I'd enjoy. Unless someone is familiar with Cypress Lake they wouldn't know this is here. Jameson grabs my hands and pulls me towards the center of the market.

19

Jameson

sends a selfie of Babygirl and me

Pops

This is her? She's beautiful, son.

Mama

You two look lovely together.

She's the one for me.

Pops

You think so?

I know so.

Seeing the smile on her face only further validates this was a good choice. After some snooping, I found out the Night Markets is something Cypress Lake started organizing a few years ago. They've got everything from small pop-up eateries to painting activities, sometimes they even have dance classes.

Cassidy has been having nightmares and I thought getting her out of the house would be good for her. Plus, it gives me another reason to be with her, to touch her. Since the break-in, I've been staying with her the past few nights. I want to be sure she feels safe, and it doesn't hurt that we can satisfy our craving for each other before we pass out, her wrapped in my arms.

Every morning I wake up to the taste of her strawberry chapstick on her lips and she moisturizes my beard, that's before I get out of bed. Waking up between her thighs is all the breakfast I need. Interlocking our hands I pull her deeper into the market, my eyes focused on where we are headed.

"Stop it right now!" Her mock anger makes me laugh as she slaps my arm. They have a live band here tonight and dancing. Since the reunion, I couldn't stop thinking about how free she was while she danced. And honestly, I can't stop thinking about how free I felt with her, either. Everything is easy with her.

She pulls on my hand, the joy in her eyes shining bright. How could I not love her? My eyes go wide at my own realization. I don't even want to fight against how soon it feels. She's it for me. And the smile she has on her face right now makes it all the more real.

I let her curves lead the way as she sways her hips to the beat. We jump and dance, enjoying the band that has some amazing covers and original music. The music changes to something we can really dance to and I waste no time pulling her into me, my hands grabbing into the softness of her stomach before she rolls her ass against me. The feel of her ass pressing into me lights my body up, knowing I'm the one that gets to hold her, to call her mine. She grinds into me as I hold her, my dick doesn't care that we are in a crowd. It responds instantly to her movements. An aching throb as we dance, not missing a beat she rolls her hips and smirks at me before she turns to face me. There's no way she can't feel the hard-on I'm sporting, she rubs herself against me and her devilish smirk tells me I'm not wrong.

"Can I touch you, Cassidy?" My voice is thick with need, but I want to be sure she's okay with blatant PDA.

In response, she throws her arms around my neck, reaching on her toes to give me a deep and sensual kiss. Her warm tongue runs at the seam of my lips and I open for her, inviting her in for more. Our tongues dance as do our bodies, there is no competition and no need to rush. She leans back slowly, looking up at me with those dark-honey colored eyes, her lids are heavy and her mouth holds a satisfied grin, plump from the kiss we shared.

She turns back around, swaying her hips as we dance as if there isn't anyone around—no band, no dancing couples—just *us*. I run my hands around her waist, right below her breasts. Gently, I squeeze the underside of one as I grip her wide hips with the other. Dropping her head back against my chest, I can see that she has her eyes closed, her mouth parted slightly as a soft murmur leaves her lips. She gives me her body fully, to touch and tease and worship.

Lifting her arms up toward the sky she wraps them around my neck as she softly runs her nails back and forth on the back of my head. I run my fingers along the underside of her breasts before teasing her peaked nipple through the material of her dress and the whimper she releases makes my knees buckle. My dick aches behind the zipper of my pants and I consider taking her from behind in the back of the truck. My hand strains as I dig my fingers into her hip a bit more, thinking about having her spread open for me, her moans would drown into the music.

Spinning her in my arms, her head stays back as she laughs and I quickly pull her body into mine. Knocking her off balance a bit, she falls into me and my eyes watch her pink tongue travel along the bottom of her lips.

She pulls out her phone, one that has a crack running right down the middle, I watch it slip through her fingers and I snatch it up. Not wanting it to hit the ground and incur more damage.

I swipe down her screen and click the camera button, angling it in front of us. I watch her smile reach her eyes as I say, "Take a picture with me, Babygirl." I snap a couple pictures, one of us smiling and another with my tongue peeking out, pressing it against her cheek.

She snatches her phone back, giggling as I drop my head to her shoulder and nuzzle my face in her neck, taking in the heady vanilla scent of her and hear one more snap of her camera.

"Can we get something to eat?" she whispers in my ear, still swaying to the music as she grinds her pelvis into my thigh. Fuck, this woman is every wet dream I've ever fucking had. My hands skim down her curves, squeezing at the fullness of her waist.

"Yeah, Babygirl." I place a small kiss on the space between her neck and ear as she pockets her phone. "There's a new place here tonight that I think you'll really love."

Her hand is small and warm within mine as I lead her to the late night brunch spot I read was going to be here. I learned quickly how much this woman loves breakfast and even though I can't cook it myself, I will gladly take her to every single breakfast eatery I can find.

Syrupy sweetness wafts in the air, growing stronger the closer we get to the spot we came here for. The hot pink food truck is parked just north of the center of the market where all the music is. Bubble letters are written across the front in cursive that reads Bangin' Brunch Bites, the white background making it appear neon.

A woman with the same color hair peeks through the window and greets us with just as much spunk. "Heya! Welcome to Bangin' Brunch Bites, where every bite packs a punch and sass comes with a side of syrup! Let me close up this order and I will be right with you guys!"

When I look at Cassidy, she is buzzing with excited energy that matches my own. As she looks over the menu I watch her dance and shimmy her shoulders as her eyes land on options I assume she wants to try.

We decide to get a few different things so we can try all our favorite sounding menu items: sweet potato biscuits with hot honey fried chicken sliders, strawberry stuffed french toast bites, mimosa coolers, and a few other small plates we couldn't say no to. Which is how we both end up gorged out on a picnic blanket under a tree with twinkling lights hanging above our heads from a low hanging branch.

My eyes find her lips and I watch her lick off a bit of frosting from some strawberry filling. I can't help but stare, my eyes glued to how her loose curls frame her face. Cassidy is leaning back on one of her hands as her upper body rocks side to side listening to the music that plays throughout the market while the band takes a much deserved break. Her legs are crossed at the ankle but her feet tap along too. The look of contentment that plays on her face, her lips turned up softly at the corners, makes her all the more beautiful.

"See something you like?" Her question is flirty and dripping with a lust I want a taste of, which is exactly what I do when I lean over and kiss her.

Her lips are soft against my own and I pull her bottom lip between my teeth. Her eyes light up then soften before closing slowly, the feeling of her soft lips drives me to open the clip she has her curls trapped in and I quickly tangle my hands in her hair. Gifting me with a low groan as the vanilla scent of her lotion around me. The tastes of strawberry and mango from the mimosa linger on her tongue. She moans faintly and that's all I need to haul her into my lap. Her thick thighs rest on either side of my legs and she hovers over me just enough. Fuck that, I want to feel all of her on me. I grab two handfuls of her ass and lower her completely.

"Mmm." She hums before I'm back to kissing her.

"See something I like and want," I say, responding to her earlier question as I bite gently on her neck and she hisses. "That's it Baby, give me all those pretty sounds. I want every last one of them." She grinds down against my hard cock to the rhythm of the music and I return her moan with my own.

I press my hips into her as she rolls against me and drops her head back. Cassidy is a sight to behold and I don't plan on ever letting her go. She leans down, resting her forehead on my own and our heavy breaths mingle together as we both try to calm ourselves. She takes in a breath and releases a shuddering exhale before she laughs a bit and says, "We should save this for later, yeah?"

"Definitely" I agree with her, my ragged breathing now calmed somewhat.

I don't want our interaction getting anymore heated out here. No one gets to see her break apart but me. "You're right, Babygirl, let's go. Looks like the band is getting back on the stage."

She stands, smoothing her shirt into place, and I follow her back to the center where the music thumps and the light pulses to the beat. The rest of the night is perfect, we dance until sweat glistens on our skin and then make our way back to the car.

Halfway back to her place when she turns the music down and faces me. "Tell me about this house! I know you've been working on it for a long time now but I haven't seen it yet."

My hand has been rubbing her thigh as we drive and I squeeze it just a bit at my excitement. The house is almost done and I love that she wants to see the hard work we've put into it.

"We've got a couple more weeks to go but we are in the final stretch. Then I need to fly out to the second house and make sure the team is on top of things. Actually"—he pauses for a moment, contemplating his next words before continuing—"if you are up for it, I would love to show you." She nods her head and I make the next left, taking us to the house I still don't have a name for.

"I didn't realize the new property would take you further from Cypress Lake." Her voice is small in her question. It may sound like a statement but I can hear the concern in her voice.

"I need to fly out there soon to check on the progress. I promise you, had I known that I would have been running into *you*, I may have passed up on it. It's a full flip, unlike this one that I plan to rent out to tenants as a short-term rental," I say, hoping that quells the anxiety that's rippling off of her. I pull her hands into my lap, rubbing my thumb back and forth as we get closer to the property.

We pull into the driveway and I jump out of the driver's seat to get her door. Noticing she no longer reaches for the handle when we park has me puffing my chest out a bit. Once we make it in the house, I turn on the lights and rush to adjust the security system before it starts going off.

"Here, let's start this way." I walk her through the kitchen and living room, pointing out the areas I'm especially proud of as well as the spaces that still need work but telling her the ideas for it all nonetheless.

Once we make it to the backyard, I share my plan to make a social gathering oasis, one for large groups as well as more intimate moments, along with a full outdoor kitchen. Seeing her eyes sparkle at my hard work brings me so much pride. Anders and I have worked on this for a while, not including all the work we did with the design and draw-ups.

"It's really amazing, Jameson. Seriously, it's beautiful. You guys have done an amazing job." Her praise sends me to a new level.

"I love it and I've gone back and forth, but the more and more I think about it, the more I know it will be a great rental and in the end, will make us money."

Briefly, the thought of hiring a management company crosses my mind. But staying here in Cypress Lake with Cassidy means I could manage it myself. It wouldn't be hard to find or build new properties for the area. The vision of starting a new unit in Crews Construction and Consult flits across my mind and a thrill runs through me.

"You're amazing, do you know that?" I set down my phone and keys on the counter in the kitchen before looking back at her. "I'm going to run to the bathroom, I'll be right back okay? Hopefully, Anders hasn't turned off the water on me." I laugh as I head back to the front bathroom.

Keeping this house as a rental property is the right move. I'll have to really think through this management portion for Crews, maybe talk about it with Anders over a beer. I want to have all my ducks in a row before I tell her I plan on moving here permanently. Staying here with my Babygirl feels more and more like a reality. Now, more than ever.

20

Cassidy

General HOES group chat

Ben & Jerry's emergency

B

Oh no…

Lo

What's wrong babe?

I knew they did great work but this is stunning. My eyes widen as Jameson walks me through his hard work and I'm completely blown away. There is a pool table off to the left of the entrance of the foyer and I may not know how to play, but I would be down to let Jameson teach me. As I walk deeper into the house there are concrete spheres that have a cutout inside for what seems to be a space for speakers. They lead into the sunken living room which makes the entire room feel cozy and intimate. I take the two, wide steps down and my eyes land on the inky-black brick fireplace that is from floor to ceiling, framed by what feels like a wall of windows. The windows make the entire backyard feel like a piece of art..

The rooms haven't been staged yet, they're just empty rooms that are waiting for furniture and nicknacks but this kitchen is one made for chefs to do their thing. The dark cool-gray concrete floor fades into wide planks of stained wood that reminds me of the color of rolled tobacco. The countertops match the polished concrete flooring.

It's a dream here, and also a nightmare.

As soon as Jameson heads to the bathroom, my one big insecurity rears its fugly-ass head. I wasn't expecting for it to be so...done. My eyes are misty at the in-my-face reminder that, unlike this house, Jameson isn't a permanent fixture here. Not to mention the other house that he has.

We haven't discussed what we are to each other but everything points to us being an *us*—he's mine and I'm his—at least I hope so. He said he liked being mine, but does that mean we are together? I would know if we talked about it. *Fuck*. What if I'm not? What if this is just another reminder that I'm not someone's first choice, just like with my parents.

I close my eyes and take a deep breath. Right as I raise my arms to rub my temples a ping sounds for a text notification. My eyes snap open and land on the phone. Jameson's phone. And no matter how much I wish I didn't see the text, I did.

I can't wait to see you this weekend, love you *winky face with tongue out emoji*

My eyes land on the words, on that stupid fucking emoji, instead of the name. It has to be a girlfriend or... no. Absolutely not. There has to be an explanation; I refuse to jump to that type of conclusion when he has given me no reason to not trust him.

"Hey, Babygirl." Jameson comes back into the room but halts mid-step after seeing my face.

I can feel the tears well in my eyes thinking of the text message and how quickly he will be leaving once this house is fully renovated with tenants living in it. And I just—fuck this. Fucking, fuck this. I wipe my eyes with the back of my hand, streaking the brown mascara under my eyes as he starts walking towards me again, quicker this time. "What happened? Are you okay?"

I blow a breath and take him in, already missing his warmth but I won't leave here without knowing. "I was waiting for you to come out of the bathroom and you got a text," I say to him, pointing to his phone with my eyes and then back to him. "I didn't mean to look but it was a reflex and—"

His worried expression doesn't leave, but a layer of confusion warps his face as his eyebrows lower. He picks up his phone and opens his messages. I watch as a short-lived smile curves his lips before his eyes are back on me.

"I promise you, this isn't what it seems. It's Alma," he says, as if that explains anything at all. Maybe it should make sense but right now, it doesn't. My emotions war with one another, not understanding any of this. "She's my eighty-seven year old girlfriend, more like an adopted grandmother at this point. You accidentally gave me Alma's number the night of the reunion."

My eyes widen at his explanation and I'm so glad I didn't let it become something bigger than what it was. He brushes his fingers over my own that are resting on the counter but I can't stop myself from slowly pulling my hand back. *He's leaving, Cassidy.* I take in another deep breath, prepared to lay it all out.

"The house is beautiful," I start, needing to try my best to explain myself, to explain my feelings.

"Baby, I promise that there is nothing going on with Alma. Just an occasional true crime marathon. I'm actually flying out to be with her for a surgery she needs. I meant to tell you earlier." He chuckles, trying to clear the nervous energy I'm putting out. "That's not all, is it?"

"It's a dream here but it reminded me that you don't live here." My nerves start to get to me, knowing that I will be going home alone tonight. Knowing that this could possibly be the end and that thought makes tears well up and fall down my cheeks. "You don't live here and I can't be a second choice in someone else's life. In *your* life. This has all been incredible, but you are leaving Cypress Lake in a couple weeks," I say, when internally I'm yelling, *you're leaving me in a couple weeks.*

I loosen a heavy breath and try to get a handle on my emotions so I can continue, but now my nerves are a bit rattled at the thought of not having a future with Jameson, of not having more time with him. "Why would you go and make me fall in love with you if you didn't plan to stay?" My voice raises at the end and that's when realization hits me. I love him. I love him and I just shouted it at him.

"I love you Jameson. And...well, you know how my parents treated me or more so, their lack of treatment all together. How they were never home and left me to my own devices. I was alone constantly until I found Paloma and Janelle, until I moved into my grandmother's house. My parents spent more time being infatuated with one another and their jobs than ever trying to love me," I say, swallowing down my nervousness and raising my hand, pausing him before he speaks.

"Before you say anything, I need you to take this weekend as you visit with Alma and think about what *you* want. Because I know I want you. I want you all the time. But I can't live with the thought of you moving here for me and regretting it. I think I need some space to sort out my feelings about all of this." I wave my hands between us. "And a weekend apart isn't going to kill us. Right?"

"Is that what you really want? Space?" he asks me, his face still stunned from my confession, but the hurt in his eyes breaks something inside of me. I grasp his hand in mine and look up at him.

"You are incredible and everything I could have ever asked for…"

"I feel a 'but' coming," he says, and he's right.

"*But* I know that if you don't take the weekend and make the best decision for you, and what you want your next step to be, then one of us is going to end up resenting the other and that is the last thing I want. I want a lifetime with you Jameson."

"If space is what you want, then I'll give it to you, Babygirl," he says and pulls me in for a hug that envelops my whole body, squeezing me tight in an embrace that feels more like a goodbye.

Without warning he lifts me with ease and deposits me on the kitchen island. Given that there isn't any furniture, I don't object. "There are so many things I want to tell you but I…I don't want them to feel disingenuous after everything you've said. What I will say is what I feel for you trumps every other desire. I could never grow to resent you, Babygirl. I need you to know that I want a lifetime with you too. I can't leave without you knowing I feel the same." He squeezes his strong arms around me once more and I pull back the sniffle before squeezing him back. "I promise you, I will figure it out but this is not the end for us, I won't let it be."

The moment I lock my door I release the gut-wrenching scream I'd been holding onto since my eyes couldn't mind their own damn business. I knew that this was too good to be true but I'm trying to hold out hope that this will blow over and he will come back to me.

He has to.

I press my back further into the door, sliding down the front of it, I try to hold back the tears that are begging to be released. Space. What the fuck is wrong with me that I asked for space? That's not really what I want, but he needs this. He needs to be able to decide what he wants without the worry of losing me... if that's even a worry of his. What if he finishes this weekend and realizes I'm not worth it? Maybe he goes back to the house and realizes all he needs is another property to focus on? My eyes burn from trying to hold back the tears and I feel ridiculous because I'm arguing with myself about something I asked for.

Taking a deep breath I remind myself that I don't need to ramble on excuses, repeating myself over and over. What's done is done but I can't shut off the questions and thoughts, my brain working overdrive to try to make sense of it all while trying and failing to keep my heart protected. I slam my eyes shut, willing back the sting of oncoming tears. What was I thinking, getting into a situationship with a man who doesn't even live in the same state as me?

It's just like my parents all over again. My parents' real child was their job, they nurtured it and tended to it but seemed to have forgotten I existed. They were never home long enough to be bothered with me, their own fucking daughter. That's the true problem here and my heart breaks because I wanted this so badly. The thoughts almost shout at me and I can't stop the laugh that tumbles from my mouth. A self-deprecating, soul-crushing laugh.

The reality is that I'm not even in a relationship with Jameson. We never discussed if we were exclusive or not. So how can I be upset with somebody if the lines weren't drawn up in the first place. *Because I love him.* He weaseled his way into my heart and I have fallen head over heels for him.

Tingles sweep up the back of my neck and across my face at the embarrassment; I've never felt so foolish to have fallen in love with someone so quickly, someone who may have no plans of staying around to begin with. Wouldn't he have said that? Maybe he would have if I didn't cut him off, too nervous at the possibility of rejection.

I clutch my hand to my chest, attempting to breathe past the pain. My mind reminds me about the way he looks at me, the way he talks to me, the way he makes me feel like I am his entire world. I see his handsome face from the reunion in my mind's eye, urging me to make sense of something that my heart wants so badly. Only to find out that I was just a visitor in his life, a passing glance. It feels like an "I told you so." I lean my head back against the door and breathe, because though my mind wants to make me feel like a fool, my heart tells me otherwise. It tells me to take a moment and let the pain pass because this isn't over. Not by a long shot.

Standing up from the floor, I reach into my back pocket to grab for my phone that was vibrating just a moment ago. The *crunch* sound I hear next isn't a pleasant one. "Dammit!" I yell, my voice snapping given my frustration. It was already worse for wear but now I can't see anything on the screen.

I don't have the energy for this right now. It was such an incredible night, dancing with him in the middle of the market is something I won't ever forget. The way we swayed as he wrapped his strong arms around me made my heart pitter-patter like we were at prom. Two kids finally having the chance they wouldn't give themselves all those years ago. The freedom I felt as we tasted treats from the little tapas place within the market's walkway. It was the perfect night with the perfect man, my man.

Those words summon a new swarm of hurt and it coats my skin. How am I supposed to forget him if he decides not to come back? And why in the hell did I say I want space when I know damn well I don't? I didn't ask for space for me alone, I take in a deep breath as I remind myself. I want to be sure he doesn't just give up on the work and traveling he loves so much.

My feet feel like stone as I walk to my bedroom. Pulling on an old raggedy shirt that's three sizes too big and almost sheer from the fabric thinning with the amount of times I've washed it, I walk into my bathroom. Not bothering to turn the lights on, I do my skincare routine before wrapping my hair up in a satin scarf and climb into bed. My heart aches and I let out a forceful breath, attempting to clear my mind as I do; I pull the covers high up under my chin for some sense of comfort. I hope that asking for space, for both of us, was the right move. As I take in deep, cleansing breaths, my brain finally settles while listening to the fan's soft sweeping sound and I fall into a dreamless sleep.

Stretching my arms above my head, I roll over in bed. Not wanting to get up, knowing I have a meeting with Anderson to get the library completed today.

My phone is broken to pieces after the crunching from my ass; sliding down the door now feels a bit dramatic and my poor phone paid the price. Not only that, but I don't have the time to order a new one. I'm not too worried about it since I will mostly be working down in the bar for the weekend and I can take my calls there. Anyone who needs to reach me can get a hold of me there.

A few knocks rattle at the front door. "Be right there!" I yell from my room as I stand. Pulling on a pair of black leggings, I walk down the hallway seeing Paloma has already made herself at home in the kitchen.

"Hey, babe! I tried to call you but it went straight to voicemail. I figured you may want a pastry and cafecito since I was picking something up for myself and the crew. It's going to be a busy day," she says, handing me a small paper cup along with a guava and cream cheese pastry.

Taking a hearty bite of the flaky deliciousness, I hum my appreciation as my tongue darts out licking at the powdered sugar that coats the top. "Yeah, I broke it last night. I'll get a new one after the bachelorette party," I say, my voice solemn, sipping at the sweet but very hot coffee.

"I spoke with Anderson this morning and he is going to meet us downstairs in"—she looks down at her phone, checking the time—"about thirty minutes, so we better get on it. Luckily he has all the materials and measurements from the original remodel. He brought a few guys to get everything finished quickly. How was your date?"

I nod at her to follow as I make my way to my bedroom, I pull the dresser drawers open as I look for one of the many Shaken Tropes t-shirts I own. I pull a purple one over my head and look at my best friend who is sitting on my bed, waiting for me to spill the details.

"The date was incredible, Lo. We danced all night at the Night Market and tried out so much good food. It was a dream date and he is a dream man. Oh! And he showed me the house." My voice dips and Paloma's brow furrows as she watches the joy drain from my face.

"The house is beautiful. He has a real winner, but it's almost done and that means he is almost done here," I continue, sliding off the leggings from earlier and replacing them with a pair of loose-fitting boyfriend jeans that are distressed at the knees. "And it's just... Lo, he doesn't live here and I know that he would be willing to move here for me, but I can't have him feel that pressure, not from me. You know?" I ask, but not really asking her, just saying it out loud for someone to hear me. "I want him to really want to be here. Not just for me. I don't want resentment to grow. And I may have shouted that I love him." I continue to adjust my clothing, not wanting to look up at her.

"Woah! You what?" she yells, excitement coating her voice. "I'm so glad you finally told him because girl... Did he say it back? Of course he said it back," she answers the question immediately.

"Actually, no. I didn't let him finish speaking before I interrupted him. He said, I mean the world to him and this is what he wants too but—"

"Now you're worried he isn't going to come back?" My shoulders slump slightly as she has logicked it out. "He loves you, I can see it in the way he looks at you and how he takes care of you. He's coming back,

Cass."

"Yeah, that's what my heart says too." Pressing my sock-clad feet into my sneakers, I lace them up and snatch a quick sip of my cafe con leche. "Fuck! It's still hot."

Paloma laughs and I squint my eyes at her. "You are always in a rush to finish it," she says.

"Hush, they make it so good! I just want a good taste." I chuckle and it feels good to laugh after how last night ended. "Come on, let's head downstairs."

We open the door that leads to the bar and I can see that Anderson is already walking around the parking lot as his guys pull out the equipment they need. We decided to close up the bar tonight so the guys would have plenty of time to work with such short notice, and Anderson promised us that the transformation would happen despite the tight timeline.

Paloma sets out bakery goodies and coffees on the bar so the workers can all grab what they want as I unlock the front doors.

"Hey guys! Thank you so much, I know this is a lot of work for a weekend." Each of them waves me off, smiling as they grab for a pastry and white paper cup.

Anderson reaches out and gives me a side hug as he also sips at the hot liquid. "It's not too big a job, we've had worse. We have the blueprints and everything we need. It'll be an easy job for everyone here," he says, taking a side step so he is facing me. "What's going on with your phone? I tried to call you so you knew we were on the way."

For a man of few words, he's got a lot to say today. "I broke it last night. I'll get a new one once the bachelorette party is done. I'm not leaving this place until I absolutely need to."

He nods his head and pats my shoulder before walking over to his team. I'm not sure if he notices the tiredness in my voice or the longing that I'm sure is in my eyes. His best friend is all I can think about and having Anderson here, now that I know Jameson co-owns Triple C, makes the situation that much harder. I have a few last minute follow-ups with inventory to get done, so I take this as an opportunity to get to it and make my way back to the office.

Anderson and the Triple C Crew made quick work cutting all the boards and already had a few bookshelves up by the time lunch rolled around. Paloma ordered sandwiches and pasta salad and made sure to serve the guys drinks as I finished up in the office. Without a phone I was way more productive than I normally am.

My hand hovers over the phone in my office as I consider calling Jameson. I half hoped that I would have gotten a call from him today, but I did ask for space and he wouldn't know that I broke my phone last night. Shaking my head, I stuff my hands in my pockets and leave the office, locking the door behind me.

"Holy shit!" The words fall from my mouth and I take in the library that is almost fully complete. What the hell! They're fast.

"We are almost done. Just need to wrap the areas where the shelves meet, add the crown molding, and add the caulk to all the seams of paneling," Anderson says to Paloma.

"I'm sorry, what did you just say?" she snickers, knowing damn well she heard him. He eyes her before shaking his head. Ignoring her antics, he walks over to his team to discuss the last bit of details and she bursts out laughing. I walk up next to her, bumping her shoulder with my own.

"He was talking about *cocking* the seams, you'd know." I nudge Lo and her fake gasp chokes her laughter. "I'm gonna clean up here, why don't you run out and get the few pieces of decor we still need?"

I may have been in the office most of the day but I'm bea. *Work needs to get done so that this weekend runs smoothly*, I think to myself as I reach for the broom.

21

Jameson

How am I going to kick Helen's ass at our bowling league all wrapped up like this?

You're not! You'll need rest.

Bowling can wait.

Bowling waits for no one, youngin'.

This is not how I was expecting our night to end. I wanted to lay myself out and tell her—tell her how much I love her and want to be with her—but it didn't feel right. Not when she asked for space. When I tell her I love her, I want her to know that it's the truth and not because I'm trying to convince her.

And she isn't wrong in how she feels. It's only been a short time since I started thinking of moving back here and though I've pretty much made up my mind, I didn't consider putting everything behind me. Before her, I would already have a new project lined up, but I don't want another project that takes me further away from her. The last thing I want to do is jump into this without having all my ducks lined up. Hurting Cassidy is not a part of a decision I plan on ever making and being apart from her, even just for a night, hurts in a way that crumples my heart.

Rubbing my hand in a circle against my chest, I think of how her parents basically ignored her and how they were so dense they couldn't care to see what their absence was doing to their daughter. It's not a feeling I want her to ever associate with me. I pull my shoulders up to my ears in a deep inhale and remind myself again: giving her space will allow her to see just how true my feelings are.

I can already feel how tight and stiff my body is going to be in the morning from Anders' hard-ass couch. I could have gone to a hotel, but after calling Anders and telling him everything that happened tonight, he told me his couch was always open to me no matter how much I hate it.

He blew my mind when I shared about her wanting space, because he agreed with her. Told me that if Cassidy is where my future lies then I need to tie up all the other loose ends and do what needs to be done. He said, "what's a couple days in the grand scheme of forever" and he has a point.

So I'm going to take this weekend. When I'm done visiting with Alma I'll come right back to her. Because though I love my work, I love her more. This isn't a fling and I hope she knows that, she's meant to be my girlfriend. That title feels so small in comparison to what I want with her. She's my future and her struggles from her past are getting to her and we are going to fix that, she will always be my first choice.

Turning on my side, I fail in my attempt to get comfortable. I have a flight to catch at six in the morning but I don't see sleep in my future anytime soon. I shift again, not finding a single spot of softness. Why spend so much damn money on a couch, if you can't even kick your feet up in comfort?

Huffing a breath, I grab the remote off the coffee table and click on the television. Flipping through the channels, a true crime show fills the screen. Alma has turned me into a crime show junkie.

I didn't realize I fell asleep until the alarm from my phone blares beneath the lumpy pillow my head rests on. *These really are made for looks and not comfort,* I think to myself as I stand and stretch, feeling as if I've been sleeping on bedrock instead of a gallery sofa. He needs to burn this fucking couch and I plan on bringing the matches.

Opening my text thread with my girl, I ramble off a quick text before pausing over the send arrow. *She wants space,* the little voice inside my head reminds me. For a moment the thought of deleting the message crosses my mind, but it's only for a moment before I press send. I know she would rather know I was getting on the plane safely than to give her the space she asked for.

> I know you said you wanted space, I wanted to let you know I'm heading to the airport.

> See you in a couple days, Babygirl.

It's too early to hear from her, so I don't wait for a response and start getting my things together.

> I'm heading out! Take good care of my girl.

Anders

> I will J. I'm already at the office getting some things loaded in the truck. Safe travels. See you in a few days.

> And buy a new couch. I'm going to have a cramp in my back for the next fucking week.

Fuck, I'm a grouch. It feels strange to be in such a nasty mood as opposed to my normal, jovial demeanor, but I can't help it. Even the drive to the airport does me no good. I know what I need. My hands tangled in chestnut curls and strawberry kisses.

It's been a few hours and still no text from Cassidy. I know she wanted space and it's a busy day. But still. When I check our text thread I can see that my message isn't marked as delivered. I scrunch my forehead up in confusion before I rattle off a text to Anders to make sure everything is alright. He should be at Shaken Tropes by now.

> Hey bro, you at Shaken Tropes?

Anders must already be on his phone, putting in a delivery or something when my text comes through, because his bubbles pop up immediately.

Anders

> She broke her phone. Get on the plane, she's
> not going anywhere.

I really hate when he anticipates what I'm going to say and when he's right. I slide into my window seat and remind myself that I will give her this weekend, give her the breathing space she thinks she needs so badly, and come hell or high water I will get her to listen to me and then she will never be rid of me.

The flight was smooth and I made it just in time to give Alma my love before she's wheeled into surgery for her heart stent. If Alma had family this may have gone differently, but since the night I text her phone in error, we hit it off. I wanted to be here for her because I care for her and because she deserves to know that someone is out here waiting for her.

Putting in my headphones, I turn on the audiobook I've been listening to. I've been eyeing the books on my girl's bookshelf and listening to the ones I see her pick up often. She goes back to the pages for comfort, no matter if it's a spicy book or a mystery. This one happens to be a spicy one. Some magic system romance—once I've convinced her that she's lost her mind, I have a few new things I plan on doing to her, inspired by this particular novel. I just have to get her to see she's not just the first option, she's the blueprint.

I've always been a relationship guy, wanting to settle down with someone rather than skip around. She is smart and quick-witted, open and unapologetically herself. She makes it easy to share details about myself, wanting her to know the deepest parts of me.

Cassidy takes care of those she loves, wanting to see the best in everyone. Watching her run her business, how she truly invests herself in all of her patrons no matter if they're a one-time customer or a regular. She is simply a wonderful person. I'm not blind either, if she's in the room I can't take my eyes off her. I haven't since the reunion and I don't plan to.

Alma comes out of her surgery doing well. The surgeon gives me a wave to go back to see her and I follow the blue tiled floor towards her room. Ever since that first night after the reunion, when Cassidy gave me the wrong number, we've kept in touch. She doesn't have any living children and her husband passed away nearly fifteen years ago. She was alone, until she decided I was hers too. I huff a laugh remembering her text message back to me. She's amazing and has become someone really special to me.

"Hey, Girlfriend." She laughs at the nickname I've called her since texting her instead of the curvy woman of my dreams. "How are you feeling?"

"Oh, I'm gonna be just fine, suga'. I'll be back to clearing the pins at bowling nights in no time." Her voice shakes a bit from both the drugs wearing off and her old age. "You tell me what's got you so heavy?"

It's amazing how quickly she picks up on things. "Alma, don't start. I'm here to check on you. Not unload my problems onto your plate."

"Hush boy and tell me what's going on with that woman of yours," she says. Her voice holds an all-knowing quality that I haven't yet wrapped my mind around.

"Well, it's your fault really!" I say. She barks a laugh until she looks up at me, though I'm joking, I'm also somewhat serious.

I fill her in about our conversation at the reunion, our date, I even tell her about the break-in. "She's an incredible woman. Beautiful, smart, and caring. Owns her own bar called Shaken Tropes, it's all based on her favorite romance books. She's everything I could have wished for in a woman, more than anything I could have dreamed really."

"Then what in the hell are you doing here?" she chastises me.

"I wanted to be here for you."

"I'm not going anywhere. I love you and I am so glad you are here with me. But you've got to make her see. If you really want to be with her, she needs to know you're all in."

"I don't ever want to make her feel second best or a non-factor, like her parents did, but she wanted space. So that's what I'm giving her. Then I've got this property that is just south of you I need to check in on," I say to her, letting my innermost thoughts speak for me.

"That property is clearly running just fine without you considering you've only been there once," she replies matter of factly.

"Yeah, I guess you're right. I'm only popping in tomorrow to sign off on a few things for the realtor. A couple that is expecting their second child was in the area and loves it. I wanted to surprise Cassidy with the news that our personally designed backyard would have some new owners."

"And you still can."

"First I'm going to snap a picture with the family. I know she would want to see," I reply. Almost sad that I couldn't bring Cassidy with me I add, "She wants space, Alma."

"She doesn't want space, boy! She wants you. A woman like her wants to be seen and understood. She doesn't want to think you'll fly away like a bird once the weather changes." She ponders, grabbing the large hospital cup of water and taking a sip before continuing, "She needs to know you've got roots growin', and right now even though you may be workin' on it, it doesn't look like you do. You're so head over heels for her that you could trip over your own two feet. You need to make this right!"

I let Alma poke at me a bit more. We eventually settle into a comfortable silence as Morgan and Penelope's—from Criminal Minds—flirty banter fills the room. Before I know it, it's time for Alma to get some rest, visiting hours having been over quite some time.

Leaning over I press a kiss to her grayed hair and say my goodbyes. I promise Alma I will be on a flight back to Cypress Lake tomorrow—I will pick the earliest option—and will stop in to see her before I go.

She shakes me off and tells me to video call her before I board the plane. Her steely gaze stays on me long enough that I agree before I leave to get some rest at my hotel room for the night.

I'll get some work done in the morning before I check out and make my way to the airport. I'm ready to get back to my Babygirl. It's time I talk some sense into her. I get busy downloading a few more audiobooks before falling asleep.

22

Cassidy

"Alexa, play 'Another Sad Love Song' by Toni Braxton."

I stick my hand in my back pocket on instinct, reaching for the broken phone that isn't there. Maybe I should have bought a new one. I know I asked for space, but damn do I miss him. How do I know if he's tried to call without having it? I don't have time to get wrapped up in what-ifs and questions that I don't have answers for right now.

The bachelorette party is tonight and there are so many little things I need to get done. Paloma and I brought in temp staff to help with the night. We want to focus on the girls having an amazing night and don't want our regular customers to feel forgotten about. We announced this night on our social media platforms, letting our followers know that tonight would be about Dancing in the Library. I really wanted all our patrons to feel comfortable and that meant letting everyone know that it may not be their cup of tea if they want a relaxing night of reading.

Pulling out the outfit I picked out for the festivities, a grin blooms on my face. I'm so excited to be branching out in this way and it makes me think about how badly I want to turn this apartment into an event space. We would be able to do so much up here. With how large it is, we could totally break this up into three different spaces that could be used all together or individually for different parties. I may need to seriously consider looking for my forever home sooner than later. I could totally see Dancing in the Library being a *thing*. Clapping my excitement, I cannot wait to share this with Paloma. I grab a notebook and jot the idea down, not wanting to forget it.

Sliding on the black distressed jeans that are shredded right above my ankle, I button them before I slide my arms through my soft satin blouse, the color of bloomed thistles. I gather the material in the front and wrap each side around, tying it at the back. I smooth my hands down my sides as I take my reflection in; I love a good wrap top or dress and purple is just my thing. I slip the gold grouping of dainty necklaces around my neck, clasping it at the back. Lastly I slide on a thin gold band on my fore finger. The ring is something I always wear. I saw it in my gran's jewelry box and she gifted it to me when she realized I couldn't take my eyes off of it.

My chunky black sandals are waiting at the door leading down to the bar, I slide them on and make my way downstairs. I want to help Paloma get everything set up but as I close the door and turn around, my eyes take in the space.

I blink rapidly, staring at the already decorated bar. The library looks vibrant with new couches and tables. The area is blocked off a bit to make it feel a bit more VIP for those who either want to sit and read during the afternoon hours or dance the night away in the evenings. There are also a few chaise lounge chairs set up in a circle with a couple small round tables for the bachelorette party. It gives them a private space to sit down and catch their breaths from dancing or to enjoy a cocktail. This is insane, it looks incredible. There is a buzz of excitement that I can feel; I cannot wait to welcome everyone in.

Rounding the bar, I laugh at the ice cube trays that Paloma ordered for tonight. Some are wings for "Big Wing Span" and others are tiny dicks. She created a new drink for the bride called Up All Night and made cream and espresso dickcubes, mimicking the real deal. Popping one out of the silicone mold, I hold it up to give it a good look before popping it in my mouth. *Hmm, they got girth.*

"Tonight is going to be amazing," I breathe out to no one but myself.

The bar is quiet aside from the door swishing open. The citrus and bourbon scent I've missed so much wafts towards me and I don't need to open my eyes or lift my head to know who is standing in front of me right now. I do anyway, needing to see him.

"What are you doing here?" My mouth drops open in a gape. How can someone get better looking after only a weekend? It takes great effort from me not to combust from the joy I feel now that he's back so soon and here, with me.

"Hey, Babygirl. I missed that beautiful face of yours." He sits at the bar but keeps his hands and lips to himself.

At the thought of kissing him my eyes dip to his mouth and quickly shoot back up. Before I deep-dive into any of those wants I need to know this is a good visit, an I'm-moving-to-Cypress-Lake-and-never-leaving visit.

"I tried getting a hold of you a couple times this weekend but decided to let you be, to give you space," he says the last word as if there will never be space between us again. "And I may have heard about your phone from an oversized birdy."

A grin slowly curves my lips before I impishly respond, "Oh, did you?"

"Mm, I did. So I made sure to make a pit stop before I came here."

I'm not sure where he was storing it, but he pulls a medium-sized white gift bag from behind his back and sets it on the bar in front of me. He nods his head for me to grab the bag, and I do, needing to know what he's got inside of it. A rectangular box with a picture of a smart phone is on the front. Pulling it out, there's a heavy-duty, light-purple phone case as well. "Can't have you breaking your phone again," he jokes, and my eyes are still wide as I hold this gift, *a very expensive gift.*

"This is—It's too much!" Though I can't let it go because it's perfect. The phone is my favorite color as well.

"Don't even think about giving it back. This is for you and you need it. Plus, it's already registered to your number and you can't pull a fast one on me and give me the wrong number again." His eyes are wide as he looks at me, almost daring me to put the phone in the bag.

"First you thrust yourself into my life and now you buy me a new phone? Next you'll expect me to text you all the time," I jest.

"That's been my master plan all along, Cassidy. You'll never be rid of me." He places his arms on the bar leaning into me and I do the same. I want to be closer to him.

"Oh, and one more thing. I've missed you so damn much, beautiful, and I want to introduce you to someone really important to me."

My grin grows into a full megawatt smile at hearing that—knowing he has missed me as much as I have him. I lean over, looking around his frame to see who he brought with him. Maybe I missed them, but there doesn't seem to be anyone else here. "I've really missed you too, Bulldozer. But there's no one else here."

"I want to introduce you to my Alma," he says her name with so much love, with the same softness I use when I speak to my grandma.

He still has not fully let me in on his decision but with the small moment we just shared this feels like he's back for good. The bar is quiet aside from the soft music playing in the background. Staff hustle around us, all in their own worlds as they wrap up last minute preparations.

"Can we talk somewhere more private?" Jamesone asks.

Fuck. This can't be good. He wants to let me down easy and doesn't want me to make a scene by bursting into tears in my own bar. Maybe he bought me the phone so we could try long distance. Fuck. I take in a small breath not wanting to get myself worked up before he says it himself and I roll my eyes at my own thoughts.

"Yeah, we can go to the office," I say, as I open the counter and walk around.

He follows close behind me. Once we are in the office I close the door and offer him a chair at my desk. I take the seat next to him rather than behind my desk, not wanting this to feel like a business transaction.

"So, um, how is Alma?"

His lip quirks up at one side. "She's doing well," he says as he pulls out his phone, tapping on the screen before I hear a video call chime.

"Hey, Honey." A soft voice comes through the line. "Have you made it back to your lovely girl yet? I was starting to think you got *preoccupied* and wouldn't call."

"Yeah, Alma, I got her right here." He talks to her in a gentle voice, the same voice I would use with my own grandma, one I need to call. He hands me the phone.

The old woman smiles warmly at me, her deep-brown eyes are soft and her voice is a quiet whisper as she speaks, still talking with Jameson as if it was him looking at her and not me. "She's stunning Jameson. She's everything you said and more."

Taking in the space around her, it seems like she's in her hospital room still. My eyes note the collar of the hospital gown and monitors near the back of her bed. I wouldn't be able to tell though, her jet black hair is straightened in a braided top knot pillowed at the top of her head, not a single hair out of place. Her lipstick, a crimson red, enhances her golden tawny skin. She looks like royalty and I say a little prayer that I'll look as good as she does when I'm her age.

"Cassidy, meet Alma. The love of my life." His voice is mocking me now, "My eighty-seven year old girlfriend who likes Criminal Minds and bowling on Saturdays."

"Don't you start boy, you're supposed to be making up. Ignore him, lovely. It's a pleasure to finally meet you." My lips fold in as I try to hold back my laugh.

"It's really nice to meet you, Alma, though I wish it were a better circumstance. How are you feeling?" I ask her.

"I'm feeling good, better the moment I get to lie in my own bed away from the looky-loos in here."

"I'm sure you will be home in no time!"

"And I can't wait for it. I'm ready to scrub the floor with Helen." She puffs her chest out best she can and continues. "She is my, um, bowling buddy. Nevermind Helen... Listen dear, he's a foolish man who is head over heels for you, suga'. Now that I know he has made it back safely and I've met you, I think I'm going to get some rest," she releases a yawn before saying goodbye along with asking me to hear him out. Jameson ends the call, setting the phone down on my desk and looks at me.

"I don't want to be anywhere else, Babygirl." His voice is light, welcoming me into a conversation. "After visiting Alma I realized how foolish I was to leave without telling you fully how I feel. After talking with Alma she made me see I was missing something, and that something was telling you I'm not going anywhere. The house I'm renovating may be temporary but this, what we have, is not.

"Remodeling, nomading myself around, those places aren't my home, *you are*. Wherever you are is where I'm going to be, I need you to hear me in that. I need you to know that I am not leaving you. I want it all. I want the anger, the jokes, the dancing in the middle of the market like no one is there. I'm so sorry I didn't make that more clear to you, that was never my intention." He grabs both sides of my face, looking into my very soul before he continues, "I love you Cassidy Heart. You're the blueprint... always have been, always will be. Every curve. Every dip. Every smirk. You're it for me."

"I'm so sorry I didn't give you the chance to speak. That I didn't listen to you. I just—" His words stop me, realizing he just told me he loved me, and he doesn't give me another second to think and say it back before he pulls me onto his lap .

"I'm so sorry." My apology is muffled now that my face is mushed into his chest. I breathe in his scent, willing it to fill me and be a balm to my foolishness. "I can grovel, if that's what you want."

His chest rumbles with laughter as his hand slides up the nape of my neck and into my hair, pulling my head back in a sharp angle so I can look at him eye to eye.

"I want you on your knees, but not to grovel." His voice dips low, so low that it hits my panties. Like he never left. I'm weak for this man and now that I know what a fool I was, I need to make up for the lost time even if it was a short couple of days.

"We don't have much time before your party starts but I need to take you upstairs. Show you just how much I missed you." My body trembles at his words. I know we don't have enough time to do much of anything, but having his hands on me is all I can think about at this point.

23
Cassidy

I never want space again.

Bulldozer

Good, because I don't plan on giving you any.

We barely make it up the stairs before he's lifting me into his arms. I wrap my legs around his waist and grind against him the best I can before his lips are on mine again. Fuck he feels so good. Everywhere his hands touch my body responds with growing heat and moans fall from my mouth.

He pushes the door closed behind us and locks it with one hand before it's back on me. Grabbing handfuls of my ass he walks us to the bedroom. I untie my shirt and drop it on the chair nearby. Next, I'm tugging at the back of his shirt wanting it off so I can feel more of him. Needing to feel more of his skin on mine. He lets me pull his shirt off and I throw it to the side, not caring where it falls as he devours my mouth. He backs into the room and I prepare myself to be put down but he turns, placing my feet on the floor as he backs up towards the bed and looks at me with hooded eyes filled with lust. "On your knees, Cassidy."

I comply quickly, dropping to my knees in front of him as my mouth waters at the thought of pleasuring him. I drop my head back and take in his form from this angle. He looks like a Greek god dipped in gilded onyx. My heartbeat picks up at the sight of him as he pulls his belt free from his pants in one swift movement. Why is that so hot? The anticipation skyrockets my heartbeat. My fingers flex at the need to unbutton his pants but he does it for me. Slowly unzipping, he pushes his pants down his legs and is left in nothing but a deep-green boxer brief. His erection is thick and pulses beneath his grip as he strokes himself through the material. "Show me how sorry you are, pretty girl."

He peels his boxers off and his cock springs free as he leans back against the bed, I crawl closer to him. Taking him in my hand, I stroke his thick shaft slowly and watch as a small bead of pre-cum shows. I swirl my tongue around his head, tasting its salty flavor before I lick him from the base of his shaft back to the tip. Taking him deep in my mouth, I hollow out my cheeks and enjoy the feeling of fullness.

"Fuck, Cassidy, you feel so good." His words spur me on as I suck him deep into my mouth. His cock bumps the back of my throat and I swallow it down greedily, hearing him take in a quick breath. His moan follows and I continue, softly gripping his balls, kneading them as I bob my lips on his dick. I take him in deeper as his hands find my hair, gripping it and pulling me free of him. "If you keep this up I won't last another minute."

"Mm, we always have round two." His grip loosens slightly and I take him in my mouth again as he hisses from the sensitivity. "Please," I beg him, it's the only word I can find to express the deep need I have for him at this moment. The want I've been holding on to has been building since the first night I danced with him.

He doesn't wait for me to beg before he stands, lifting me from under my arms and tossing me onto the bed. His hands find the buttons of my jeans and make quick work of unzipping them as he slides them with my panties over my hips. His gaze starts at my full breasts that sag slightly to the sides from their weight to my soft belly as it flares to my wide hips. I'd close my legs if I was a shy woman, but I'm not. I'm proud of my body and watching him fully take me in turns me on even more, so I spread my thighs further apart.

An invitation.

That's all it takes for his control to crumble and his mouth is on me. Drinking in my juices as his tongue laps at me, fucking me with it. I'm ready for him and thank God he knows it. He climbs up my body, kissing every space he can. He kisses my ankles and up my calves, biting at my thigh as if he didn't just feast on me like a starved man. He places soft, wet kisses on my stomach before grabbing handfuls of my breasts, taking each one into his mouth. He sucks in my brown areola and before he moves over to the next one, he thrusts into me. Slow and deep, he eases into my wet heat, filling me, and my mouth drops open in ecstasy.

"Just. Like. That, take every single inch of me." He pushes deeper on every word until my clit is pressed against him and he grinds into me.

I lose sense of space and time at the feeling of him. He works my breasts, massaging and kissing them. Nipping softly at my nipples as he thrusts into me. Every single inch of him feels like forgiveness, feels like an awakening. He lifts my leg, placing it over his shoulder for a better angle, and the action crumbles my resolve. My orgasm builds with each thrust until he brings one of his hands down, pinching my clit and sending me sailing over the edge.

"Oh my God, Jameson."

His thrusts become rampant as he pumps into me, finding his own release as I climb to another one. My next orgasm is quick, hitting me and breaking me into a million pieces. His weight drops on top of me, kissing me gently before he rolls off the bed and makes his way to the bathroom. He comes back with a warm cloth and cleans me up before I go to relieve myself. When I walk out of the bathroom his eyes are on the clock.

"We gotta get ready, Baby. Can't have you missing the party you're throwing."

We both shower quickly, not able to keep our hands to ourselves but knowing time is no longer on our side. I make quick work of diffusing my hair and pinning the front up. My curls at the top fall to the sides, framing my face, while the back stays full and long.

I see Jameson's gaze follow my movements as I pull on the wrap dress I set out earlier this morning. I wasn't fully certain what I wanted to wear tonight and I'm glad I have a back-up option, considering my top and jeans are now laying haphazardly on the floor. It's a deep emerald green with a low v-neck, showing my ample cleavage and tying at the smallest part of my waist. There is a small pull on the side that allows me to gather up the fabric, giving it a more sexy look and an overall more flattering fit on my body. Adjusting the front wrap, I smooth it down. It didn't look like much on the hanger but adding my curves into the mix, I look like a vixen. That's exactly how I feel when I catch Jameson's eyes still on me from the mirror I'm standing in front of.

His head hangs low, his eyes watching me as his deep-brown locs hang in his face. He rolls his shoulders back, the muscles there tensing and moving as he takes long purposeful steps. Eating up the space between us, my eyes devour him as I watch him approach me from behind in the floor-length mirror. There is a glint in his eyes that forces me to keep contact. Fuck, this man is incredible and I'm trying not to drool on myself.

He stands behind me now, grabbing my hips and pulling me into him so I'm standing between his legs. My chest rises faster as he reaches his arm around my chest, wrapping it along the front of my throat as he cups my shoulder, securing me in place. Hugging me as he pulls me against him, leaving no room between us. The feel of our bodies pressed together does delicious things to me even after he thoroughly ravaged me less than an hour ago.

I can feel a thrum pulsing low in my core as his locs fall forward cascading like a curtain, the heat from his body warming me. My breathing completely stops as a warm breath coasts on the shell of my ear, followed by his nose skimming the curve of it, and I shudder with anticipation. His other hand wraps around me and he palms the softness of my stomach, pulling me deeper into him. At that moment the length of him presses against my ass while he grazes his teeth where my shoulder and neck meet, and my body goes molten when he bites down and sucks.

"You're so beautiful it hurts." His hand ghosts along where my thighs touch, inching closer to my pussy that is already growing wet for him. He runs his thumbnail up my slit on the top of my burgundy mesh panties and the sensation steals any thoughts I was contemplating. His laugh is a deep chuckle as he whispers in my ear, "You look like Christmas, maybe I should unwrap you."

Fucking hell. I want nothing more than for this man to do just that. My head drops back leaning against his hard chest and I moan at his exploration of my body. His fingers dip inside my panties then, giving me a long stroke, then he fills me with one of his long, thick digits. He *tsks* at me when my eyes close and I snap them open just as he says, "You know I like you keeping those eyes on me, Cassidy."

I meet his gaze in the mirror and watch as he swirls his fingers along my clit. His eyes meet mine at the same time as he pulls his hand free of my panties, righting them before he swirls his tongue around the same finger covered in my juices.

"Get your shoes on and let's get out here before I strip you bare and fuck you senseless again." His voice is low and husky. He slaps my ass and I yelp from the sharp, brief pain, happily doing just as he says.

By the time we make it downstairs, the night is in full swing. Thank God for business partners who think ahead. Paloma and Brianna have the drinks flowing for the bride-to-be, Candice, and her sister, as well as all the other bridesmaids.

The girls are all dancing, enjoying the music as they sway and throw their hands in the air. Dancing in the library just like she asked, and I couldn't be happier that we were able to make it happen.

As Jameson wraps his arm around me, pulling me near to him, I realize this is what I have been waiting for my entire life. My friends and the man of my dreams. I just didn't realize they were all so close to me. This is exactly where I am meant to be. He hands me a Long Island iced tea, kissing me gently on the neck as he whispers his *I love you's* in my ear. Something I don't think I will ever tire of hearing. I turn to him, "I love you so much, Jameson." And kiss him back.

I never need confirmation I'm his first choice when I'm the only one he's looking at.

Paloma pulls me away from him, tugging my arms as she brings us both to the center of the bachelorette party and we dance the rest of the night away. At least as long as Jameson can keep his hands off me. I smile to myself knowing I'm in for a long night and a whirlwind of a lifetime.

Epilogue

Jameson

SIX MONTHS LATER

Paloma

All set!

Anders

Perfect! I'll be there with the grannies soon.

Paloma

Don't call them grannies. LOL

Anders

That's what they are.

Thanks guys... Anders you're a fool.

Hand in hand with my Babygirl, we're standing in front of the house I hope to completely renovate. It's in rough shape and I know I'm probably going to need to do a lot of convincing for Cass to agree. We moved in together shortly after I showed up at the bar from my visit with Alma all those months ago.

Once we finished the remodel in Cypress Lake, we ended up naming it the Emerald Hideaway House since it had so many dark-green touches in the cozy home—it felt *right*.

The first person I wanted to show was my Babygirl, and I did. She fell in love with the place, and though I planned to make it a rental property, it felt like a great place for us to begin our life together.

Right after, I launched a property management unit on the consulting wing of Crews, and it's been great. Starting something new, something that is already making a profit for us feels incredible and is giving me a focus right here at home, in Cypress Lake with Cassidy.

But right now, standing here, I'm hoping this wasn't a mistake because Cassidy isn't budging and it's beginning to make me nervous thinking she hates it. The house overlooks the town's expansive lake. It has enough square footage to become a four or five bedroom home with three bathrooms, two being large enough to have a primary bedroom and full en suite. I viewed the floor plan earlier this week and have been waiting for it to go on the market. And now that it's about to, I'm ready to make the purchase but not before she gives me her approval.

She doesn't know it yet, but this is going to be our forever home. There is a large kitchen inside with good bones, one that is large enough I will be able to add two kitchen islands. We started taking cooking classes down at the Night Market and it has become something we both really enjoy. I want enough space to cook whatever recipes we dream of along with enough countertops I can spread her open on and have my own meal.

"Are you sure?" her question lingers in the air. "Can we think about it?"

My plan is contingent on her agreeing. I know I'm not supposed to put all my eggs in one basket but with her, the basket overflows and I don't have to be concerned with what-ifs, not with her.

"I'm sure, Baby. We have to make this decision now. They are letting me look at it a day before it launches on the website and I know it will be snatched up quickly." She nods her head, not saying another word but stepping closer to our forever.

"Okay." She turns to look at me, her smile beaming brighter than the sun. "Let's do it! I know you can make this house incredible."

I take her by the hand, bringing her closer to where the front porch will be. As she reaches for the door, I stop her. Holding both of her hands in mine, I bring her attention back to me, needing to feel the warmth of her gaze.

Getting a degree in architecture didn't prepare me to build a life, it only gifted me the ability to learn to build a house—a physical structure. But this woman, *my woman*, has shown me that loving someone is the foundation of a great home.

With her hands in mine, I rub small, gentle circles over them with my thumbs. Watching her eyes light up as she takes me in is an all-consuming feeling, it heats my entire body. Which is exactly why nerves aren't on my radar, there is nothing to be nervous about when it comes to the future I hope to plan with Cassidy.

"Babygirl, you're the love of my life. I want to build more than just this house with you, but our lives. When I saw you the night of the reunion, I hoped God wasn't playing a joke—giving me another chance. I would have never imagined a missed connection would lead me here, with you. I will do everything in my power to show you what unconditional love looks and feels like. I want to be a part of making every single one of your dreams into reality." I smile softly at her.

I bring my hand to her cheek and stroke her tears away with my thumb. I pull out the black velvet box that has been burning a hole in my pocket and open it before getting down on one knee. "But first you have to make one of *my* dreams a reality. Will you make me the happiest man in the world and become my wife?"

I watch her eyes widen, tears pooling as she gasps, silent joy filling her eyes. "Jameson." My name falls from her lips in a whisper as she finally locks her gaze on the ring and it sends me back to breakfast this morning. She made blueberry waffles but all I wanted was a taste of her and have her I did, spread out over the kitchen island.

Nothing at the jewelers matched what I wanted for her so I put in an order for a custom piece. I told him I wanted something that was strikingly beautiful and one of a kind, like her. Her engagement ring is a gold band that wraps around the base of the pear-cut diamond, giving an appearance that it's floating. I almost wish I brought her matching wedding band with me so I could claim her right here as my wife.

Her tears fall as she dips low, meeting my gaze she holds my face and kisses me before giving me her answer. "Yes! Yes, I will marry you, Bulldozer! Oh my fucking God, yes!"

Cassidy launches herself fully into me, almost knocking us both into the bushes. If I didn't have a foot planted, I'm certain we would have both been picking leaves out of her hair.

Throwing her arms over my shoulders and tugging me into her, she kisses me with abandon and I do the same, pouring all my love into this one kiss. Tasting her like it is the first time because it always feels like the first time. Cassidy is the blueprint to my very soul and I want to be sure she knows that wherever she is, she's my home and my very reason for breathing. I take the ring out of the box and slide it on her finger before opening the front door and walking in with her. She's so consumed with the ring that she doesn't look up until all our friends and family scream in excitement.

"Congratulations!" Everyone yells, popping confetti. It flies everywhere as my future wife's shock stuns her into silence, that is, before Paloma and Janelle run to her. Cass wraps her arms around them with tears in her eyes as she grins up at me with a look full of love.

Paloma was a huge part of this, getting the house ready. Anderson too. He picked up the ring for me before he shuffled off to pick up Alma and Lee.

Alma is sitting in the soft chair we brought over for her, next to Lee, Cassidy's grandma. They hold each other's hands with pride. I'm scared of the day they become close friends, but right now, all I can see is Cassidy. Soon-to-be Cassidy Bennette.

The grannies' smiles of approval are all I need to gather my Babygirl back in my arms, her back to my front as she looks out at our friends and family.

"Yes, a thousand times, yes."

Claiming His Luna

EXCERPT FROM JAMESON'S AUDIOBOOK

She never imagined she would be here, within her own pack lands, surrounded by the same wolves who had always been their enemies. Low growls were the only sounds within the quiet of the room, now that she was alone with *him*. Inara's tan fur was soaked from the rain but she refused to shift back, refusing to allow him even a glimpse of her naked flesh simply because she knew he *wanted* it.

His dominance thickened the air in the room, she wouldn't admit it but her core warmed with need from the feeling of it. It prickled against her skin in both a warning and a vow. Inara's wolf had a mind of her own, if it was up to her we would be at his feet, completely bare to him.

Ready to be ravaged.

Will you hush! I don't want to deal with your thoughts. She attempted to hush her wolf.

And why not? Look at him, he's the perfect male for us.

Inara internally rolled her eyes at her wolf's words but she did just as she suggested—she took in her fill of Enzo, the alpha who just claimed her pack as his own. His legs stood wide, his tree trunk muscular thighs clothed in worn jeans. Her gaze followed up his form to the arms he had crossed over his wide naked chest and thick biceps. Enzo's hands flexed under her scrutiny and when she made it to his handsome face, a smirk

285

tugged at his lips.

If she could slap his face, it would make her all the more happy.

And then get on our knees.

Will you be quiet!

He tsks Inara, effectively cutting off the inner struggle with her wolf before he spoke, *"Let her speak her mind, Mate."*

Inara's eyes go as wide as saucers as realization blooms over her.

"I love how your wolf thinks," his deep voice is dark with desire.

How? How is he in my head?

A whine falls from her mouth the longer she holds her wolf back, the longer she sits here staring at the wolf who calls her his.

"Shift for me, baby." Enzo commands, watching her shake her head, refusing him once again. "If you make me force you, it's going to hurt. Stop being a brat and *fucking shift."*

His alpha command pressed against her and she knew what he said was true, the command traveled over Inara's fur like a sickness. Coating her in a nausea that curdled her stomach. For a minute, Inara considered staying in her wolf form and making him force her to shift. Knowing that it would only deepen the rift between the two of them even further. When she looked into his eyes, watching the burning frustration behind them, Inara decided otherwise.

Normally it wouldn't be difficult to shift back into her human form, but the beast within her was pleased being in Enzo's presence. The anger coating her fur held on to whatever it could to stay in control. Inara closed her eyes and took a deep breath, imagining the voluptuous figure she had when she wasn't within the skin of her wolf. When she opened her eyes, Inara's gaze snapped to Enzo's and his eyes were molten as he and his wolf took in her shapely form.

She's fucking stunning—her thighs are thick and paired with wide pup bearing hips we can't wait to grip our hands into. Her soft belly sits just above a triangle of brown curls and he does his best to hold back, swallowing our desperation for a bit longer. Gods, her breasts. They hang in heavy teardrops with large brown areolas and darkened nipples, my wolf longs to have our teeth sunken into them. Image after image flutter through our mind as he showed me in explicit detail just how he would suck them into our mouth, how he would lave his tongue around her blackberry peaks. My wolf's eyes track the light sway of her waist length dark brown curls as she switches her stance, uncomfortable under our stare. No. Not discomfort. Want.

She wants him, he along with his wolf can smell her arousal from here. Ours. Ours. Ours.

His wolf chants.

"You need to leave." Inara finally spoke and the beast inside Enzo thrashed against him from her rejection. "You are *not* staying here, not with me." Her voice was slightly above a whisper, speaking to him as though he's a wild animal. It's an attempt to calm his wolf, but it does the opposite because that's exactly what we are.

Wild.

With a speed Inara was unprepared for, he pressed himself against her. Pushing her until the back of her knees hit the bed, forcing Inara to fall back. *My submission is what he's after... but I'm not entirely sure I'm ready to give it to him so easily.* Inara's wolf tuts at her foolishness.

He scents the air around her, licking his lips as he does. His wolf all but growls at her while he grinds his length against her. "If you think for one second that I'm sleeping on that floor and not in this bed with my cock sunk deep into your dripping cunt, you my love are a fool."

287

"In your fucking dreams. You won't be getting anywhere near my pussy."

"Every gods damn night." Enzo growled, knocking her legs open with his own. "Every night I'll be right here worshipping you, claiming you, knotting you until you damn sure know who you belong to."

He dropped between Inara's thighs like a beast ready to devour his prey; the gleam in his eyes told her that he wasn't ever letting her go after this. Not when he called her his *mate*. Inara's eyes dropped for just a moment. The width of him made her mouth water and her sex clenched in anticipation.

Inara looked down her body at this powerful man down on his knees before her, desire and danger mixed within his golden eyes. His wolf was battling for control and something about the view snapped the last thread of her resistance.

"Just this once." She said, "Just tonight."

Enzo pressed his nose into the apex of her thighs, nuzzled into the curls between her legs. "If that's what it takes for you to believe this isn't forever, baby, then so be it. Just know, once I have you, you'll never be rid of me. You are *mine*."

He licked into her pussy, tasted her and growled at how fucking incredible she tasted. Enzo lifted her leg over his shoulder and sucked on the sensitive bundle of nerves there. He gripped her thighs, spreading Inara wider as he nestled between her legs, wrapped his arms around her thighs and tugged her body into his. Absolutely ravishing her.

"Oh my gods, Enzo." Inara moaned his name as if they'd always been a part of one another. Her voice was a song and now there's nothing that could stop him from making her his. Nothing but a no from her lips.

She swore he wouldn't be sleeping in her bed and she was right, there won't be any sleeping in this bed tonight. Her wetness coated his face as he pulled one arm free from around her leg and plunged two fingers deep into her dripping cunt, pumping them into her as she moaned his name.

"That's right, baby, give me those delicious fucking sounds. Your wolf deserves this." Inara's back bowed off the bed as he pushed another finger into her sopping pussy, he curled his fingers and massaged the spot inside her that would send her carrening over the edge. Enzo worked her into a climax so high that when she came down, she was certain she would break apart. Enzo kissed his way up her soft belly and heaving breasts as he moved his fingers over her clit. Pressing his thumb hard over the sensitive nerves there she whined. Once he was over her, he nudged the head of his cock at her needy entrance.

Rather than sliding himself into the only place his wolf urged him to, he held himself back.

Where we need him, Inara. Her wolf whimpered.

"Why are you—don't stop. Please don't stop." Inara pleaded, begging him to continue.

"I need to feel you come around my cock, baby." Enzo groaned as he rubbed his hard length from her clit to her sex. He enjoyed the sight of her sweat slicked skin far too much. Loved how the blush darkened her chest, neck, and cheeks. She bucked against him, the thought of needing to beg for her release was almost too much, but she was close. So. Fucking. Close. *Please.*

Inara's wolf begged, needing a release after all that's happened. Needing the closeness of her mate. *Please Inara, please. He's our mate. They were made for us.*

"Please." She whispered, a pitiful meowl but he heard it nonetheless.

Enzo pressed the tip of his dick further into her and the width of it burned in the most delectable way. When he pulled himself back, Inara cried out from the emptiness. "Fuck. Please Enzo. Please fill me with your cock."

"Look at how you beg so pretty for me," before Inara could say anything more he thrust into her, filling her wet heat completely. This time when he pulled back, he thrust into her again, hard, quickening his pace as the leud wet sound of their skin slapping together bounced off the walls of the bedroom.

Her toes curled and the walls of her pussy tightened around him, pulling him in deeper. *"Fuck, you feel so good baby. So perfect for us. Let me see you, Little Wolf. Come out and play."* Enzo's wolf growled into their linked minds, he spoke directly to Inara's own wolf. When she looked at his face this time, she could tell her own wolf had pushed her way through because she could see his eyes in vivid detail though still a dark golden yellow, now had a green ring around his pupil. He looked fucking magnificent.

Enzo, or maybe his wolf, dropped his head down to her breast and as he pounded into her he sucked a deep rosy peek into his mouth. He sucked so hard his cheeks hollowed out and she screamed out in ecstasy. His tongue licked slow languid circles around her areola, getting the taste of her just like he showed me he would.

She felt him swell inside her, deeper, harder he plunged into her warmth. Enzo's knot was stretching her until she cried out, her voice hoarse with lust. The pressure was borderline unbearable but it felt so fucking good she couldn't imagine telling him to stop.

"You're so perfect. Such a good fucking mate taking my knot like you are." Inara preened at his words, pressed her breast up into his chest as her back bowed.

The thick base of him pressed deeper, pain and pleasure mixed together until she couldn't tell if she needed to run or beg for more.

"Don't even think about it, Little Wolf. You are ours now. Always." His wolf voice growled out, speaking directly to Inara's wolf as his knot stretched her, locking them together for hours to come.

"Please Enzo, come with me." Inara moaned. He dropped his face into her neck and she turned her head, giving him better access as her breasts bounced from Enzo's hard thrusts.

"Going to come, baby. Going to fill up this perfect tight little pussy." And though the words warred within her, there was nothing more she wanted than to feel his come fill her completely.

"Yes. Fill me. Please. Oh my gods." Her nails lengthened and she dragged them down his back as he roared his release. Filled with lust, Enzo sank his canines into her neck—branding her with his mating mark and locking their fates forever.

If you enjoyed this excerpt from Jameson's audiobook, and you want Nicole to actually write Claiming His Luna, make sure you tell her how much you need it on her socials and maybe she'll listen.

COMING NEXT

Second Swing

Cypress Lake isn't just a place—it's a feeling. For Clinton and Paloma, it's where old wounds resurface... and where new chances begin.□

To keep up date with Nicole Devonne and all things Cypress Lake Reunion, subscribe to her newsletter or follow her on socials. Find all the information at nicoledevonnebooks.com

Acknowledgments

Thank you God, for being a steady current during the days where the waves felt like they were going to take me under.

To my husband: Thank you for showing me everyday that true love isn't fictional, it's alive and very real. There were so many times I wanted to throw in the towel and be done with it all. You were my constant cheerleader and reminded me that I can do hard things. Thank you for believing in me and seeing me despite the lack of caffeine and my many episodes of wanting to pull my hair out and toss my laptop. You're the real MVP, Big Dawg!

My daughters: I hope one day, when you are old enough to read this, you know how much you inspired me to believe in myself. Not just to show you all that you can achieve your dreams, I can also achieve my own. I love the three of you with my entire being. You three are my reasons—my whys.

Mom & Dad: You've always been my cheerleaders whether I could see it or not. I currently can't see what I'm typing from all the tears so let me make this good. I learned my work ethic from both of you; you inspired in me a love of reading and desire to create worlds. I love you both infinitely; thank you for showing me I am capable of so many things even when I don't believe in myself. I could ask you both not to read any of this but I think you would do it to spite me... so enjoy and don't make it weird!

Sissy: Even though we will never read each other's book recommendations (lol) you always have my back whether you get it or not. I admire you so much and I love you!

My safe people—Isa, Alex, and Annie:

My real-life Paloma, my duet partner and best friend, Isa: I cannot even begin to describe what you mean to me. You pushed me to join a community that changed my life and then you joined me shortly after. You were my very first alpha reader before I even knew what the hell rhat role was. Thank you for seeing me, every time, every day. I hope to always sing loudly and off-key with you!

Alex: I don't know if I can get through this without crying, God I'm a sap. Thank you for being my person, my platonic soulmate, for always understanding me even when I didn't have the words. You have been such a blessing in my life and we are in this thing until we have our shared porch and are old and senile.

Annie, my soul sister: I'm so glad we connected. You just...get me. The stars aligned and connected us, even if we are so far apart. Thank you for brainstorming with me, for horses, for our Brian's, for getting me through some of the toughest parts of my year and never judging me. I love you so much!

Taylor, Sydney, DeAnna, Fay, Sarah, and Genna: I want to thank each of you for your guidance, feedback, and genuine friendship. I would have been absolutely lost without every single one of you. Each of you have been a guiding light on my path to becoming an author and I am so grateful to have your friendship.

Thea, my cookie: Thank you for being sunshine even when you felt dark. You truly light up my days. Thank you for all the late night calls and voice messages, for random brainstorms sessions and show recommendations. You are a wonder and I am better with you in my life.

Joyce: My God, thank YOU! This book would not be where it is without you. You gifted me a road in which I journeyed to become more confident in my writing, eventually taking a chance on myself and saying *yes*. I now get an eye twitch when I write the word THAT (lol). Thank you for empowering me, pushing me, and urging me forward in areas where I felt too small. Working with you has made me a better writer and has given me confidence I didn't have before connecting with you. Thank you for loving Cassidy and Jameson as much as I do!

Pia, thank you creating such a beautiful cover and being apart of this journey. I came to you for advice and somehow took the small amount of information I gave you to make my dream cover. I appreciate you so much, more than you'll ever know.

To my readers: Thank you for taking a chance on my debut novel and for reading Cassidy and Jameson's love story. Whether you loved the book or not, you took a chance on me and I am so grateful to you.

About the Author

Nicole is a stay-at-home-mama, born and raised on the West Coast of Florida. You can find her bundled under a blanket with her kindle, reading a steamy romance, or writing her own swoon worthy characters.

When she's not lost creating a new story, she's trying new food spots with her husband, playing mermaids with her littles or sneaking away for thrifting and iced coffees with her teen.

She is a self-proclaimed beverage goblin who is easily snackfluenced. Nicole will admit that chicken tenders, caesar salad, and fries are her grumpy moods worst enemy.

Made in the USA
Monee, IL
06 June 2025

18989102R00184